**GIDEON'S RAID**

In this jubilee novel, George Gideon, Commander of the C.I.D., plans the most audacious raid in the story of the Met. If successful, it will wipe out the organisation responsible for eighty per cent of London crime.

From the beginning, the project hits snags. First, Gideon finds the whole operation whisked out of his hands by the Chief Commissioner. Then, when a midnight call from a supergrass brings the shattering revelation that every detail of the raid has been 'leaked' to the other side, the top brass turns to Gideon again, and puts him in command of what has now become a high-risk salvage operation: a desperate attempt to catch London's most dangerous men before they have a chance to run for cover, thus escaping justice forever.

**About the author:**

William Vivian Butler celebrates a double jubilee with the appearance of GIDEON'S RAID. Apart from being the twenty-fifth adventure in the Gideon series, it also happens to be his own twenty-fifth book.

His first detective novel, GUY FOR TROUBLE, was published in 1945, and in the forty-one years since then, he has written a wide variety of crime books, both fiction and non-fiction. In 1982 he received a special Edgar Allan Poe award from the Mystery Writers of America.

GIDEON'S RAID is the fifth novel he has written following in the footsteps of John Creasey, the original J.J. Marric.

William Vivian Butler lives in Surrey and has two children, Carol and Nigel.

# Gideon's Raid

---


**J.J. Marric**

as told by William Vivian Butler

CORONET BOOKS
Hodder and Stoughton

First published in Great Britain in 1986 by Hodder & Stoughton Ltd

Coronet edition 1987

*The characters and situations in this book are entirely imaginary and bear no relation to any real person or actual happening.*



**British Library C.I.P.**

Butler, William Vivian
Gideon's raid.
I. Title II. Marric, J.J.
823'.914[F] PR6052.U875

ISBN 0 340 41367 0

Printed and bound in Great Britain for Hodder and Stoughton Paperbacks, a division of Hodder and Stoughton Ltd., Mill Road, Dunton Green, Sevenoaks, Kent TN13 2YA.
(Editorial Office: 47 Bedford Square, London WC1B 3DP) by Cox & Wyman Ltd., Reading

To
NORAH BUTLER

with thanks for all your interest,
in all my books, over all these years
– Bill.

Contents

# 1 Caged Tiger

Kate Gideon patted the pillow beside her invitingly.

"For Heaven's sake, George, forget about that stupid raid and come to bed. It isn't November 1st for a whole week yet, and even when it is – "

She broke off, not wishing to put any more pressure on what was already a very sore point.

Gideon, though, finished the sentence for her.

"And even when it is," he muttered bitterly, "the whole business is nothing to do with me, and I'm virtually under orders to stay away from the Yard." The mutter became first a growl, and then a roar, as he added: "During the biggest operation in the whole history of the Met!"

Thrusting his hands deep into the pockets of his dressing-gown, he began pacing up and down the bedroom. Even though he was wearing bedroom slippers and walking on thick carpeting, his footsteps sounded as loud to Kate as the tramp of a marching army.

She folded her arms and lay watching him. Her grey-blue eyes looked calm and mischievous, and revealed nothing of her secret anxiety about him.

"I was going to say you'll wear the carpet out," she told him. "But the way you're going on, you're not doing the floorboards a lot of good either."

This was true enough. The house – a red-bricked semi-detached in Harringdon Street, Fulham – had been built in

1885, and the boards were vociferously protesting their age with a continual squeaking.

Kate expected, at the very least, that George would respond with a rueful grin; but his thoughts were miles away, and he hardly even glanced in her direction.

"Ah, well," she said, painfully aware that she was talking to herself. "If you will insist on behaving like a caged tiger, I suppose the only thing to do is go downstairs and fetch you a bone."

Not even a grunt coming from her husband, she slipped out of bed, put on a rose-pink negligee, and headed for the door, moving with that languorous grace that never deserted her, no matter how trying a situation might be.

Half a minute later, she was down in the kitchen, preparing a hot toddy – a mug of milk liberally laced with brandy. George had never required anything like that to help him sleep in the past; but he had needed one every night lately, and would probably be wanting two or three a night before long. There was still a full week to go before November 1st.

Kate frowned to herself as she heated up the milk in a saucepan, and then went into the living room to fetch the half-bottle of Martell's Three Star from the back of the drinks cabinet. They were nearly out of the stuff, she noticed. Not surprisingly, really. George liked a very occasional whisky, but hadn't normally much use for brandy. They only bought a half-bottle of it a year, and most of that went into the Christmas pudding.

Suddenly she found herself laughing. What, after all, was she worrying about? Needing a spot of brandy before he dropped off to sleep hardly meant that George was on the point of breaking up! It was just that it was so *unlike* him.

During all the years that he had been Commander of the Criminal Investigation Department at Scotland Yard – and it was only just short of twenty-five years now – he had never had the slightest trouble in sleeping the sleep of the just. Even though he had been under pressure on countless occasions – often, in fact, under multiple pressures, with crises cascading on top of him from all directions, as he battled relentlessly through some nights of rampaging crime – George had always possessed the ability to remain calm, unshakeable as a rock amidst the torrents of panic. She had known him to pace a room when he was trying to solve some tricky problem. She had never known him to do it compulsively, just to relieve nervous tension: but quite obviously, that was what was happening now.

The milk was hot in a moment. Kate poured it into the mug, added the brandy, and made her way back to the foot of the stairs. George's pacing was still continuing, and seemed to be thundering right through the house, and echoing all her fears.

She stopped laughing, and swallowed hard, finding herself startlingly close to crying.

Poor George, she thought. How could she stop him feeling like a caged tiger – when, to all intents and purposes, that was exactly what Scotland Yard had made him?

★ ★ ★

It had begun seven or eight months before, when Gideon had calmly suggested a raid on three major criminals and their associates. It was an audacious suggestion, because the criminals in question were so big that they were believed to be responsible, between them, for eighty per cent of all the organised crime in London. One of them was Barry Mayne, a Cockney gangster who had established a Mafia-like hold on vice and prostitution rackets in the inner city areas. Another was Jeremy Kemp, a social-climbing tycoon who owned a string of West End theatres, but whose real profits derived from one of the biggest drug rackets in British criminal history. The third was Arturo Salvados, rumoured to be the master-mind behind nine out of ten major bank robberies.

The trio – known to the underworld as "the Big Three" – worked in close liaison with each other, so one thing was obvious from the start. The raid would have to be a precision-timed combined operation, synchronised so as to attack the three leaders, their chief henchmen and all their operation centres simultaneously. The utmost secrecy was also necessary, because, as Gideon grimly pointed out, "Top criminals pay top bribes, and a cop who gave *this* show away would be a rich man for life."

The plan for the raid had been submitted to the Assistant Commissioner (Crime), Alec Hobbs, with whom Gideon sometimes walked a difficult diplomatic tightrope, since he was not only his immediate superior but also the husband of his youngest daughter Penny. On this occasion, though, there had been no difficulty at all. Alec had realised at once that this was a bold, imaginative stroke that would deal a body-blow to London crime, and had lost no time in putting it to the Chief Commissioner, Sir Reginald Scott-Marle.

Scott-Marle, usually a cold, aloof individual, had for once been quite emotional. He had burst right into Gideon's office and shaken his hand, not once but three or four times over.

"Masterly, George, masterly. There's nothing else that I can say. We've been playing cat-and-mouse with this choice threesome for quite long enough. It's time we pounced – and to do it on all three of them at once, in a single night, is clearly the right, and, indeed, the only way. There's – er – just one point on which I'm afraid I must take issue with you."

Scott-Marle's manner changed as abruptly as though the sun had gone in, and a chill wind had started to blow straight from the Polar regions. He was suddenly more than cold and aloof, but icy, almost hostile. He tapped the document that Gideon had submitted as cautiously as though it might explode in his face.

"What you've suggested here, as I understand it, is a C.I.D. operation."

Gideon stood his ground.

"Is that surprising, sir? I do happen to be the C.I.D.'s Commander."

Scott-Marle smiled, so faintly that it could be described as frostily.

"I realise that, of course, but there's something you must realise too. The Yard has changed, George. We've flushed out all the watertight compartments. The days of thinking departmentally – let alone acting departmentally – are over."

Gideon grunted. He needed no telling about the wind of change – sometimes it seemed like the gale of change – that had been blowing through the Yard. C.I.D. men had been put under uniformed ones, and vice versa, in section after section. But he had deliberately ignored it on this occasion. He had intended that this should be *his* raid, and he had wanted to hand-pick the men for it himself; men that he had known for years and could trust implicitly. And from the very nature of things, the men that he knew best were in his own beloved C.I.D.

He doubted, though, if that argument would cut much ice with Scott-Marle in his present mood. So he simply said: "I take it, then, that you want me to adjust the proposal to bring in Uniform."

That was when the blow fell.

"I don't want you to do anything more about this at all, George," Scott-Marle said flatly. "You've made your contribution – a momentous one, as I readily admit. You've galvanised us into launching what could be the most devastating raid in police history. But to make sure of a hundred per cent success in co-ordinating all our resources, I'm putting a man from Uniform in charge of the operation. You know him, I expect, although he's only recently joined the Met: Commander Wally Warburton."

Gideon swallowed hard. He had thought it quite likely that the whole project would be vetoed, but it had simply never occurred to him that it would be peremptorily whisked right out of his hands. He struggled to fight down a sense of outrage, and to view the thing dispassionately.

He did, in fact, know Warburton, but not very well. He had come to the Met from the Nottingham force a year or so before, had risen from Superintendent to Chief Superintendent in six months, and had been made a Commander in another three. He was a youngish man, as young as Gideon had been when *he* had first been made Commander, and in some ways, he was not unlike a youthful version of Gideon himself: a pugnacious, thrusting man who made the corridors ring with his barked commands. He didn't have Gideon's massive presence, though. In fact, he was rather slight in build, and had a high-pitched voice: his bark was far closer to a yap than a roar. On the occasions that they had met, Gideon had been rather irritated by him; but that was neither here nor there. No one could question his ability, his energy and his enthusiasm – and what counted more?

"A – um – a very good choice," said Gideon, with only the slightest hesitation.

Scott-Marle smiled, a shade less icily than before.

"I'm glad you agree, George. Warburton's a first-class man. I'm confident he'll do an equally first-class job. He's being relieved of all other duties so that he can concentrate on the raid from now onwards. I'm giving him *carte blanche* to co-opt anyone he likes on to his team. And he's also being given a whole floor of the building – floor seven – as headquarters for the operation. It's vital that nothing should go wrong, and when you're dealing with villains of the calibre of Mayne, Kemp and Salvados, the slightest slip might wreck the whole show. So I've told Warburton that I fully expect the planning and preparations to take months."

Gideon's eyebrows shot up.

"Months! But surely that means a very big risk of something leaking out?"

Scott-Marle wasn't smiling now, even coldly. His face was suddenly grim.

"Don't imagine your point about secrecy hasn't been taken, George. I've given instructions that the men co-opted on to floor seven duties should be treated almost as though they were on a jury. They are not to reveal anything about the operation, even to their closest colleagues elsewhere in the Yard. They'll not even be using the same canteen as the rest of us. And I'm having a special telephone system installed on the floor, to prevent anything being accidentally overheard through a switchboard mix-up or a crossed line. I'm even taking Home Office advice on whether we can install 'scrambler' phones throughout the floor."

Gideon tried hard not to look as dubious as he felt. Accidental leaks weren't the real danger, he told himself; human nature was. How many of the dozens of people on floor seven would be proof against the temptation of the enormous bribes that would be on offer, once a word was whispered that a raid was being planned against the Big Three? *He* would have been able to hand-pick totally reliable men. But Warburton, with his very limited time at the Yard, would have to take people on hearsay – or trust.

The more he thought about all this, the less he liked it. It looked as though the opportunity of a lifetime – of the Met's long, proud lifetime – was being stupidly thrown away. But there wasn't anything he could say about it that wouldn't sound like sour grapes; petulant objections born of resentment, hurt pride . . .

And then suddenly Gideon's pride received its most damaging blow yet.

On his way to the door, Scott-Marle turned, and added casually:

"Oh, just one more thing. I'm afraid you will have to consider yourself outside the security barrier. That may seem a bit outrageous, seeing that you're the instigator of the whole thing – but I want Warburton to feel he's in full command, and if you were on the scene, even in an advisory capacity, he might find it a – er – a bit unsettling. The last thing I want is for him to be constantly looking over his shoulder, so to speak – even at you. All right?"

He was gone without waiting for Gideon's reply, which was perhaps just as well. Gideon was inwardly seething.

And at some level inside him, he had been seething ever since.

He had obeyed orders, of course. In fact, he had savagely over-obeyed them. Not once during the long months of the spring and summer had he ventured anywhere near the forbidden seventh floor. On the innumerable occasions when one or other of his men had tried to pass on some rumour about what was happening up there, he had stopped the would-be informant with a curt growl, or, more often, an outright roar. He had not even let Alec Hobbs confide anything to him, except for a single whispered, "The big show's on November 1st."

He had tried to burn off his feelings about the raid by

burying himself in his work – and there had been no shortage of grave cases to occupy his time and attention: the appearance of one of the most sensational mass murderers since Jack the Ripper, to give only one example.

The policy had partly succeeded. Gideon found himself forgetting about the raid for long stretches of the working day. He was even able to force it to the back of his mind when he returned from work in the evening and had supper or watched television with Kate. It was the end of the day that was the trouble. Then, suddenly, just when he most needed to relax and switch off, all his suppressed fury surfaced, and drove him to this restless pacing and prowling.

Tonight, he was not only furious about the raid. He was furious with himself, for giving way to such a childish sense of resentment. Feeling exactly as though he was trying to brake a lurching, skidding lorry, he somehow forced himself to a standstill, and when Kate came up to the bedroom carrying the hot toddy, she was startled to find him lying on the bed, grinning up at her half-triumphant, half-shamefaced.

"Thanks for the bone, love," he said, accepting the drink. "Rare and juicy as usual."

The grin grew.

"I've been thinking. I'm long overdue for some leave. How would you feel about coming with me on one of these winter breaks to Bournemouth?"

Kate's heart leapt. It was a long, long time since George had suggested anything like that, right out of the blue. It took her back thirty years or more, to when they were first married and their first baby hadn't even been thought of – days when they'd often made crazy, spur-of-the-moment decisions to drop everything and go somewhere, just for the hell of it . . . Not that those plans had always materialised. Police emergencies – the endless call of duty – had frequently led to heartbreaking last-minute cancellations. But sometimes it had worked out. Sometimes they'd gone. And the result had been magic weekends, unforgettable even after three decades.

A moment's reflection, though, told Kate that it wouldn't

be a magic weekend this time. Not with George feeling banished at a crucial point in the Yard's history –

"It's a marvellous idea," she said. "But let's face it. All that will happen is that you'll catch your death of cold pacing up and down, up and down the prom."

Gideon's grin changed to a glower, a sure sign that he knew she was telling the truth.

"I give you my solemn promise, love, that I won't pace a *yard* – " he began, but broke off. Even half-jokingly, Gideon didn't like making promises he couldn't keep. And he had suddenly realised that given no work to do, nothing to think about but that bloody raid, he might be impossible to live with – and the weekend break could turn into a wit's-end nightmare for both of them.

He searched for something to say, but then realised that there was no need to say anything. Those serene grey-blue eyes of Kate's seemed to see right through him, and told him that, as always, she knew it all. He wished to God that *he* could feel serene, could beat this gnawing frustration, restlessness, anxiety –

That was when the plugged-in telephone beside the bed broke into his thoughts with a piercing *pheep*. He glanced at the clock on the Teasmade. Nine minutes to twelve. Almost certainly an emergency call of some kind. Few of their friends would ring – or, rather, *pheep* – as late as this.

He picked up the receiver, and the next moment, found himself gripping it so fiercely that the flimsy plastic threatened to buckle in his hand.

"George? This is Alec. Listen. I've got a crisis on my hands."

It sounded like it, too. Hobbs's voice was usually cool and calm, even in an emergency; it could get as cold as Scott-Marle's. But now it was hoarse and shaking. For a terrible moment, Gideon thought he was speaking from home, and that there had been an accident there.

"Is Penny okay – and George?" (That was his baby grandson, named after him.)

"No, it's nothing to do with them. I'm here at the Yard – the raid HQ, seventh floor."

Gideon's own voice became for a moment cold.

"If you're going to say anything about the raid, sure you've got clearance from Scott-Marle?"

Hobbs's reply shook him so much that despite his fierce grip, he nearly dropped the phone.

"He's here beside me, George, and it was he who ordered me to ring."

Suddenly Alec seemed to slip out of both his accustomed roles. He wasn't remotely like the smooth, polished Assistant Commissioner (Crime) – or Gideon's quiet, rather correct son-in-law. He became much more like a real son: a son in dead trouble, appealing for help. Sounding a lot younger than his forty-odd years, he finished, in a torrent of words:

"The raid's been blown completely. We had a call from a supergrass about an hour ago. Apparently there's been a leak – and a big one. Mayne, Kemp, Salvados – all the Big Three have had tip-offs. They know the whole raid plan in detail, the timetable, the officers being used – the lot! There's just one point in our favour. They think they've got a week's grace, so may not move for a few hours, at least. Sir Reginald and I reckon that if the raid can be carried out straight away by completely different personnel, whose integrity is beyond suspicion, there might just – *just* be a chance of saving the whole – "

He broke off so abruptly that it was obvious that the receiver at the end had been suddenly snatched away from him. Scott-Marle himself came on the line, sounding tense, terse, embarrassed.

"In a nutshell, George, I'm asking you to take over; to bring in your own hand-picked team as you originally intended – and carry out the whole raid now, tonight. It's asking a lot, I know. But are you willing to try?"

Gideon hesitated just for a moment.

Scott-Marle wasn't exaggerating. He *was* asking a lot – and Gideon would be asking still more of his men, dragging them out of bed in the small hours and pitchforking them straight into a desperate battle with the most dangerous criminal organisations in London – organisations already alerted, trigger-happy, on their guard . . .

But, being Gideon, there was, of course, only one answer he could make.

"I'll be round right away," he said. And putting down the receiver, he jumped off the bed, once again moving with all the ferocity of a tiger.

There was a slight difference, though, this time, thought a smiling Kate as she watched him.

He now looked like a tiger bounding out of its cage.

# 2 Takeover Team

Before Gideon had finished dressing, the telephone pheeped again.

This time it was Alec Hobbs.

"George. Sir Reginald doesn't think it would be a good idea for you to come into the Yard through the main entrance. The place may be being watched, and the people we're up against can make connections faster than a bank of computers. There's the danger of inside leaks, too. It only wants a whisper to get out that the great Gideon has been seen arriving dramatically at midnight, and rushing straight up to the seventh floor – "

"Huh!" Gideon grunted. "I should think a lot more whispers would get out if the great Gideon is seen blundering about outside the canteen entrance, stumbling over dustbins in the dark."

Hobbs remained deadly serious.

"Not the canteen entrance, George. There's a door the whole seventh floor team have been using, at the back of the building. Listen. You park your car in Old Pye Street, then walk down a little alley – "

He gave precise instructions, which Gideon listened to, glowering. The idea of hole-in-the-corner stuff like this being necessary at the very entrance to Scotland Yard –

He finished dressing at top speed, grumblingly permitted Kate to re-do a too-hurriedly-knotted tie, and a second later, the front door was slamming behind him. His shabby, but spacious and comfortable, Rover sped him to Victoria Street in less than twenty minutes, and it was just a quarter past midnight when he turned into Old Pye Street, at the rear of Scotland Yard. A solid October downpour was falling, and he had omitted to put on an overcoat, so that he was very wet and not in the best of tempers when he came striding up to the special side door.

His anger melted, though, at the sight of Scott-Marle and Alec standing in the doorway waiting for him. Never before had he been welcomed at the Yard by a reception committee consisting of the Chief Commissioner and the Assistant Commissioner (Crime)!

Oblivious of the rain, they stepped out of the doorway and came up to him. Scott-Marle was wearing an overcoat, hat and gloves, and was clearly on the point of leaving. His face, brightly lit by a bare bulb over the doorway, was expressionless, except for a faint, wry smile.

"Hullo, George. Thank God you've come," he said. "As you can see, I'm off home. Not to sleep, I assure you. I shall be waiting by the phone until this business is over. But – " the smile became almost diffident – "this is going to be a night for snap decisions, and I think you'd rather make them without having me breathing down your neck. I kept you out of all this to give Warburton a free hand. The least I can do is clear out and give *you* a free one now."

This was so unlike the usually cold, dictatorial Scott-Marle that Gideon was taken aback. After a second's reflection, though, he understood. Scott-Marle knew that he would be making this raid an old-style, full-scale C.I.D. operation, running right against the official policy of bringing uniformed men in at every stage. He was willing to turn a blind eye, but would find that easier to do at a distance, like Nelson with his telescope.

He slipped off a glove and held out his hand. Gideon was surprised at the strength and warmth of his grip.

"Good luck," he said brusquely. "I'm afraid you'll need it. But if anyone can save anything from this shambles, I know you can. Alec, take George up to the seventh floor and fill him in on all that's happened. And remember, from now on, what he says goes. Consider every order he gives to be automatically underwritten by me."

With a final nod at Gideon, Scott-Marle turned and left – so rapidly that it was as though he was making an escape.

Hobbs managed a smile as he and Gideon went inside the building.

"In other words – you're my boss again, George. Like old times, isn't it?"

Alec had been Gideon's Deputy Commander only a few years before, and it was Gideon himself who had persuaded Scott-Marle to promote him.

Gideon returned the smile. For some reason – perhaps because the shock of the débâcle had worn off, perhaps because responsibility had suddenly been taken off his shoulders – Alec was looking much more like his old self. Though there was still just a hint of desperation in his voice as he said:

"Don't expect to find anything going on upstairs, George. As soon as we heard that the secret was blown, the whole raid was officially abandoned, and the operations room closed down. We even sent the night staff home who were manning the telephones here. A panic measure, maybe, but who knows? One of them could have been responsible for the leak – or part of it, anyway."

They had reached the lift doors. Alec pressed the button, and they opened at once. Gideon was no longer smiling. He always hated witch-hunts inside the Met, but knew that a big one would have to be started: the biggest, probably, there had ever been.

"How many Yard personnel were involved in the raid preparations?"

Typically, Hobbs was ready with the precise facts and figures.

"One hundred and twenty-three all told. One commander – that's Wally Warburton, of course. Five chief superintendents. Six chief detective superintendents. Sixteen other supers. Twenty-nine inspectors – "

"All right, that'll do to be getting on with," Gideon said. "Was anyone outside the police force in on the plan?"

"We had criminal contacts all over London, of course, reporting movements of the Big Three and so on. Any of them could have guessed that a raid was pending. But they couldn't have known the whole plan – and it was that which was leaked. Every detail of it, from A to Z. So it's got to be an inside job."

"And probably from a pretty high level inside, from the sound of it," said Gideon.

Alec grimaced.

"It looks as though I should have said a hundred and twenty-five were involved," he murmured wryly. "I was forgetting Sir Reginald and me."

The lift stopped, and in a grim, tense silence they stepped out of it together and strode down empty, silent corridors to a door labelled, rather strangely:

TARGET EIGHTY
OPERATIONS CENTRE
Commander: W. Warburton
POSITIVELY NO ADMISSION EXCEPT TO
AUTHORISED PERSONNEL

"Target Eighty?" wondered Gideon. Then he realised. That must have been the name for the whole raid operation, probably suggested by the claim he had made in his original report: that it would eradicate, in one fell swoop, the gangs responsible for eighty per cent of London crime. It was ironic, really. Such excessive caution had been used over the raid that even its codename hadn't been whispered outside the seventh floor. And yet the net result had been the most devastatingly total leak in police history. There was a lesson there somewhere, but he couldn't think what.

Still grimly silent, he followed Hobbs into the operations room. The place had a Marie Celeste air – as though it had been not merely deserted, but abruptly abandoned. Very abruptly, from the look of it. Out of the battery of telephones arrayed along a table down one side of the room, two had been left off their hooks; the receiver of one of them was still emitting a faint, bleeping protest. There were three plates of half-eaten sandwiches in sight, and sundry cartons of cold, congealing coffee. One carton had been knocked on its side, probably by the sleeve of someone leaving in a hurry. Papers for a yard around it were stained and sticky.

"What on earth happened here?" asked Gideon.

"The night staff received two shocks in quick succession," Hobbs said. "Me telling them to pack up and go home, and Scott-Marle telling them they might all find themselves suspended pending a full inquiry. A bit drastic – but Scott-Marle and I were feeling pretty shell-shocked ourselves. That call from the supergrass knocked us for six, as you can well imagine."

"Who did he actually call?"

"The Chief Superintendent on night duty. He immediately telephoned Warburton at his home. Warburton rang me. I rang Sir Reginald – and the three of us came straight here. Sir Reginald took Warburton aside. I don't know what they said to each other, but Warburton turned right round and went home. Scott-Marle told me that the whole operation was obviously washed up, and that he was going to close it down. It wasn't until the night staff had gone that he came out with the idea of calling on you."

Gideon frowned round him at the deserted room, noticing particularly the maps and charts that lined the walls, detailing the complex ramifications of Target Eighty. They showed that there were policemen on watch in doorways and stake-outs all over London, keeping various aspects of the Big Three's organisations under surveillance. And, of course, there was a concentration of watchers keeping an eye on the movements of the Big Three themselves. The operations room must have been receiving an all-night flood of reports from these men, some by telephone, some by radio. (A second table, as long as the one with the telephones, was a radio reception centre.) What had happened when it was all so dramatically shut down? Had all these watchers been left reporting dazedly to dead lines?

Alec noticed Gideon's puzzled look, and answered his unspoken question.

"Scott-Marle told me to contact all the men on surveillance duty that I could reach, and give them the same message: 'It's all off – pack it in'," he said. "His theory is that if everyone connected with Target Eighty is told the whole thing's abandoned, then whoever leaked the details of the raid *will be bound to leak the fact that it's now called off.* If he does it straight away – there's no guarantee, of course, that he won't wait till morning – then Mayne, Kemp and Salvados will relax, and be sitting ducks for you."

Gideon nodded, rather dourly. That made a lot of sense, he supposed, but he couldn't help feeling dubious. If the stake-outs were all abandoned now, and the whole complex machinery of surveillance had been abruptly dismantled, it meant that *his* men would be operating completely in the dark – hoping that their quarries hadn't been tipped off, or smelt a rat and done a bunk, during the hours that would have to elapse before he could mount his own raid.

One more item worried him.

"Surely, by abandoning Target Eighty so abruptly, you're giving away the fact that we know about the leak?" he said. "Doesn't that put your supergrass's head on the block? Who is he, by the way?"

"One Rene Renalto," Hobbs told him. "Shifty mobster, Barry Mayne's right hand man. I reckon he aims to take over as London's top villain himself once the Big Three are out of the way, and thinks we'll be willing to turn a blind eye to his activities because he's so obligingly grassed on everyone else's. He's wrong about that, of course. But as long as he's risking a knife in the back on our behalf, it would be unkind to disillusion him."

"Very," grunted Gideon. He hated the idea of coppers buttering up slimy supergrasses, but was far too shrewd not to realise its great, even crucial importance in modern policing. "Let's hope he doesn't wind up with a knife in his back tonight!"

He walked across to the long table with the phones, and sat down heavily behind one of them. "This all right to use?" he asked.

Hobbs nodded. "They've installed a battery of electronic

safeguards on this floor. Whatever caused that leak, it wasn't bugging or phone-tapping."

Gideon stared at the phone for a couple of seconds before picking up the receiver, collecting his thoughts. Not that they needed much collecting. He had decided, back in the car, whom he would call on for this very special raid: three chief detective superintendents who had worked with him for so many years that they were not so much colleagues as lifelong friends – Riddell, Honiwell and Lemaitre.

Tom Riddell was the obvious choice to tackle the smooth, social-climbing drugs king, Jeremy Kemp. For a year or more, Tom had been collecting evidence against Kemp, and in Gideon's opinion, it had been a major blunder not to include him in the Target Eighty team. Probably the reason was Riddell's nerves. A large man, once as formidable and commanding as Gideon himself, Riddell had thinned startlingly and was now gaunt and haggard, with "nervous tension" written all over him. A couple of years before, framed by planted evidence and subject to a police inquiry, he had suffered what amounted to a breakdown and had gone missing from his home for two days. It had taken a major confrontation between Gideon and Scott-Marle to stop him being suspended outright. But Gideon's confidence had proved more than justified. Before the end of his "disappearance", Riddell had not only dramatically recovered from his breakdown: he had cornered and arrested the man who had framed him, Sid Stannet, one of the biggest vice racketeers in London.* There was no doubt about it. Tom was still a good copper, one of the best in the force; and taking part in a history-making raid like this might be just the boost he needed to put him back on the road to being his old self.

*If* his nerves didn't crack, of course . . .

Gideon decided that he had no time to worry about "ifs" like that. Riddell needed a break, and he needed Riddell. That was all there was to it. He dialled Tom's number, and

* *Gideon's Law.*

the next moment, the telephone was ringing in the semi-detached in Wimbledon where the Chief Detective Superintendent now lived. There was a long pause, and then Vi, Tom's little bird-like wife, answered, with a high-pitched "Hullo" that resembled a startled cheep.

"Hullo, Vi," said Gideon. "This is George. Listen. Get Tom to come down to the Yard as soon as possible, will you? By one a.m. at the latest."

The cheep became hoarser, higher.

"He's not in any trouble, is he?"

Memories of the fraught Stannet affair obviously came flooding back to her.

"No trouble," Gideon assured her. "But don't expect him back before breakfast. And by that time, he'll be needing a big one – sausage, bacon and eggs, I shouldn't wonder. It's going to be quite a night – "

Vi was beginning to protest that she hadn't anything but muesli in the house when Riddell himself took over the phone.

Gideon didn't mince his words.

"Listen, Tom. You've probably heard rumours that a big raid was pending. Well, for reasons I won't go into, it's been brought forward to tonight. I'm in charge, and I want you to take over the part of the operation aimed at Kemp and the whole drugs ring."

"Kemp!" Gideon could almost hear Riddell's start. "But I was taken off that case months ago."

"Well, you're back on it now with a vengeance," Gideon told him. "Your orders are to lead a raid on Kemp and arrest him personally. You can take as many men as you need. We'll be assembling half the force before the night's out."

"But, George – "

"No buts, Tom. It's diabolically short notice, I know. And I can't guarantee that Kemp and his henchmen won't be to some degree prepared. Things could become very hairy. But if you can pull it off, it'll be your biggest success since Stannet – probably the biggest of your career. Think you're up to it?"

"Up to it!" said Riddell. "Just try to keep me away!"

He sounded so enthusiastic that Gideon rang off, chuckling. That sounded just like the old Tom, he thought.

He wasn't to know that at the other end, Riddell was trembling so violently that it was all he could do to replace the receiver.

* * *

There was nothing tense about Gideon's next call. It was to Chief Detective Superintendent Matt Honiwell, one of the most comfortable, reassuring personalities in the C.I.D. A large man with a mop of curly brown hair, Matt had a warm friendliness about him that made women automatically think of him as cuddly. This wasn't just a pose. Matt did in fact have a sympathetic nature: too much of one for a copper at times. He tended to get involved with people, and could easily become over-involved – haunted and harassed by the human problems inevitable in so much police work. There was another side to him, though. With hardened criminals no one could be harder; and few men had a better record at making major arrests. Gideon had earmarked him for tackling the bank raid master-minder, Arturo Salvados, who would probably be the most elusive of the Big Three.

He repeated to Matt most of what he'd said to Riddell, including the warning that it could be a hairy night. Typically, Honiwell started to try and reassure *him*.

"Ah, well. Between us, we've been through so many hairy nights it's a wonder we don't have beards down to our ankles! I reckon we could survive one more, don't you?"

"With luck," Gideon grinned. "See you soon, then. Before one, please."

The grin faded before he dialled the next number. He had decided that the man to tackle the toughest target, the gangster Barry Mayne, was his oldest associate in the force: Lemaitre. Lem, a lanky Cockney with a sharp tongue and an agile brain to match, was Chief Detective Superintendent in charge of one of the roughest manors in north London. He and Gideon had once been detective sergeants together, and at that time had been hot rivals, showing equal promise. Lemaitre's subsequent career had been hindered by two things: his lack of respect for authority and his compulsive habit of jumping to conclusions. Many a time, Gideon had been forced to rescue him from the consequences of making wrongful arrests. There would be no risk of that happening tonight, though: the raid was bound to be backed by watertight evidence against all the villains, laboriously collected over months. What was wanted was quick, decisive action – and that had always been Lem's forte.

Gideon was not too happy about ringing him, for the simplest of reasons: Lem was working all-out on a harrowing case, and liable to be dog-tired. He was in charge of the inquiry into the Stocking Strangler – a murdering rapist who had claimed five victims in just nine weeks, all within Lem's manor, and mostly in one district of it: Warnham Green. The inquiry hadn't been going well; Lem was having to battle with hostile reporters and TV interviewers almost every night – he had been on the TV news that very evening, assuring the nation for the thousandth time not to panic because an arrest was imminent. Poor Lem. It was a shame to disturb him. But Gideon guessed he'd never be forgiven if he left him out of a major exercise like this . . .

Lemaitre came on the phone instantly, suggesting that he hadn't yet gone to bed. If he was desperately tired, he didn't sound it. His voice was as cheerful as ever. His agile brain was obviously wide awake, too.

Once Gideon had explained that the raid was on tonight and that he was in charge of it, Lem had no trouble guessing the rest.

"So there's been a ruddy leak or something, the whole caper's blown up in the Big Brass's faces, and they're calling on you, as per usual, to get 'em out of the mess! You're a born muggins, Gee Gee. You know that, don't you?"

Anyone else talking to Gideon like that would have been silenced by an earth-shattering roar. But Gideon had long accepted that nothing would ever stop Lem being Lem. He just growled: "Never mind what I am. Just see that you get yourself round here sharpish – at the latest, by one! Oh – and Lem."

"Yep?"

"I ought to warn you. I'm putting you in charge of the Barry Mayne part of the raid. And since, as you've guessed, there *has* been a leak – "

Lem finished the sentence for him.

" – Barry's boys could be waiting for us, and trigger-happy into the bargain. Not to worry, Gee Gee. Even a shoot out will seem a picnic after nine weeks on the bleeding Stocking Strangler. And I've been wanting to take a crack at Barry for years. You know me. Always did have an eye for the Mayne chance . . ."

Lemaitre paused, expecting Gideon to laugh, or at least chuckle. Instead there was as total a silence as if the line had gone dead.

Gideon had, in fact, stopped listening to him. All his attention was concentrated on Alec Hobbs, who was standing beside him, grim-faced, obviously the bearer of bad news.

With a brief, "See you at one, then," to Lem, he slammed down the receiver, and said to Alec:

"What's happened? Don't tell me another call's come from that supergrass."

"No one will ever hear from Rene Renalto again, I'm afraid," Alec told him. "He's just this minute been found, in his own garage drive, hunched over the wheel of his car – with exactly what we predicted, George: a knife in his back. I'd guess the choice of weapon was symbolic – to show what the Big Three thought he'd done to *them*."

Gideon nodded. His face was as grim as Alec's now.

"So they know *we* know about the leak. Let's hope to God that's all they've discovered – or guessed," he said. He had an uncomfortable feeling that another of his predictions was going to prove all too true.

They *were* in for a hairy night . . .

# 3 Midnight People

With that, Gideon and Hobbs got down to work in earnest. Soon, from that derelict-looking operations room on the seventh floor of the Yard, orders went out which caused lights to spring on in hundreds of policemen's homes all over London, as men of all ranks – superintendents, inspectors, sergeants, constables, mostly C.I.D. but a few from Uniform – received the summons to report to the Yard and be ready to join a top-secret emergency operation. No one was told what the operation was. But they all gathered that it was something big – very big. Hearts were beating fast. Overcoats were being scrambled into with feverish haste. Cups of coffee, hurriedly made by loved ones, were being downed at a gulp, choked over, or left untouched as hundreds of nearly simultaneous dashes were made through hundreds of different front doors, out into the pitiless downpour of that sodden October night.

Also out and about during the rain were three people, none of them remotely connected with the police or the impending raid, who were nevertheless destined to play a major role in the dramas of the night.

No one would have been more surprised to hear that than the first of them, Henry Jones. Henry had never played a major role in anything throughout his twenty-four years of life – except in his daydreams. He had played a starring part in those all right, and always the same part: stepping out of the darkness, sometimes with a dazzling Roger Moore smile, sometimes with a threatening Charles Bronson stare, just in time to rescue a girl from the clutches of some attacking yobbo – or yobbo gang. In his dreams, Henry could knock out six toughs as easily as one. As a matter of fact, he probably could have seen off a gang quite easily in real life. He was tall and powerfully built. With his fair hair and rather rugged features, he should have been quite attractive to the opposite sex. But his tragic history – his father had died when he was seven, and his mother had promptly gone off with a lover, leaving him to be taken into care – had given him psychological scars that would not heal. He often gave the impression of being a mental defective, although in fact, when his brain power wasn't seeping away into fantasies or his confidence being gnawed at by despair, he could be quite sharp and shrewd. Such moments, though, were rare. For the most part, bumbling and shy, he spent his life drifting from place to place and job to job, and these days from job centre to job centre. He kept himself to himself so much that he had no friends or even acquaintances. He really came to life only long after dark, in his own company, when he roamed the streets looking for an opportunity to fulfil that ever-recurring daydream: to step out of the night and be a hero to some desperate girl.

There was a crazy logic behind the dream. If a girl was desperately grateful to him – best of all, if she actually owed him her life – then surely there should be no barrier between them. The heavy, numbing feeling that all women hated, rejected, despised him would go. He would be a hero to her, wouldn't he? She'd be bound to kiss him, fondle him, maybe even want to sleep –

At that thought, floods of adrenalin poured into Henry's stomach, and it felt as though he no longer had a brain in his head; nothing but a seething skullful of churning sexual fantasies. Just dreams, of course – but every one of those dreams could become reality, he knew, if only he could do his rescuing act. Just once. Flushed and quivering, he stepped out of a shop doorway into the streaming rain as exultantly as Gene Kelly about to do his classic "Singing in the Rain" routine, and set off briskly down Northcote Road, a grim street of terrace houses not far from Warnham Green police station.

A policeman on duty nearby watched him curiously as he went. Henry was known to the local bobbies quite well: he had been pulled in twice for suspicious loitering and once for being a Peeping Tom. (A couple had been making rather violent love, and he had mistaken the girl's gasps and groans for strangled cries for help.) On none of these occasions had he explained what he was doing roaming the streets in the small hours; he had muttered something about finding it difficult to sleep and liking to take walks.

He had noticed the very odd look the policeman gave him, but thought nothing of it. He was never surprised to find himself being hated and despised. He didn't read the papers or watch much TV, and had no idea that he was a natural suspect in the case of the Stocking Strangler, who was currently terrorising that very neighbourhood.

And was, in fact, at that precise moment, turning his blue-black Metro into the further end of Northcote Road, not a hundred yards from where Henry Jones was striding.

* * *

The policeman hardly even glanced up as the Metro swept past him. There was nothing remotely suspicious about the pleasant-looking young man behind the wheel. Clive Exton was an expert at not arousing suspicions, least of all police ones. His work behind the counter at a travel bureau had given him a lot of practice at dealing with people smoothly, and his smiling, assured persona rarely cracked, even when the darkest killer urges were developing behind it.

He was, for instance, smiling now at everyone and everything – at the policeman, at the streaming rain, and at the curious figure of Henry Jones, striding along lost in his daydreams and utterly impervious to the rain.

"Poor soul. Obviously half mental," he told himself. "Be lucky not to be pulled in as a Strangler suspect."

The thought amused Clive Exton. His smile grew. He started chuckling to himself, but then stopped abruptly. When he was alone, his chuckles sometimes had a habit of getting out of control, turning into silly giggles that could go on for hours. He didn't understand why that happened, and didn't like it when it did. He suddenly realised that he had slowed down to walking pace. Hell, that was stupid. Any moment the cop would think he was kerb-crawling. He hurriedly stepped up his speed to thirty, and turned a corner into Northcote Square.

He was still smiling, still calm and assured, as he glanced about, looking out for a solitary walking girl. There weren't many around these nights, because of the reign of terror that he himself had created.

However, there were bound to be one or two about. There were always one or two, especially around midnight, when there were still lights in the bedroom windows of most houses, still plenty of cars and even lorries roaring by, and they thought they were relatively safe.

Sure enough, a few seconds later, Clive spotted a girl walking quickly across the straggly patch of grass in the centre of the square. In the cold, orangey light of the square's lamps, she looked young and pretty, though her face was largely hidden by the plastic mackintosh turned up round her cheeks. All he could really see of her was a mass of long, chestnut hair, totally unprotected against the rain, and large, dark eyes staring straight ahead of her.

She seemed lonely and desperate, Clive thought. He'd be doing her a favour, sending her out of the world for good.

The simplest approach would have been to stop the car, and ask her if she'd like a lift. He could even have warned her that the streets weren't safe with the Strangler about. But Clive Exton didn't operate in that way. His method was always to leave the car parked somewhere, and follow his victim on foot, pouncing on her as soon as they reached some sufficiently dark and deserted spot. Almost any dark spot would do, because his technique was swift and involved little or no noise. First he donned a stocking as a mask, to make sure his victim didn't spot his features – which could be dangerous if he was interrupted before he completed the kill. On reaching the girl, he would whip a second stocking out of his pocket and twist it round her neck until she lost consciousness; rape her while she was weak, gasping and powerless to resist, and finally pick up the stocking again and complete the strangulation. The whole terrible business rarely took him more than eight or nine minutes. Within a quarter of an hour at the most, he was usually back in his car, driving away, smiling and humming to himself – and finding it harder than ever to repress those giggles at the thought of how easy it had all been . . .

The girl had now reached the end of the strip of grass. And suddenly she was playing right into his hands, crossing the road and heading towards a dark alley leading off between a bank and a closed and shuttered bingo hall.

Excitement mounting inside him, belying his cool, confident air, Clive parked the car on the far side of the square; felt in his left-hand trouser pocket to make sure that the two stockings were there, and then stepped out into the torrential rain. He was glad about that rain. It would drown the sound of his footsteps as he crept along behind the girl, and would get into her eyes if she tried to peer behind her. The only trouble was that it drenched his clothes. The sweater, T-shirt and jeans that he was wearing felt in seconds like clammy rags, and his socks squelched inside his shoes as he padded softly into the mouth of the alley. It wasn't completely dark in there; the thick low rainclouds above were bright orange in the reflected glow from the thousands of London street lamps, and sent enough light back downwards for him to be able to see the girl ahead very clearly.

She was walking quickly, glancing neither right nor left, let alone behind her. That was strange, he thought. Surely any girl in her right mind would be throwing fearful glances behind her in a dark spot like this. Hadn't she *heard* about the Stocking Strangler?

* * *

Judy Moss certainly had heard about the Stocking Strangler, but had very little room in her thoughts for him at that moment. Clive Exton's guesses about her had been uncannily accurate. She *was* feeling lonely and desperate – more so than at any other time in her life.

Judy was one of those girls who are one hundred per cent dependent on men, and had been one hundred per cent lost since her boy friend, Stan, had packed up with her, which he had done on the very eve of her twenty-first birthday, just a fortnight before.

She had been living with Stan at his flat, really a dowdy maisonette, which was situated just off this square. When the row had started, Stan had turned vicious and began sneering at her – a side of him Judy had never dreamed existed before. Stunned, unbelieving, she had grabbed all the belongings that she could lay her hands on, and stormed out through the front door. On the very doorstep, she turned back, hoping he'd come, or at least call, after her. But all he did was savagely slam the bolts on the door behind her.

Judy had rushed home to her parents, who had just retired from running a small newsagent's business, and lived on the other side of Warnham Green. But Mr. and Mrs. Moss were a straitlaced couple, strict Baptists both of them, and highly disapproved of their daughter "living in sin". Life at home throughout the past two weeks had alternated between freezing silences and flaming rows. Judy couldn't stand it, and had taken to long night-time walks to think things out and "find herself", as she rather grandly put it. "Well, please God the Stocking Strangler doesn't find you first," Mrs. Moss had told her, over and over again. Judy had taken some notice of the warning. Up till now she'd been back home well before eleven. But tonight she had had a very severe shock. All this while, she had been nursing the hope that she and Stan would make it up, and in a day or two, she would go back. An hour or so before, she had finally summoned up the courage to revisit the maisonette. All her knocking and ringing had produced no reply, but she still had a spare key in her handbag, and had opened the front door and gone in. Apart from everything else, she had a lot of bits and pieces she wanted to collect, and she started roaming round, looking for them.

It wasn't long before she found a lot of bits and pieces that weren't hers – or Stan's – and the terrible truth dawned on her that during the past two weeks, another girl had moved in and taken her place.

There was no sign of Stan or the other girl now, and suddenly Judy worked out why. Stan was a sales rep, and his company – Warmelite Double Glazing – had their big annual sales conference in Brighton this week. He liked to go down there with a girl. Last year she had gone with him; it had been the start of their romance. Now it looked as though he was starting off with the other girl, whoever she was, in the same way.

Well, good luck to her, that was all Judy could say. Good luck to her, and good riddance to him . . .

Forgetting about her bits and pieces – all she wanted was to be gone out of the place at all possible speed – she rushed out of the maisonette, slamming the door behind her and striding out into the night as though all the devils in hell were after her.

By the time she reached Northcote Square, she was a little calmer, and her ferocious stride had slackened to a quick walk; but her eyes were still wide and staring, and her thoughts a dark mixture of anger, resentment, bleakness and despair. As she crossed the road and turned into the alley, she did, for a moment, remember the Strangler, and the folly of being out alone, in this of all areas, so late. But her bitterness slashed through all sense of caution. What the hell did it matter what happened to her now?

It was at that moment that she heard a soft, squelchy step behind her. *Right* behind her . . .

She spun round, and saw a stocking-masked face so close that she could feel the man's breath on her cheeks. Cold, clammy breath, filtered through the mass of sodden stocking. Not that she had time to feel anything for more than a micro-second. In a flash, a second stocking was whipped round her neck, and would have cut off all possibility of her making a sound – if the man's fingers hadn't been wet from the streaming rain. As it was, the stocking slipped and slithered in his grasp, and Judy, stunned and shaken though she was, managed to kick, struggle – and give out one half-choked scream.

It wasn't much of a scream, and didn't carry far; but it did reach the ears of one man walking round the square, at the end of the alley.

It wasn't surprising that he heard it, because he had been listening for such a sound for just about all his life.

A girl, thought Henry Jones. A girl in desperate trouble, fighting for her life! Hardly able to believe his luck, he sprinted across the pavement of the square and dived into the mouth of the alley.

# 4 A Big Case?

Two miles west of Warnham Green, in Hammersmith, exactly the same midnight downpour was falling – and two more people were travelling through it, headed for high drama, although neither of them had the slightest inkling that anything unusual was going to happen.

Detective Constable Brian Fullerton was not one of the men selected to take part in the impending raid. He would have been difficult to contact, in any case. He and his wife Maggie had been spending the evening having dinner with friends, and were now rather sleepily driving home to Ovaltine, biscuits and bed. They had had a little altercation a few minutes earlier. Their friends, Dave and Julie, a couple whom the Fullertons had known for years, were now very much wealthier than they were. Dave, who was almost exactly Brian's age – thirty-three – had just been appointed advertising manager of his firm, and although he hadn't been unkind enough to mention the salary he was getting, it was obviously far, far beyond a detective constable's pay. Julie had asked rather smugly when Brian would be getting promoted, and the remark was still rankling with Maggie when they had started the drive home.

"Well – when *are* you getting promoted?" she had snapped at her husband, only to receive the reply she always got – a dreamy smile, a shrug and a murmured: "When I get the man I'm after, darling. And it won't be just a stripe I'll be given then. I'll have bought myself a ticket to the top."

Maggie groaned. There were times when she hated that dreamy smile of Brian's. Whoever heard of a dreamer getting anywhere in the police force?

"And just how long have you been after him now?" she demanded. "It's two years to my certain knowledge. It could even be three! If only you'd – "

She broke off. She knew it was no good expecting him to give up the biggest thing in his life: the secret file of evidence he had been painstakingly collecting against a major criminal – someone so big he had never even told *her* his name . . .

All she knew for certain was that the criminal was a very rich and prominent person, and that no one had the slightest suspicion that he *was* a criminal – except Brian, who had happened to see something or someone suspicious when he had been driving past the criminal's house in a police Panda.

Laughed at when he had tried to report the incident, Brian had become obstinate. Since then, he had spent nights on end keeping a lone watch on that house, noting down all the callers, and surreptitiously questioning neighbours. He had to be very careful, he told Maggie. If his quarry ever suspected *him*, he'd be as good as dead, from that moment.

In his day-to-day work Brian was a pretty mediocre policeman, and knew it. But once he got home, and to work on that file of evidence, he became a changed man – excited, eyes gleaming, the criminologist of the century! There were times when he infected her with his excitement; when she believed that he *was* on to something – as well as someone – big. But there were just as many occasions when she wondered whether he was wasting his time, and all his chances of promotion, on a crazy fantasy.

He was looking at her now, out of the corners of those dreamy eyes.

"Trust me, pet. I know what I'm doing," he whispered.

Maggie was about to snap back that it was time his superiors knew what he was doing too. Not that Detective Sergeant at Hammersmith police station who was always so rude to him. Someone high up, like Chief Detective Superintendent Honiwell. He'd commended Brian in the past for the work he did on one case. She was sure *he'd* listen –

But she changed her mind about arguing any more tonight. It was late. They'd both had a long day, followed by an exasperating evening. Better to let it go and get to bed.

They had arrived outside their home now: No. 184 in a long row of 1920s terraced houses. It wasn't bad, as old terraced houses went, Maggie told herself. It had been modernised throughout, brightly painted, fully double-glazed – and Brian, in one of his less dreamy moods, had created a masterpiece out of the miniature front garden: a grotto of rock plants surrounding a little pool, in which swam three large goldfish. A house to be proud of, she'd always thought. But Dave and Julie had spent half the night talking about the house they were planning to move to on a luxury estate, and of course it couldn't be compared with anything like that.

Maggie peered at it sadly – not that much could be seen of it from the car tonight. Water was streaming down the windscreen as though the world had turned into a gargantuan car wash.

"Good job we brought our umbrell – " she was beginning when suddenly something very odd happened. The moment he'd stopped the car, Brian turned and clutched her arm. Fiercely.

"Look hard, pet. At the front door," he whispered. "Do you see what I see?"

Maggie did look hard – but all she could make out was a square of light, distorted by the myriad raindrops beading the car window.

"There's a light in the hall – but then we always leave one on, because of – "

She broke off, her heart pounding as she suddenly realised what he meant. The square of light was twice the size of the glass pane in the front door. To let out that much light, the door *itself* would have to be open. Someone must have smashed the lock, broken in –

Things happened fast, after that. So fast that it was hard for Maggie to take them in.

One moment Brian was beside her. The next, he'd breathed a soft "Stay here – and don't move until I shout." The next, he had opened the door on his side of the car, and crept out on to the road. The next, he was round the car.

Maggie opened the door on her side, and had a clear view of Brian sneaking up the little path past his wonder of a mini-garden and reaching his own doorstep. The front door was ajar, as she'd guessed – in fact, it was about three-quarters open. Brian kicked it back on its hinges, and strode inside.

It must have been less than a second after that when she heard him shout: "Stop! I warn you, I'm a policeman – "

Then came the most terrible moment of Maggie's life. Two shots rang out, one straight after the other. As sick and shaky as though the bullets had ploughed into her own body, she staggered out of the car and was more than half-way across the garden when she heard three more sounds, equally ominous. A low groan. The thud of a body falling – and almost simultaneously, the crash of the kitchen door slamming at the back of the house, as someone made a frantic getaway.

Maggie rushed through the front door, and was suddenly giving a low groan herself. She had almost stumbled over the body of Brian, lying in the doorway of the little room he called his "study". There was blood everywhere, and he was staring lifelessly at the ceiling, obviously completely unconscious. But thank God, he was still breathing. Loudly, in fact – with a curious sound that was half-way between choking and snoring.

She went down on her knees beside him, terrified to touch him in case she made his injuries worse. It was difficult to see through the tears which were flooding her eyes, but it looked as though one bullet had hit him on the edge of the chest, near his right shoulder, and the other one had badly grazed his right temple.

Maggie blinked furiously and wiped her eyes. One thing more she could see now, very clearly. The study had been ransacked. The drawer where he kept his all-important file had been yanked from the desk and was lying on the floor, and the file itself had gone.

So Brian *was* on to Someone Big; and that Someone Big had found out about it. That thought kept running through Maggie's mind as she rushed to the phone in the hall, and dialled 999.

When the operator asked her which service she wanted, police, ambulance or fire brigade, she answered Ambulance, and then told the ambulance people that a terrible accident had happened. She decided against ringing the police station. She didn't want Brian's superiors to be mixed up in this too soon. They were stupid small-fry and probably wouldn't even believe her story. The only thing to do was to go above their heads, to –

Desperately Maggie flicked through the pad of telephone numbers kept by the phone. When Brian had worked on that case with Chief Detective Superintendent Matt Honiwell, Matt had given him his private number to contact in case of emergencies. After some frenzied flicking – made all the harder because her hand was shaking so much that she could scarcely hold the pad – Maggie found the number, and dialled it frantically.

She just caught Matt Honiwell in time. The phone rang in the hall of his cosy Bayswater flat when he was heaving on the second of a pair of Wellington boots, preparatory to going out into the downpour in answer to Gideon's summons.

It was alarmingly close to one, and it never paid to keep George waiting, so Matt wasn't too pleased to be telephoned at that moment. But being Matt, he somehow managed to keep his voice calm and friendly.

"Mrs. Fullerton? Ah, yes. I remember your husband well," he lied.

Fullerton? Brian Fullerton? Ah, yes. Suddenly he *did* remember him. A very odd detective constable. Dreamy. Looked more like an artist than a copper. But he had been brighter than he looked – had, in fact, spotted a clue that everyone had missed . . .

He had no time to do any more remembering. Maggie Fullerton was suddenly filling his head with a torrent of words, describing the arrival home, the open front door, the shots –

"Shots?" yelled Honiwell. "How is Brian?"

It was typical of him to use the constable's Christian name.

Maggie stammered out that there was blood all over him, and struggled to describe his wounds.

"Have you rung the police station? Sent for an ambulance?"

"An ambulance, yes. But I – I haven't called Hammersmith police station, where Brian works. I decided to ring you instead."

Matt ran a hand through his mass of curly hair.

"Nice of you to think of me," he said mildly. "But *why*?"

Maggie's reply was only just coherent.

"You're the only one who can help. This case – it's too big for the others."

"Too big?"

Matt was still battling to grasp the situation when something happened that was all too easy to understand. Maggie suddenly shouted: "Oh – my God! Brian – he's – he's *stopped breathing* – "

And she rushed away from the phone in the direction of the study, leaving the receiver swinging on its flex. Matt heard dull thuds as it banged against the wall in the Fullertons' hall, and terrible background sounds of Maggie sobbing and calling to her husband. Who did not, of course, reply. Who might never be replying to anything she said again . . .

That was enough for Matt. He hung up the phone, deeply troubled – even haunted – by what he had heard. He dialled Hammersmith police station, a number which he knew by heart; obtained the Fullertons' address (which Maggie had forgotten to give him) and decided to get over there straight away.

Netta, the woman he had lived with for twenty years and who was now at last his wife, stood watching him worriedly.

"Matt. Don't forget George wants you at the Yard."

"This is more urgent," said Honiwell. "A detective constable's been shot. In his own home. May be lying dead. For some reason, his wife rang me."

He headed for the door, calling over his shoulder:

"Ring George, will you? He's in a special ops room on the seventh floor, I think. Tell him I'll be along as soon as I can."

Then he was gone, leaving Netta staring at the phone. And wondering how on earth to tell the Commander of the C.I.D. that the man he had ordered to report sharp at one would be "along as soon as he could".

* * *

At that moment, in a little semi-detached in Wimbledon, the wife of another of Gideon's men was having much more serious worries.

Vi Riddell knew every one of Tom's moods like the back of her hand; and she knew the one he was in now painfully well. He was behaving almost exactly as he had done before his near-breakdown a couple of years ago.

When Gideon had asked Riddell if he felt up to playing a leading part in the raid, he had shouted: "Up to it? Try to keep me out of it!"

But he had hung up the receiver trembling from head to foot, and for several minutes had sat, slumped in a chair in his pyjamas and dressing-gown, shaking like a shell-shock victim.

Vi had hurried into the kitchen and rushed him a cup of tea, very hot, very sweet and very strong. At least that had got him back on his feet, but Vi didn't like the way he strode up to the bedroom without a smile or a word of thanks, and slammed the door behind him.

He had emerged fully dressed, and putting on his breezy act again.

"Cheer up, Vi. This isn't a funeral. Not mine, at all events, though it could be Jeremy Kemp's. I'm off to arrest him. Part of a mammoth raid on the Big Three and all their works. Could be the biggest break I've ever had. Is that the time? I must go. As the old song says, night, night, sweetheart, see you in the morning . . ."

He gave her a peck of a kiss, and the next moment, was through the front door, and getting the car out of the garage, whistling in the streaming rain.

Vi was almost sobbing as she watched him drive away. That over-brightness of Tom's was the worst sign of all. It meant that he was liable to crack at any moment. And he was facing one of the biggest challenges of his life . . .

For several seconds, she hovered by the phone, half-inclined to ring Gideon and warn him. She decided against it, of course. Tom would never forgive her if she spoilt the night of his big break. All she could hope and pray was that it wasn't the night of his big breakdown . . .

* * *

Over in north London, Gideon's third raid-leader, the spry Lemaitre, was looking at himself in the mirror and rubbing Brylcreem into his now rather sparse black hair. There was a broad grin on his face, if anything could be described as broad about his sharp, almost spiv-like features.

"Better look my best for Gee Gee's big bonanza," he said to his French wife, who had once been a bubble-dancer in night clubs, and still went by her 1950s stage name, Fifi. She folded him a freshly ironed handkerchief for the breast-pocket of his natty, dazzlingly pin-striped suit.

He patted it briskly into place, and blew a kiss at her, still grinning. He had been dog tired when he had come home tonight, but was now in a positively ebullient mood, already making plans for the raid on Barry Mayne, and looking forward to a night of action that would show George Gideon what old Lem was made of, once and for all.

There was another reason for Lemaitre's cheerfulness. After the long weeks of fruitless, frustrating battling with the case of the Stocking Strangler, it was a profound relief to be tackling something different, and to be in a situation where he could win.

"Just think of it!" he said aloud, partly to Fifi but mostly to himself. "A whole bleeding night – without hearing a word from anybody about the Stocking Strangler!"

That had always been Lem's trouble – jumping to conclusions.

# 5 The Big Switch

At the very moment when Lemaitre was telling himself that he would have a Strangler-free night, in the dark alley off Northcote Square, Judy Moss was being choked into unconsciousness by the stocking in Clive Exton's hands.

He had finished that part of the operation, and she was out cold, a dead weight against his body, when he heard heavy footsteps – and equally heavy breathing – behind him in the darkness. It wasn't that Henry Jones was out of breath. It was just that the excitement of being a rescuing hero at last was having a choking effect on him, too.

By the strange, ghostly reflected light from the orangey London sky, Henry could see clearly that there was a man in a stocking mask ahead of him, and a limp, lifeless girl in his arms. It never occurred to him to take cover or use caution. His only fear was that he might be arriving too late; that the girl might already be dead. Rage and anxiety mingled with his excitement to create an explosive mixture, and he hurled himself at the Strangler, his fists flying, roaring almost like an animal in his fury.

Clive Exton never for a moment lost his cool.

He tossed Judy aside as lightly as though she was a rubber dummy filled only with air, and sidestepped as nimbly as a matador. Jones charged past him as clumsily and mindlessly as any bull. And before he could recover himself or turn back, Henry found himself being seized by the back of his T-shirt and propelled, with a strange, cold, maniacal force, towards the side of the alley. A high wall came looming up through the streaming rain, which was bouncing off it as though the very bricks were hissing and spitting at him. The wall was covered with slimy pigeon-droppings and white graffiti. One word had been scrawled in such large letters that it could be read even in this dim light: KILL. The letters swam towards Henry, blurring and whirling as he struggled desperately to free himself from the maniac's grip, then finally exploding into blood-red streaks and stars as the top of his head crashed against the wall, and everything dissolved into a kaleidoscope of blinding colour, numbing pain and finally all-engulfing darkness.

Clive Exton remained totally calm as he stared down at the second person he had reduced to unconsciousness that night. His heart wasn't beating even a fraction above its normal rate. The only trouble was that he was having to fight hard to suppress that wretched giggling as he suddenly realised what a marvellous hand Fate had dealt him.

He recognised the stranger as the barmy-looking character he had seen from his car, walking along Northcote Road. He had thought at the time that he would make a good Strangler suspect. Now he noticed that he was rather similar to him in height, if not in build, and happened to be wearing the same sort of clothes – just a dark T-shirt and jeans. It was true that his own clothes were new and expensive, while the stranger's (from what he could see of them) were battered and torn; but what did that matter? Both were in such a soaked and soggy condition that the differences would never be noticed – not, at any rate, by a terrified girl who would remember nothing except maybe a wet T-shirt pressing against her as she fought for her life.

All he had to do was take the stocking off his own head and force it over the stranger's . . . and the girl would automatically assume that the stranger had been her attacker. And since he was so obviously a nut case, the police would automatically make the same assumption – and be thrown off the trail of the real Stocking Strangler for months, perhaps for ever.

"It's perfect!" Exton told himself. "Absolutely perfect!"

And suddenly, to his horror, he heard his own laughter ringing round the alley.

Swallowing hard, he managed to stop it – and immediately set to work. First, he yanked the stocking off his own head; a difficult thing to do, because the wet fabric caught in his mouth and nose and clung to his hair. Then, ringing the stocking out like a wet towel, he bent over the stranger and somehow succeeded in slipping and squelching it over his head. The stocking ripped in several places, but that couldn't be helped. Then he thought of two finishing touches. Clever, they were, in his opinion. He slid the other stocking – the one he used for strangling – into a back pocket of the stranger's jeans. Then, coolly and casually, he lifted the unconscious man's head off the pavement and let it fall. For the story he was going to tell, the stranger needed bruises at the back of the head.

Next he turned his attention to Judy Moss, the victim to whom he hadn't given the slightest thought since he had tossed her aside several minutes before. Kneeling beside her and bending low, he discovered that she was breathing normally; that meant she would soon be returning to consciousness.

He hoped she wouldn't start screaming. If there was one thing he couldn't stand, it was the sound of a woman's screams. It brought back terrible memories of his mother, a neurotic wreck who had never stopped screaming at him, night and day, for year after year –

He closed his eyes to shut out those memories. They only upset him, deep down, and started him shivering all over. He didn't know why, but like that stupid giggling, he wished it didn't happen, and struggled to stop it when it did.

Ah, the girl's eyes were open now. And she wasn't screaming. She was staring up at him dazedly through the gloom.

He tried his best to give her a winning smile, not that she'd be able to see much of it.

In his smoothest travel-agency voice, he murmured:

"How are you feeling? You've been through a terrible

experience, but don't worry. I'm here now, and I'll see that that monster doesn't come near you again."

"Y-you?" Judy Moss tried to speak, but her swollen throat would hardly let her. All she could get out was: "W-who are you?"

Clive told her his name.

"I live near here," he added chattily, "and was just driving through the square when I heard you calling for help. I got out of the car, and came running down this alley, just in time to see you being attacked by this murdering bastard." He nudged Jones's unconscious body with his foot. "He had a stocking or something round your throat, and had pulled it tight. Fortunately, he didn't see me come up behind him. I managed to seize him and yank him backwards. He lost his balance and fell, banging his head on the pavement. Luckily for me," he finished modestly. "Don't suppose I'd have had much chance against him otherwise. Rough stuff's not really my scene."

Judy half-sat up and looked round her. Then she gave a long, shuddering groan that was partly a choke.

"Christ . . . my throat . . ."

"Bound to be sore for a while," Exton told her. "But as long as you can breathe okay, I shouldn't worry too much."

She was beginning to notice him now. In fact, she was staring up at him in wonder. "Thank God you came when you did. I'd have been done for, otherwise. Don't you realise, that's the S-stocking – "

It was as though trying to say the word "Stocking" brought back the full memory of the thing itself tightening round her neck. Suddenly her throat gave up altogether. She couldn't say a word, and looked about to faint again.

Exton put a reassuring arm round her and a reassuring tone into his voice.

"I know who it is all right," he said. "And I'm going to make bloody sure that he never does this to any girl again. Do you think you can stand up? There's a phone kiosk just round the corner in the square. We can ring the police from there – and if we're quick enough, they can come and get him while he's still out cold."

With his help, Judy got to her feet, and walked beside him all the way to the kiosk. She seemed to be leaning on him both physically and mentally.

Being sneered at and rejected for another girl by Stan, threatened with the wrath of God by an icily disapproving father, and finally having the life nearly choked out of her by a maniac from the night, had not affected Judy's total dependence on men. Rather it had intensified her need for male reassurance to the point of desperation.

Only a dream man could lead her out of this nightmare of shock, pain and terror. Even the presence of one on the scene magically relieved her feeling of being alone and unprotected in a hell-pit of coldness, loneliness, menace and fear.

A handsome face, she thought Clive had, when she saw it clearly in the brighter light of the square.

Strong . . . sensitive . . . A man to feel so *safe* with, she told herself, as she watched his long, thin fingers dialling 999.

* * *

The moment Exton uttered the words "Stocking Strangler", his call was transferred to the Strangler incidents room which Lemaitre had set up at Warnham Green police station, less than a mile from Northcote Square.

Lemaitre was not there himself, of course. At that moment, in fact, he was just getting his car out of his garage to leave for Scotland Yard. But he had left very clear instructions as to what should happen if ever there seemed to be a genuine chance of catching the Strangler, and the Inspector on night duty, a red-faced, rotund and very excitable man called Dexter, was determined to carry them out to the letter.

"Leave this to us, sir," he told Clive. "You and the lady just stay where you are. On no account go back to the alley. The Strangler might be very dangerous when he comes to. We'll be with you in two or three minutes at the most." His red face almost purple with excitement, he started bellowing orders over his shoulder before he'd even put down the receiver.

Well inside the two or three minutes, police cars began arriving in Northcote Square. Within a few more seconds, Inspector Dexter was leading at least a dozen uniformed men into the mouth of the alley, some carrying torches, all armed with revolvers. Other men were busy cordoning off a big area, including the square, the alley and six surrounding streets. Anyone would have thought that the alley contained an unexploded bomb, instead of a single sprawling unconscious body.

Not that Henry Jones remained unconscious for long. His eyes flickered open when eight or nine torches were trained on his face, and then blinked dazedly down at the armoury of guns levelled at him, one or two of which were jammed against his ribs.

Before he could find his voice, Inspector Dexter barked, with heavy police irony: "Right, lad. Off with that stocking. We've been waiting a long, long time to see your handsome features."

Henry just stared blankly.

"S-stocking?"

He had no idea he was wearing one until the fact was very forcibly brought home to him by two policemen yanking it over and off his head. Before he could recover, the torches were dazzling him again, as though he was being given a third degree.

One policeman whistled.

"Henry Jones!" he said. "So it was Warnham Green's very own Peeping Tom after all."

Still totally bemused, Henry tried a stumbling protest.

"I keep telling you. I'm – I'm not a Peeping Tom."

He was shaken by the sheer intensity of Inspector Dexter's reply.

"More's the pity, Jones. There'd be a lot of girls alive now if all you did was take a squint at their goings-on. I suppose you didn't get enough kicks that way, you murdering brute."

"Murdering – brute?"

For the first time, Henry struggled desperately to remember where he was, and how he had got there. And for the first time, he realised that his head was just an empty echo chamber, in which questions rolled round and round, but there wasn't a single answer. He couldn't remember a thing except – except that he had heard some girl screaming, and gone dashing to her rescue . . .

What had happened? Had he saved her?

Handcuffs had been slapped on him now. A dozen hands were roughly dragging him down the alley towards a parked police car. But he hardly noticed any of this. His bemused, half-concussed brain was still battling with that burning question, and finally managed an answer.

He couldn't have saved her. And there'd been some terrible mistake. They thought *he'd* murdered her.

All this thinking was too much for Henry, in his present state. By the time he was slung into the police car, he had lost consciousness again. And no one had heard his final faint, but proud, whisper:

"I'm no murderer. I'm – I'm on your side. I'm a *rescuer* . . ."

* * *

Lemaitre was half-way to the Yard when Dexter contacted him through the police radio in his car, which he always kept turned on in case of just such emergencies.

He groaned when the words "Stocking Strangler" were mentioned – God, couldn't that case leave him alone for just one night? – but slowly his scowl turned into one of his curious, broad-yet-narrow grins.

It seemed beyond question that the Strangler had not only been caught, but caught red-handed, and that his sickening reign of terror was over at last. Dexter said that he had Jones in the cells, and both the girl he had attacked and the man who had rescued her were with him at the Warnham Green police station. A police doctor had arrived who was examining them to corroborate their evidence.

"I called you, sir," Dexter added, "because I felt you'd like to be here too."

"So I would," said Lem. "Be with you right away."

And he promptly swung the wheel of his car, doing an

abrupt U-turn in the middle of the street. Then he pulled up at the side of the road, and called Gideon.

"Sorry to be late for your party, Gee Gee," he said when he'd explained the situation. "But I've been working too long on the Strangler case not to want to be in at the kill."

Gideon, who needed no telling how many sleepless, agonised nights Lem had spent on account of the Strangler, instantly agreed.

"Okay, Lem," he said briskly. "I'll postpone the whole shooting match this end until two o'clock. Let's hope *everyone's* made it by then."

It was as though there was a hoodoo on his plans tonight. Lem had to go on the Strangler trip. Matt Honiwell was off on an equally grave emergency and hadn't been heard from, except for that message that he'd be along as soon as he could. And of Tom Riddell, there had been no sign at all – even though a desperately worried Vi Riddell had assured him on the phone that he had driven off, heading for the Yard, all of fifty minutes before.

Fifty minutes. And at this time of night, with the roads empty, the drive from Wimbledon could easily be done in half an hour, and by a good driver, in under twenty . . .

Lem's cheery Cockney tones broke in on his thoughts.

"I'll be there by two, George, don't you worry. This is an open-and-shut case now, if I ever heard one. The Strangler slipped up and let his victim give one scream. A passer-by heard it, and arrived on the spot just in time to save the girl. *And* he knocked that bloody villain out cold as mutton. When Dexter got there, he was still out cold, with the stocking mask still over his head and the other stocking – the one he used for strangling – still in his pocket. If that isn't watertight evidence against him, what is?"

Gideon chuckled. Normally he chided Lem on jumping to conclusions, but this time he had to admit that it looked as though he really was on to a certainty.

"By the way," he said, "do we know the identity of the Strangler yet?"

Lem sounded as chirpy as ever.

"We certainly do, Gee Gee. Once that stocking was off

his face, half of Dexter's men recognised him instantly. His name's Henry Jones, and he's well-known as a neighbourhood weirdo. Simple type, though I wouldn't say actually a mental defective. Walks the streets all night long, loitering about in alleys and so on – he was pulled in once as a Peeping Tom. I hate to admit this, but believe it or not, I had him at the top of my list of suspects at one stage of the case, and was going to have him followed. Then, like a bleeding idiot, I changed my mind and crossed him off the list. I could kick myself when I think of the lives I could have saved."

"What made you cross him off?" asked Gideon.

There was a pause, and then Lem said, rather too hastily:

"Something someone said, I think. What does it matter now, anyway? The main thing is – the Strangler's got his stockings in a twist at last! See you at two, Gee Gee . . ."

The radio went dead. Gideon very thoughtfully slid off the headphones and turned back to the busy operations room, where under Alec Hobbs the last minute preparations for the raid were proceeding fast and furiously.

Just for a moment, though, Gideon had no interest in the raid.

He was thinking of something Lem had been too kind to remind him about . . . something he had said himself during one of the many agonising sessions he had had with Lemaitre during the Strangler case.

"For God's sake, Lem," he could remember roaring. "This man we're up against is one of the shrewdest and cleverest murderers in criminal history! One thing's for certain: he's not going to turn out to be some half-baked Peeping Tom . . ."

So *he* had been largely responsible for Jones's name being crossed off the suspect list . . . and for all the killings that could have been prevented if a proper watch had been kept on him.

Never again would he blame *Lem* for jumping to conclusions, Gideon thought grimly, and forced his mind back to the raid with great difficulty, because it was burdened by an almost unbearable sense of guilt.

* * *

Guilt was also something Tom Riddell was feeling at that moment, as he slid his blue Ford Escort into its accustomed parking place at the rear of Scotland Yard.

He knew the route here, every detail of it, by heart. He had driven along it every morning and every evening for years.

Why, then, had he taken all those wrong turnings? How in God's name could he have wound up, lost, in that crazy rabbit-warren of streets round Vauxhall Bridge and Clapham?

It had to be his nerves. That was the only answer. He must be verging on another crack-up.

Shouldn't he go straight to Gideon and admit it? It was obvious that he was in no state to take part in a major raid.

And yet . . . And yet there was a way out. He could pretend that it was his car, not something inside his brain, that had broken down . . . and if he walked in, smiling briskly and at his smartest and brightest, he had no doubt that he'd be believed.

Yes, that was the course to take, he told himself. If he put on a good enough act, there was even a chance that he'd fool himself – and forget those terrible doubts that were gnawing away like an army of rats at the last shreds of his self-esteem.

Riddell opened the door of the car, and half-stepped, half-blundered out on to the concrete of the car park. The downpour had stopped at last, and the fresh damp air was as stinging as a wet rag whipped round his face. He took huge gulps of it, and the next moment, found himself striding towards the back entrance of the building – the one everyone reporting to the seventh floor had been requested to use.

He'd remembered that instruction, hadn't he? So there couldn't be all that much wrong with him, could there?

Knowing in his heart that he was clinging to straws, Tom Riddell stepped through the swing doors and made his way to the lift.

One feeling he clung to felt a lot stronger than a straw.

If *Gideon* thought he was up to it, then he *must* be, he kept muttering, all the way up to the seventh floor.

And by the time he arrived there, he was – at all events, to all appearances – himself again.

# 6 A Likely Story

Gideon was so relieved to see Riddell that it never occurred to him to question his story of the car developing engine trouble.

"Just the sort of thing that would happen tonight, Tom," he grumbled. "There's a jinx on this raid, I'm beginning to think. Lemaitre has had to go and deal with a development in the Stocking Strangler case – though thank God, it's the development we've all been hoping and praying for. Matt Honiwell has also been called out on some urgent business or other. Everything seems suddenly to be more important than the biggest round-up of top criminals ever known!"

"Well, anyway, I'm here at last," Riddell said, with all the enthusiasm he could inject into his voice. "And believe me, I'm raring to go!"

Gideon grunted.

"Glad to hear it, but I'm afraid there'll be no going yet. I've postponed the zero hour until two." He glanced at his watch, and saw that it was just 1.10. "But it'll take you all of forty minutes to get fully briefed on your part of the operation, and to brief your men. Alec – give Tom a run-down on what we've planned against Kemp, will you?"

Hobbs came forward at once, cool, smiling and almost – if not quite – as unflustered as usual.

"It won't come as much of a surprise to you, Tom," he said. "All our knowledge about Kemp's headquarters and his leading henchmen are based on the facts you dug up before you were taken off the case. We want you to direct a three-pronged attack, so to speak: a raid on the buildings at the back of the Playhouse Theatre in the Strand, where (thanks to you) we suspect there's a store of hidden drugs; a raid on the Theatre Museum in Wardour Street, which you believed was the HQ of the whole drugs operation; and a raid on Kemp's flat in Bayswater. I suggest you take personal charge of the third raid. Kemp was seen arriving at that flat just after eleven p.m. Of course he may have left since – "

Riddell had suddenly forgotten his nerves. The fact that the information he himself had supplied was proving so useful gave his confidence just the boost it needed. He even found himself questioning his superior quite sharply.

"But surely, if the flat's under surveillance, we'd know if he had left!" he almost barked.

Hobbs shrugged and turned to Gideon.

"Shall we tell him the whole thing, George?"

Gideon came across the room.

"It's hardly fair to keep him in the dark," he said, and explained, as briefly as he could, about the call from the supergrass, the abandoning of Target Eighty, and the closing down of all the stake-outs.

Riddell suddenly felt the room starting to sway round him.

"You mean – the whole raid's been leaked, and Kemp's expecting us?"

"Not if our plan has worked," said Gideon. "We're hoping that he, and all the Big Three, will have been told by now that we've abandoned the whole project, and be lulled into a sense of false security. Just for this one crucial night."

"But if they aren't – " Riddell began.

Gideon folded his arms and thrust out his chin, looking suddenly a towering, almost Churchillian, figure.

"If they aren't," he said, "then, as I warned you on the phone, Kemp & Co. will be prepared for an attack, and things could get very hairy. You can see why I wanted you in on this, Tom. It's a pretty desperate situation – and I had to have old hands in charge whom I could trust implicitly. There aren't many that I trust more than you."

The old Gideon magic worked again. With a major effort, Riddell pulled himself together, and his brain – basically one of the shrewdest in the Met – started working at full pitch.

"Kemp used to have another flat – a secret one he shared with a mistress in Pimlico," he said. "If his suspicions have been aroused, he just might have done a moonlight flit there. With your permission, I'll make this a four-pronged raid, and include that too."

"Permission granted," said Gideon with alacrity, and Riddell went striding off to find and brief his men, looking and feeling one of the most commanding men in the room.

Even though the room was still – very slightly – swaying . . .

★ ★ ★

Meanwhile, in that small, brightly painted terraced house in Hammersmith, Matt Honiwell was also struggling with his emotions.

He had arrived there half an hour before to find Maggie Fullerton in near-hysterics, and the unconscious detective constable showing as little signs of life as a waxwork dummy, except for the blood pouring out of him. After ripping up sheets and pillowcases to fashion crude bandages and somehow succeeding in stopping the flow, Matt had rung the Fullertons' doctor and had sounded so important that the man had rushed here, with just a coat over his pyjamas. The ambulance that Maggie herself had sent for arrived simultaneously. By that time Fullerton had resumed his stentorian, snore-like breathing, and the doctor had given an encouraging verdict.

"Thank God, the bullet missed his lungs, and the loss of blood was stopped before it became disastrous. As for the wound to the temple – that's not too serious in itself, little more than a graze. But the shock from such a jolt to the brain – that's harder to calculate. He's breathing strongly, though. That's a good sign. Barring complications, I'd say he has an excellent chance of pulling through."

The doctor looked round in some bewilderment.

"But surely this is a police matter? I must make a report."

"I'd be grateful if you would," Matt said, gently. "And don't worry, Doctor: I *am* a policeman."

"He's a Chief Detective Superintendent," Maggie said, with a pride that was somehow pathetic in the circumstances. "One of the top men at the Yard." She added, even more pathetically: "This isn't an ordinary crime. It's a very special case, you see."

"*Very* special," said Matt. He didn't know what she was talking about, but his confirmation of her boast seemed to do Maggie good. She was calmer suddenly, hope replacing the hysteria in her eyes.

The ambulance men lifted Brian Fullerton on to a stretcher. They had difficulty manhandling it out of the study through the microscopic hall, and past the equally microscopic front garden. One of the stretcher-bearer's feet landed up in the goldfish pond, which was overflowing after all that rain.

"Where – where are you taking him?" Maggie demanded.

"St. Giles Emergency," they told her. St. Giles was a big new hospital on the far side of Hammersmith.

Maggie then turned to Matt.

"Shouldn't you be ringing the Yard?" she said.

"What for?" said Matt.

"To arrange for men to watch over Brian. He'll need protection every moment once that Someone Big sees his file."

"Come again?" said Matt, confusedly.

That was when his emotional struggles began.

Standing there in the dripping front garden, with the water from the overflowing pond swilling around their feet, he, the doctor and the ambulance men were treated to a shrieking tirade about the secret file on a Master Criminal which Brian had been building up for year after year, and how, after finding Brian lying wounded, she had discovered that the file had gone. To Maggie this was a dramatic top-level emergency. She obviously felt that the Chief Commissioner should be alerted immediately. And Matt's ever-sympathetic nature told him that in her place, he would probably have felt exactly the same.

But he wasn't in her place, and couldn't help taking a down-to-earth, logical policeman's view. A detective constable building up a file on one of the biggest criminals in London? A likely story, he thought. Surely it was much more probable that Fullerton was escaping from his lack-of-promotion frustrations through excursions into private fantasies! That would fit in with what he knew of Fullerton, who was too dreamy a type to make much headway in the force, and had stayed a detective constable for a good ten or twelve years.

Against that, of course, there was the fact that constables' houses didn't usually rate a burglary bid by armed bandits – and it *did* look as though the file had been the object of the raid.

Maggie, then, was right up to a point. Fullerton obviously had been collecting evidence against a pretty vicious criminal – but probably it was only some tinpot local villain. It was hard to believe that a constable, even a shrewd one, working entirely on his own, would have the knowledge, or the opportunity, to build up a wealth of usable material against anyone in the really big league.

There was an outside chance that Maggie was also right about Fullerton being in danger. The local villain might just decide to try and get at him in hospital, although he'd be an unusually reckless one if he did. It would maybe be a good idea to contact the local police and order them to keep St. Giles under a bit of extra surveillance – but the situation didn't really call for anything more.

That was how the common-sense, police side of Matt Honiwell was reacting. But the human side of him was aware only that here was a distraught wife in desperate fear for her husband, who was already an unconscious, bleeding victim of vicious assassins. He had to do a bit more for her than that, he told himself, and suddenly decided what he could do.

"Cheer up, Mrs. Fullerton," he said. "This much I'll promise you. The moment Brian arrives in that hospital, there'll be a policeman by his side, and one will be there twenty-four hours a day from now on."

In thinking that would pacify Maggie Fullerton, he was making the mistake of the night.

She paused there, but only to allow the stretcher-bearers to pass her, and carry Brian into the ambulance. Then she started again.

"*One* policeman? Not even armed?"

Matt sidestepped that one neatly.

"Oh, he'll be armed. With a walkie-talkie – keeping him in constant touch with the police station just round the corner."

He'd forgotten he was talking to a constable's wife.

"The police station isn't round the corner. It's a mile and a half away."

"But less than a minute by police car."

"What good will that do if a gang breaks in – and takes over the ward?" Maggie's voice was shaking as much as her small, thin body. Her face was just a white blob in the darkness, but her large dark eyes, wet with tears, glistened almost luminously in the reflected glare from the ambulance's headlamps. "You don't believe my story, do you? You think Brian's a dreamer and just makes everything up. I was wasting my time calling you – "

"I didn't say that – " Matt began, but then fell silent. He couldn't deny that she had come pretty near the truth.

The doctor suddenly spoke up.

"I'm afraid I can't stand about any longer, shivering in my pyjamas," he said. "And that husband of yours, Mrs. Fullerton, needs to get to hospital quickly. I wouldn't delay matters any longer, if I were you."

"But he's going to leave Brian totally unprotected – "

One of the ambulancemen was back now, and joined in.

"If this gentleman is a top brass Yard man, like you said, lady, surely he knows best. Anyway, we've got to drive your husband off now. Are you coming with him or aren't you?"

Maggie jumped into the ambulance. The door closed behind her and it drove off. But despite that closed door and the ever-widening distance between them, Matt could still hear her screaming:

"One constable – against the heaviest mob in London! That's murder! They'll kill Brian, I tell you – before the night's out, they'll kill him – "

Her cries finally faded into the distance with the dwindling tail light. But that didn't stop them ringing round and round in Matt Honiwell's mind. He turned back towards the little house; thanked the doctor profusely and saw him on his way, and then began a lightning examination of the scene of the crime. He noticed that the only things that had been ransacked were cupboards and drawers – places that might have contained Brian's file, which confirmed that that had had been the raiders' main target. He also noticed that a jemmy had been used to break open the front door: sign of professional criminals at work. But that didn't necessarily indicate a major mob behind the raid. Small-time villains very frequently hired hardened pros to do their dirty work.

Matt looked at his watch. Nearly twenty past one. George would be going spare by now. There was just one more thing he had to do: ring the Hammersmith station and tell them to get an investigating team down here fast – oh, yes, and order them to send a man to St. Giles.

His call was taken by a sergeant on night duty, who obviously knew Fullerton well, and was shaken to hear the news.

"Poor old Dreamboat. Just the lousy sort of thing that would happen to him," he said.

"Dreamboat?" said Matt.

"Oh, sorry, sir. That's just Fullerton's nickname here. We call him that because he gets a bit dreamy sometimes, and has all sorts of wild ideas. Not that he's not a very good man, sir," the sergeant added hurriedly, obviously out of a belated sense of loyalty to a colleague in trouble.

Matt suddenly realised what Maggie had meant. If all the men at the station were like that sergeant, Brian's claim to be on to Someone Big would never have been taken seriously in a million years. And Maggie had said he was just like them, Matt remembered. Was the poor woman right? What if she was right about everything – and he and the rest were wrong?

Crisply and succinctly, he told the sergeant about the missing file, and his theory that some local villain must have got wind of the fact that Brian was on to him. "That's why I think he ought to be protected," he snapped, and gave his instructions about the one-man police guard. Suddenly, to his own surprise, he found himself saying: "Correction. Make that two men. One of them armed."

It was a pretty pointless gesture – two men wouldn't be much better than one against "the heaviest mob in London" – but no one in his right mind could go further to meet Maggie's demands, Matt told himself. He put down the receiver feeling a lot happier.

Not wishing to leave the Fullertons' house wide-open to any passing thug, he waited by the broken front door until the police contingent arrived, and then made a dash for his car. Somewhere deep inside him there was still a vague uneasiness, a microscopic worm of doubt. But it had been banished to the very back of his mind by the time he was on his way to Scotland Yard. If he didn't hurry, he'd be too late for the big raid – and would incur the full wrath of George Gideon. The thought of that was enough to make even the scrupulous Matt hit all of seventy miles an hour.

# 7 Wrongful Arrest

By that time, Lemaitre was in a hurry too. He had promised Gideon that he would have the Strangler case tied up and be at the Yard by two, and here it was, 1.35 a.m. already, and he hadn't even seen the man charged with the murders. All he had done since arriving at Warnham Green police station half an hour before was talk to Inspector Dexter and those two key figures in the drama: Judy Moss, who had apparently only just escaped being the Strangler's sixth victim, and her intrepid rescuer, Clive Exton, who was sitting back in his chair and beaming at everybody as befitted the Hero of the Hour.

Lemaitre didn't take to Exton. With his long experience of East End spivs and con men, he realised instantly that here was a smooth-talking phoney. But there was no law which said that phoneys couldn't act heroically at times, and he saw no reason to doubt that this was one occasion when Exton was smooth-talking the truth.

"Mind you, Superintendent," he was saying, for what seemed like the fiftieth time, "I had a great deal of luck on my side. A maniac like the Strangler probably had the strength of ten men, and if he hadn't happened to slip and fall the moment I yanked him backwards, and banged his head on the concrete – well, it would have been the end of yours truly, I'm afraid."

"And the end of me, too," said Judy, shuddering. "I can't tell you how grateful I am, Clive – "

She really didn't have to, Lemaitre thought sourly. The look she was giving him was saying it all, and a great deal more besides. And she was clutching his hand as fiercely as though he was saving her right now – from drowning!

For some reason, the sight of all this sent shivers down Lemaitre's spine. Why? he wondered. Was he getting to the age when the thought of young love turned his stomach? He didn't think so. It was just that there was something about this smoothie that grated on his nerves. It shouldn't, he told himself severely. Members of the public who dared to "have a go" were a rare breed these days – and this man had actually had the guts to take on the most dangerous criminal at large in London. He ought to be making grateful noises too.

But for some reason, whenever he tried to tell this man how much the police appreciated what he'd done, the words stuck in his throat, and all that came out was a Gideon-like grunt. "Blimey," he told himself. "I've been working for Gee Gee for so long I'm getting more like the old buzzard every day."

At that moment, the police doctor, a severe-looking man with the severe-sounding name of Laxworthy, appeared from the direction of the cells. He had been in there, examining Henry Jones, since before Lemaitre arrived at the station. Earlier, he had also examined Judy and Exton, and had pronounced Judy to be in good shape, apart from painful contusions around the neck. Exton had received only a slight graze on the left leg.

When Dexter had introduced Lem as the Chief Detective Superintendent in charge of the Strangler inquiry, Dr. Laxworthy wasted no time in coming to the point.

"Well, if you want my opinion, Superintendent, there's no question that the man is a psychopath. He claims to be suffering from amnesia about what happened tonight, and this may be possible. I suspect mild concussion, as the result of blows received on the forehead and at the rear of the skull. But it definitely does not explain his extraordinary mental state. He could hardly speak without stuttering, and kept asking if the girl – I suppose he means Miss Moss here

– had been saved. When I told him that she *was* safe and well, his next question was more idiotic still. 'Did I rescue her?' he asked, over and over again. It seems he lives in an extraordinary fantasy world, deluding himself he is rescuing girls when all the time he is strangling them."

"Perhaps he is some kind of religious nut," suggested Exton, "and fancies he is saving girls from this wicked world by sending them to Heaven."

The idea seemed to amuse him. He started chuckling, and didn't seem able to stop.

Judy actually let go of his hand. "Don't," she said, almost angrily. Then, more urgently: "Don't make a joke of it, *please.*"

Exton stopped then – in a curious way, by swallowing hard and cutting the chuckle short as though he had strangled it.

"Sorry," he murmured. "Didn't mean to upset you. Probably the reaction."

"It's no wonder," said Judy, and took his hand again.

Lem felt the shivers down his spine returning. This phoney was beginning to act more and more like an outright weirdo, he noted. But he brushed the thought aside. Something far more important was bothering him – what seemed like conflicting evidence.

"Did you say, Doctor, that Jones had bruises on his forehead, too? How could that have happened if he fell backwards on to the concrete?"

Before the doctor could say anything, Exton rapidly intervened.

"I think I can explain that, Superintendent. When I yanked Jones backwards, he stumbled and fell half on top of me. He could have been facing in any direction when he hit the ground, and I think he rolled over when he did so. It's pretty hard to be sure. The rain was belting down, and in that part of the alley the water was gushing like a torrent. He's lucky he wasn't half drowned."

The doctor nodded.

"Thank you, Mr. Exton. That explanation certainly meets the case. A man falling on to a concrete pavement under those conditions might well have sustained multiple injuries to the head. There is no saying what odd stones, cans or other objects may not have been swirling about in the water too. Well, I think I've completed my task and will be off now. Or would you like me to dictate a report before I go?"

"It can wait until the morning, Doctor. What you've told us will do to be getting on with. Thanks for your help and good night." Lem glanced at his watch. It was nearly a quarter to two. He had to be through here in five minutes and not a second more.

"Now I'll see Jones," he said, and headed towards the cells. But Dexter, red-faced and excited as ever, stopped him.

"Just a minute, sir. I've prepared a release for the Press. If you'd just read and initial it – "

Lemaitre was about to do so, when something suddenly struck him. The moment word got out that the Strangler had been caught, his phone would be ringing all night. And if the Press was told that Chief Detective Superintendent Lemaitre was away on a more urgent case, rumours of every sort would be rife. What case could be more urgent than the Strangler? It wouldn't take Fleet Street long to realise that it must be a major raid –

"No," he said sharply. "No release to go out tonight, Dexter. We'll keep this one under wraps. Okay?"

Dexter, who had obviously seen himself featuring on the front page of every paper in the morning, looked stunned and dejected.

"No release?"

"Not tonight, I'm afraid. But cheer up. Just think how lovely your face will look spread all over the London *Standard* tomorrow night. They'll be using you to wrap up their fish and chips all the way from Bermondsey to Balham."

Dexter didn't seem to be in the mood for Cockney comedy. His face as red as a "stop" traffic light, he still barred Lemaitre's way.

"One more thing, sir. Jones was really only semi-conscious when I brought him in. I haven't formally arrested or charged him. Would *you* mind – "

Lem glanced at his watch again. One forty-seven now. He *had* to get out of here –

"All right, all right, Dexter. I'll pronounce the magic words and get you off the hook," he snapped, and almost thrusting the man aside, rushed down the corridor to the cells. He had no time to get the keys from anyone, and so found himself staring through a metal grille at the hapless Jones, who stared back at him with the dazed, trapped, helpless glare of a caged gorilla.

Feeling completely ridiculous, telling a man behind bars that he was under arrest, Lemaitre went right through the official police formula. First he charged Jones with the attempted murder of Judy Moss; then he went through the long, terrible litany of the other five girls that he had raped and killed, ending with the customary "anything you say may be taken down and used in evidence" and a reminder that he was entitled to see a lawyer.

It was strange. Over the past nine weeks, Lemaitre had looked forward passionately to the moment when he would catch the fiendish pervert and be able to hurl all these charges in his face; but now that the moment had actually come, there was no satisfaction in it at all.

Jones's face, in the blue-white glare of the strip-lighting that illumined the cells, showed no hint of guilt, remorse or even fury. There was just this helpless bewilderment. It was as though nothing that Lemaitre had said sank in, except the one word "murder".

"Murder?" he echoed pathetically. "You are accusing me of murder? But I don't understand. That doctor. He told me again and again that the girl was safe."

"Judy Moss is safe," said Lem sharply. "No thanks to you."

"No thanks to me? But it must have been thanks to me. I remember now – I heard her scream, and started running towards the alley. No one will believe me, but I'm on your side. I'm a rescuer – that's all I want to be, a rescuer – "

"So that's why you put a stocking mask over your head, and keep another stocking in your pocket, ready to choke the life out of any girl you meet," said Lem, almost snarling.

"My God. You weirdos make me sick. What do you take us for? As my old father used to say – pull the other one, laddie. It's got bells on it."

He turned to go. It was eight minutes to two . . .

Jones's dazed protests rang out behind him as he strode off along the stone corridor that led away from the cells.

"But I've never strangled anybody in my life. I wouldn't – wouldn't know how – "

Lem swung round fiercely.

"Then how come Miss Moss swears that you had that stocking round her neck – and Clive Exton swears that he pulled you away from her only just in – " he began, and then broke off suddenly, his thoughts whirling.

That second stocking had been found in Henry Jones's pocket, so Dexter had said. If he had been interrupted in the act of strangling – had fallen back and been knocked unconscious, then surely *he* couldn't have put it there?

There was something wrong here; something that needed to be looked into.

Not that, in Lemaitre's opinion, it needed to be looked into tonight. A mild discrepancy in the evidence, that was all it was. The case was still open and shut. It was just that it couldn't be slammed quite as shut as he'd hoped. It was more like a piece of holiday baggage, locked and strapped up for the journey, from which somebody had spotted a shirt-tail hanging out . . .

In any other circumstances, he would have tried to sort the matter out straight away. He would have gone back to Judy Moss and Clive Exton and questioned them exhaustively. He would have asked Dexter if he was *sure* the stocking had been found in the pocket, and so on. But there was no time for that now. No time for anything, except a quick exit and a promise to be back first thing in the morning . . . by which time he expected to have crowned his career by cleaning up the Barry Mayne gang once and for all.

Without a glance back at the man he had "arrested" – surely one of the oddest arrests on record – Lem returned to the room where Dexter was waiting.

"Right," he snapped. "Jones has been formally charged, and, just for the record, admitted nothing. I'm off now. Got to be at the Yard, or they'll have my guts for garters. But I'll be back tomorrow – nine at the latest. And I want a full written report of the arrest, and all the circumstances leading up to it, on my desk by the time I arrive. Okay?"

Dexter looked more aggrieved than ever. He'd obviously expected praise and congratulations, not enough work to keep him busy till dawn. But Lem was in too much of a hurry to put that right.

He looked round for Clive Exton and Judy. They were nowhere to be seen.

"I thought you'd finished with them for the night," said an even unhappier Dexter. "Mr. Exton had his car outside and offered to drive Miss Moss home. I said that would be all right. Shouldn't I have?"

Lem said nothing. There was no logical reason he could give why it shouldn't have been all right. He could question Exton about that stocking business tomorrow, and certainly wouldn't have had time to ask him anything now. But that queer shivering sensation down his spine was back, stronger than ever, stronger than it had been all evening.

Forcing himself to ignore it, he went striding out to his car.

What *was* there about this Clive Exton that got so much on his wick, he asked himself, as the car roared away. He'd sensed at a glance that he was a phoney. He strongly suspected he was some kind of nut. And that stocking business seemed to provide positive proof that he had been telling lies about tonight.

But – but what possible reason could he have had for lying?

Lem started thinking furiously – but not for the first time in his career, he stopped too soon. Suddenly he had to swerve to avoid a lorry. With a startled yelp, he forced himself to concentrate all his attention on driving.

From then onwards, any other thoughts he had were about the tasks ahead of him, and every yard he travelled took him further and further away from realising what a dangerous situation he'd left behind.

* * *

Clive Exton had driven Judy to the police station from Northcote Square, and his car was still outside. It had seemed the most natural thing in the world that he should offer to drive her home.

She had unhesitatingly accepted. In fact, she walked out of the station still leaning against him, still clutching his hand.

"S-sorry about this," she said. "But I feel so weak."

"Who wouldn't," said Clive, "after what you've been through?"

He helped her to get settled in the seat beside him, and to adjust her seatbelt. It was obvious that only that belt prevented her from leaning against him again. For some reason, her trustfulness was no longer amusing. It was beginning to exasperate and disturb him. No girl had ever behaved quite in this way towards him before – but then, he supposed, he had never been taken for a rescuing hero before. It was flattering to his ego, but something deeper inside him couldn't cope with it, and kept wanting to tell her: "Get lost, you little fool."

"I think I'll take a day off tomorrow, after all this," she was chatting. "There'd be hell to pay normally – I work at Selsey's Supermarket in the High Street, and the manager's a brute – but when he hears I've nearly been a Strangler victim, I don't suppose even *he* will say anything."

"I should hope not," Exton murmured, with his smoothest smile. "By the way, where is your home? Didn't I hear Inspector Dexter say you're living with your parents?"

Judy made a face.

"Yes, I suppose so," she admitted reluctantly. "8, Rushmore Gardens. Just turn right, then right again, and then left."

"They'll be waiting up for you, I imagine. The police must have rung and told them what had happened to you."

"No, they didn't," Judy said. "I especially asked them not to."

"Why?"

"It would only worry them, and lead to the family row of all time."

Exton raised an eyebrow.

"I should think there'd be a row anyway, with you being back so late."

"No, there won't." Judy was putting on a look of almost desperate defiance. "Before I went out, I told them not to wait up for me. In fact, I said I probably wouldn't be back tonight at all. I've not been living at home, you see – not until these last few days. And I – I hoped – "

She found herself pouring out the whole story of how she had gone to Stan's flat, hoping that they could make it up, and found that he was away somewhere with another woman. "Aren't men *horrible*?" she finished.

"Some of them can be *very* horrible," Exton agreed. "As you have good reason to know, tonight."

"But some of them can be wonderful," said Judy. "I've good reason to know that too."

She was resting her hand against his sleeve. The very touch of her now sent dark feelings pulsing through Exton; feelings he was suddenly ashamed of and struggled to suppress, but which he knew could be as hard to control as that bloody giggle.

He was thankful that they had arrived in Rushmore Gardens, and pulled up the car abruptly outside No. 8.

"Here you are, Judy girl," he said, with mock heartiness. "Home sweet home."

He stretched across her to open the door on her side. It was all he could do now to control those impulses, but somehow, with a great effort, he succeeded – for the time being. He didn't think he could keep them under for long.

Not that that mattered, he told himself. She'd be gone soon. Gone in seconds –

But to his surprise, she made no move.

Suddenly she couldn't bear the thought of creeping into that house and upstairs to her bedroom, then lying awake and alone all night with the terrible memories of what had happened in the alley. Near-desperation drove her to a near-desperate move.

Releasing the seatbelt, and nestling up to Exton, she whispered:

"Would you think me just a cheap little tart if – if I said I'd like to spend the night with you? Not here, of course. But I've got the key to – to that flat . . ."

Clive Exton remained so silent for so long that she was sure she'd shocked him. But then relief flooded through her. It was all right. He'd put an arm round her and was actually laughing.

He was still laughing when he started the car and they drove away. Laughing so hard, in fact, that she thought he'd never stop . . .

# 8 Haunted Men

At the moment when the hurried Lemaitre was setting out for Scotland Yard, the equally hurried Matt Honiwell was actually arriving there. He was relieved to find that everything had been postponed for an hour, and he was just in time. It was three minutes to two.

Like Riddell before him, Matt was immediately handed over to Alec Hobbs for a full briefing, if "full" was the word. Matt's target was to be the elusive Arturo Salvados, the master-minder of bank raids; and there was no certainty about where he would be found, only leads and rumours. He had no less than three luxury hideouts (two of them penthouse flats) scattered around Mayfair, and other addresses as far apart as Harrow in the north and Esher in the south. All his known addresses had been under surveillance before the "Target Eighty" operation collapsed, and Salvados was believed to have been spotted arriving at the Esher one. The trouble was that another police observer (equipped with binoculars) thought he'd seen him looking down from the window of one of the Mayfair flats.

"What are the odds, then?" grinned Honiwell. "Seven to one on Esher, ten to one on Mayfair and about sixty to one on the rest?"

"Something like that," admitted Hobbs. "It'd be a lot more satisfactory if we'd been able to keep the surveillance going on all the places. We would probably have got a positive sighting by now. The trouble is that Salvados has a lot of enemies, and uses all the tricks in the book to keep them from knowing where he is. He's never more than one night in any one place, and may move from one to the other at any time *during* the night. But I think I'd trust the Esher sighting more than the other one. We had a reliable man in Esher, Shipton, and if *he* says he saw Salvados arrive, I think it's a safe bet that he did."

"Evens on Esher, then," said Honiwell. "Okay. I'll raid that place myself. Have we men to spare to carry out simultaneous raids on the rest?"

Gideon overheard that and intervened.

"For tonight, Matt, we have men to spare for everything," he said.

Matt found himself forgetting the raid for a moment, and remembering Maggie Fullerton.

"There's a woman I know who'd be glad to hear you say that," he said. "She was begging and pleading with me to send a squad round to St. Giles Hospital, Hammersmith. Her husband's a detective constable who got shot up tonight, and she's convinced some top criminal is after him, and will be raiding the hospital during the night to finish him off."

Gideon stared. Matt expected him to bark something about keeping his mind on the job in hand; but news of a C.I.D. man being shot wasn't something Gideon ever dismissed lightly.

"A detective constable? Who?"

"Brian Fullerton, of Hammersmith station. Came home tonight to find burglars in his house, and collected two bullets trying to arrest them."

"Bullets? Where?"

"Chest and head. The doctor thinks he'll pull through, but he was still unconscious when the ambulance took him off."

"And his wife thinks – "

As quickly as possible, Matt told him the rest of the story.

"I've sent two men to guard him, one of them armed," he said. "Didn't think I could reasonably do more. It's very unlikely, I reckon, that Fullerton was on to someone really big – and a two-man armed guard should take care of any small-scale villain."

Gideon nodded agreement. Personally, he'd have liked to have done more to allay the hysterical woman's fears, but Matt was right: it simply wasn't feasible to give a constable all night protection on a presidential scale, without far stronger reasons than they'd been given. He could see, though, that Matt was still bothered, perhaps even haunted, by the memory of Maggie Fullerton's entreaties, and haunted men didn't make good raid-leaders. He did his best to cheer him up.

"I expect she'll be more than satisfied by what you've arranged when she settles down – and sees the two men standing there," he said. "Especially as the night goes on, and she realises that nothing's going to happen."

It was a forecast he was to remember with a groan long before dawn.

* * *

As Matt went off across the crowded operations room, grabbing a cup of coffee and then setting off to collect and brief his men, a panting, sweating Lemaitre arrived.

Alec promptly cornered him, and started to tell him the plans for the raid on Barry Mayne's headquarters. But Lem already had his own plans, worked out to the smallest detail.

"Listen. What you've got to understand about Barry Mayne is this. He's the nearest to the old Al Capone type of gangster you'll ever see in England. Lives surrounded by cronies, hangers-on, minders, guards – a personal travelling circus that goes wherever he goes, night and day. So before you get to the man himself, you've got to wade through that lot, which could be a sight too costly in police lives for my liking. What I suggest is this. Yours truly knocks at the door, seeming to arrive alone and unarmed. I'll say I've come for a little friendly chat with Barry. He won't be too surprised. I've had many of them before."

"What, at around two in the morning?"

"No, but I can hint that I've something urgent to tell him. Then, when I'm alone with him, I could leak the news of Gideon's raid. Unfortunately, the leak will be a little too late for Barry. I signal – and the rest of the squad, who've been hiding down the street, come crashing in S.A.S. style, if necessary – through the windows!"

Alec did not know whether to be amused or impressed. Lem's combination of Cockney shrewdness and gusto, as always, took his breath away.

"How can the men outside know which room you're in?"

"I'll tell 'em to watch the windows. I'll find a way of signalling. I'll tell 'em to have guns covering the windows, too. If I can, I'll get Barry to look out of one of them. In which case, we'll have him – straight away."

"But supposing the travelling circus, as you call it, doesn't keep its distance? It could surround you, make you a hostage."

"No, it won't. Not if I can con Barry into thinking that what I've come to say is so hot it's for his flaming ears alone."

"We-ell – "

Alec looked so doubtful that Lemaitre appealed to Gideon, who had been standing nearby, listening to the whole thing.

"Let me play it my way, Gee Gee, for Chrissake. It'll save a lot of lives if you do."

Gideon hesitated. It was typical of Lem to be offering to put his head in the lion's mouth for the sake of his men. The question was whether he should let him. He decided in the end that he should. There was hardly anyone in the force better able to take care of himself in dicey situations than the wily Lem.

"All right," he grinned. "You're on. I can't resist the thought of a lot of C.I.D. men suddenly trying to copy the S.A.S."

His grin faded abruptly as he went on: "Lem."

"Yep, Gee Gee?"

"You haven't said a word about the Strangler case. Did you get that buttoned up all right?"

Lem's expression changed from breezy self-assurance to worried uncertainty. Hullo, thought Gideon grimly, another haunted man . . .

"Yes, I think so," he said briskly – too briskly to be

wholly believable. "Henry Jones is in the cells. Dexter had forgotten to charge him, so I did."

"Did he admit anything?"

"Not on your life. Kept saying he was trying to save the girl, not strangle her. Obviously a nut case. But here's the odd thing. Clive Exton, the girl's rescuer – the 'have-a-go' boy of the century – *he* struck me as being half a bleeding nutter, too. Smoothest phoney I've met in a month of Sundays, but weirdo with it. Kept giggling and couldn't stop. Not that that seemed to worry the girl herself, Judy Moss. She kept giving him the eye all the time I was there. Saw him as her knight in armour, I suppose. He finished up by taking her home. Wouldn't surprise me if they never get there, but wind up in bed together. Gives me the shivers, the thought of that. Don't know why. Maybe I'm getting old."

"Never mind about all that," said Gideon. "Did you find the case against Jones as watertight as it seemed?"

"Pretty much so," said Lem. "There's no doubt about Jones being found with a stocking mask on, and a second stocking in his pocket. Mind you, I'm not entirely satisfied with Exton's story." He went on to explain that if Jones had been yanked backwards in the act of strangling, he *shouldn't* have had that stocking in his pocket. "Not that it affects the situation materially, I suppose," he finished. "There obviously *was* a fight between Jones and Exton, and Jones got knocked out. Whether he was actually strangling Judy Moss at the time, or had just finished that bit, and was putting the stocking away prior to raping her, doesn't really matter a tinker's cuss. It only goes to show what I felt the moment I saw Exton – that the man's a born liar. What throws me, though, is just *why* he should be lying about this."

Gideon frowned. He felt vaguely that the question was important; far more important than Lem realised. But there was no time to consider it now. There was something else he was determined to tell Lemaitre – something he would not enjoy saying, but which demanded to be said.

"Lem," he began. "About the Press. Have you issued a statement yet?"

"No. Dexter wanted me to, but I said it'd keep till tomorrow," said Lem, and explained why.

Gideon nodded.

"You were dead right," he said. "If the Press got wind of the fact that something big was pending, it'd be as good as leaking the raid all over again." His manner became grave. "But I warn you. When you do release that news tomorrow, the police aren't exactly going to come in for paeans of praise. The papers are going to ask: 'If the police had reasons for suspecting Henry Jones, why didn't they keep a closer watch on him? Why didn't they take more care, and save all those girls' lives?' And they will probably start to pillory you for it." Suddenly he folded his arms, and his voice became gruff but very firm and clear. "Well, if they do, I shall come forward and tell the plain and simple truth. You were acting under my direct orders. I told you to lay off Jones – and the blood of those girls is on my hands, if it's on anybody's, because, for once, *I* did a Lemaitre and jumped to conclusions. Got it?"

Lemaitre would not accept that for a moment.

"I've got it – but for God's sake, forget it, Gee Gee. Laying off Jones was as much my decision as yours. When you said that the Stocking Strangler would never turn out to be a dim Peeping Tom, it made a lot of sense to me – and funnily enough, it still does. The more I stared into that dazed face of Henry Jones tonight, the more I kept feeling that the wrong man was behind bars. Now a fast-talking, fast-thinking weirdo like Exton – he's the geezer who ought to have been the Strangler, by all the rules. Still, there you go. Life's always tearing up the rule-book, isn't it? Bleeding unfair to all right-thinking coppers."

And he was off to organise the raid on Barry Mayne, with a final grin at Gideon, who was feeling very much less guilty and more grateful, perhaps, than ever before to Lemaitre – for being Lem . . .

Then, suddenly, he started. That important question he had thrust to the back of his mind forced itself through to the forefront. *Why* had Exton lied about that fight he'd had with Jones? What could conceivably be his motive for saying he had caught Jones in the act of strangling Judy, if in fact he had caught him a moment later, when the girl was lying unconscious and he was standing over her?

Perhaps he hadn't had a motive. Perhaps his recollections were just hazy. But then again, why should they have been? Exton hadn't had a bang on the head like Jones – and surely, the moment he tackles and defeats a human monster is something which would be etched on a man's memory with detailed clarity for life.

And yet, about this of all moments, Exton started fantasising – describing a scene that hadn't happened anywhere except in his imagination. Which raised a very, very interesting question. *What else about that rescue hadn't happened anywhere except in Exton's imagination?* He had arrived on the scene when Judy was already unconscious, so she couldn't contradict anything he said. The only other witness was Henry Jones – and pretty soon, he was lying unconscious too. Not just unconscious, but concussed, so that since then he'd been confused and pretty incoherent. No one, not even Lem, had paid much attention to his muttered claim that he "had tried to save the girl, not strangle her". The stocking mask he'd been wearing and the stocking in his pocket had spoken louder, damning him without question.

But, Gideon suddenly realised, a stocking mask could easily be pulled over an unconscious man's head – and a second stocking still more easily stuffed into his pocket . . .

The implications of that realisation were so awe-inspiring that it took a full second for them to sink in. And it was during that very second that Gideon felt a touch on the arm, and found Alec Hobbs beside him.

"Everyone's ready now, George. Will you give the word for the raid to start, or shall I?"

Long experience had taught Gideon how to switch his attention from one thing to another with the speed – and power – of a swivelling searchlight.

An instant later, with nothing on his mind except the

raid, he was striding ahead of Alec Hobbs across the operations room, and out through some big double doors at the end. These led into an adjoining room that had been used as a lecture hall before the floor had been commandeered for Target Eighty. It was a vast place, extending right across the Yard building from front to back, and could seat a thousand men. For tonight, the seats had been removed, and something like two thousand men were in there, standing in three groups: Matt and his Arturo Salvados raiding party on the left, Lemaitre and his Barry Mayne contingent in the middle, and Riddell with his Jeremy Kemp attackers on the right.

Gideon's Deputy Commander, the rather prim, intellectual Paul Barnaby, who looked more like a computer programmer than a policeman, was standing towards the rear with a supporting group of his own. Gideon had given him the job of organising auxiliary raids rounding-up henchmen, or being on hand to tackle any emergency relief that might be needed during the night.

Walking to a raised dais at the front of the room, still with Alec Hobbs in tow, Gideon had the feeling that he was a field marshal about to address his troops before they set off to storm the beaches. There was that kind of pre-battle tension in the air.

Staring round from the dais, he noticed Matt Honiwell running a hand through his mop of curly hair, and doubted if he had quite forgotten the desperate pleading of Maggie Fullerton, beside the body of her unconscious husband. He took a quick glance at Riddell, over on the right of the room. He was standing stiffly, almost to attention, yet suddenly he shot out a hand and touched the wall beside him. To stop himself swaying? Gideon wondered. Was Tom really as okay as he looked? Vi had sounded desperately worried about him on the phone . . . Finally his glance took in Lemaitre, the old, untiring Lem, looking as spruce as though he was going to a police dance. No one would ever imagine that he had just been handling a harrowing inquiry, and was on his way to one of the riskiest operations of his life.

Though the element of danger was present for everyone in the room, of course. Every man there knew that – in the words of the old Tennyson poem – someone had blundered, and that they were being sent out at a moment's notice in a desperate bid to save the day. And a lot of them probably thought that their lives were being risked just to save the Met's face.

He had to say something to encourage them – and, as always, Gideon decided that the best course was to be blunt.

"Right," he said. "I feel that all of you should know the truth, those of you that haven't realised it already. It's very much a case of 'once more into the breach, dear friends' tonight. At just after eleven o'clock this evening, it was learned from a supergrass that there had been the biggest security breach in the history of the Met. Every detail of a vast raid we'd been planning for months had been leaked, and the targets of that raid – the Big Three – were obviously ready to run for cover. I was called in, and my job – and yours – is to catch 'em quick, before they go. I'm not saying it'll be easy. It could turn out to be bloody impossible. But if you succeed, you'll be doing very much more than saving the reputations of a few brass hats. You'll be rescuing from the rubbish heap the biggest and most worthwhile attempt to clean up London that there has been in the whole of my time at the Met. In the next two hours, big-scale organised crime in this city can be virtually wiped out. *If* you act fast enough and – " suddenly the famous Gideon glower became a grin " – don't waste any more time listening to hot air from me."

He glanced at his watch.

"The raid is on – from now, precisely 2.19. Good luck to you all."

He had called for fast action, but even he was amazed by how fast it turned out to be. Before he had even walked the four steps to the edge of the dais, the room was half-empty – cleared by a lightning, yet highly disciplined dash to the doors. There was no queueing to get out; no hold-up at any doorway. The groups, each using a different exit, were away as fast as firemen rushing down poles.

By the time his watch said 2.21, Gideon found that he and Alec were the only people in the hall. Side by side, they strode back towards the operations centre, where, of course, a large back-up staff was now standing by to receive telephone calls and radio messages, and plot the progress of the raid.

"Great speech, George," Alec murmured. "Though what Sir Reginald would have thought of that 'saving the reputations of the brass hats' line – "

He stopped, startled by the abrupt change in Gideon's expression.

Now that the raid was well and truly launched, Gideon's mind had flashed back to the Strangler case – and he had remembered something that Lem had mentioned, almost as an aside. Clive Exton and Judy Moss had left Warnham Green police station together – *and Exton was driving Judy home.*

Which was fine if he was in fact her gallant rescuer. But if – if, by any chance, he was the Strangler –

Thrusting Alec almost roughly aside, Gideon rushed through the swing doors in to the operations room.

There were startled stares all round as people glanced up and saw Gideon's face.

It was George Gideon who now looked like a haunted man, as he hurled himself towards the nearest phone.

# 9 Night of Fear

Within five seconds, Gideon had been put through to Warnham Green police station. Within another five, he was through to the Strangler case incident room, and talking to Inspector Dexter.

With his card-index memory of police personnel, Gideon was able to put both a face and a personality to the name "Dexter". A fat, red-faced man, he remembered; enthusiastic and determined, but pompous and probably basically unsure of himself. Over-fond of reminding you of his achievements, and he turned crimson if anything he did was questioned . . .

"Dexter, this is Gideon," he said shortly, and could almost hear Dexter starting violently at the other end.

"Gideon! Oh, good evening, sir. You've heard about my good luck in apprehending the Strangler tonight, I expect."

He obviously imagined that the Commander of the C.I.D. had been so delighted that he was ringing to congratulate him – at nearly 2.30 a.m.!

"Yes, I've heard about it," Gideon growled. "But the person I'd like to hear more about at the moment is Judy Moss, the Strangler's victim."

He could imagine Dexter's face already reddening.

"Judy Moss, sir?"

"Yes," Gideon barked. "I understand she was driven home from the station by Clive Exton, the man who claimed to have rescued her."

From the sound of his gasping voice, Dexter was now turning purple.

"*Claimed* to have rescued her, sir? Surely there's no doubt about it?"

Gideon was suddenly roaring.

"There may be, there may not. What I want you to tell me is (a) where her home is and (b) whether she arrived there safely."

There was a frantic rustling as Dexter consulted a notebook.

"Miss Moss lives with her parents, sir, Mr. and Mrs. Moss at 8, Rushmore Gardens, Warnham Green."

"Good. Got their telephone number?"

"Y-yes, sir. It's – "

"Then ring it. And ring me back – here at the Yard – to tell me if she's home safe and sound."

Dexter started a desperate attempt to justify himself.

"I should explain, sir, that I would normally have rung her parents and asked them to fetch her, but Miss Moss expressly forbade me – "

"Well, I'm expressly ordering you to ring them now."

"Yes, sir. Of course, sir – "

Gideon hung up on Dexter, who was breathing so hard he might have been panting. He was breathing harder still when he rang back just five minutes later, with the news that Judy had not arrived home. It had taken him three of those minutes to wake her parents, who had not been at all surprised at her non-arrival: she had told them not to expect her back tonight, he said.

"This may not be as disturbing as it sounds, sir," he added. "Miss Moss was evidently very attracted to Mr. Exton. It is possible – er, that – er – "

"That he took her back home with him?" Gideon barked. "All right, Dexter. You've got his address, haven't you?"

"Yes, sir. A flat just off Warnham High Street. I've got his telephone number, too."

"Then ring it. No. Better get some men together and go round there. Break in – if necessary – and ring me back on what you find. And Dexter."

"Yes, sir?"
"Make sure you're armed."
Before Dexter could gasp out any sort of reply, Gideon had slammed down the phone. When it rang again, ten minutes later, the Inspector was calling from Clive Exton's flat – which he had broken into, and found completely deserted.
"Though there – there is one thing I should mention, sir," Dexter said.
"What?" said Gideon, and frowned. For a long, puzzling moment, Dexter seemed too tensed-up to speak. His odd panting went on, though; it sounded almost like a "heavy breathing" call.
"What is it, man? Get it out, for God's sake," Gideon shouted.
Dexter found his voice at last.
"The main bedroom, sir – it's obviously a man's room. Suits in the wardrobe – socks and shirts everywhere . . ."
"All right, I know what a man's bedroom looks like," Gideon growled. "Go on. What else is in it?"
"Stockings, sir," said Dexter, and suddenly words came with a rush. "Crossing the room, I happened to step on a loose floorboard. I found I could lift it up – and there they were. Thirty or forty pairs of women's stockings. Some of them obviously just bought, in cellophane packs, but most of them loose – and crumpled, as though they'd been used as masks, or – or . . ."
Words failed Dexter again, and he was back to the heavy breathing. At the thought of the danger Judy Moss was in, and the crushing sense of his total powerlessness to help her, words failed Gideon too.
Not that his brain stopped functioning. It instantly saw one thing very clearly. The Strangler case must now be given top priority; priority, if necessary, over the raid. A major operation had to be mounted, centred round Warnham Green, to save Judy or if (as in some dark, deep layer of his subconscious, he was already fearing) it was too late for that, then to stop Exton now, tonight, once and for all. True, Exton had a sane, cunning side that must be telling

him that if he harmed Judy, the spotlight of suspicion would be off Jones and could switch straight to him. But what chance was there of a sex fiend retaining a vestige of sanity in the presence of a girl he had already, that very night, lusted to kill? At all events, he was known now, he had a face and a name, and no matter where he fled or where he hid, a well-directed, no-holds-barred manhunt ought to be able to flush him out – fast.

The operative word, though, was "well-directed", Gideon knew. Which obviously left poor Dexter out. The only logical thing to do was bring Lemaitre back on the scene to take charge. He wouldn't much relish being pulled out of the Barry Mayne raid, just when he was on the point of slapping the cuffs on his long-term enemy, but –

"Needs must when the devil drives," Gideon told himself grimly. "And I've never known the old boy driving me harder than tonight."

He told Dexter to return to Warnham Green and hang on for further orders.

"Meanwhile, get the Strangler incident room fully manned," he said. "If it's closed down except for you, get the night staff back *and* the day team out of their beds! And circulate a description, and if possible, the number of Clive Exton's car. Someone ought to have an idea of what it looks like – it was parked outside the police station until half an hour ago! If there's any other lead that you or anyone else can think of, for Heaven's sake, follow it – quick!" The Gideon roar suddenly became a mild, placatory grunt. "Oh – and Dexter."

"Yes, sir?"

"Don't blame yourself for jumping to what seemed an obvious conclusion earlier tonight. Lemaitre and I – we both of us did the same. And congratulations on spotting that loose board in the bedroom. That could prove the key discovery of the whole case. Good night."

Dexter sounded as though he couldn't believe his ears. It was his first experience of the other side of Gideon; the side that could boost a policeman's confidence as easily as its roaring counterpart could chop it down.

He was still saying "good night and – and thank you very much, sir" when Gideon slammed down the phone, and strode across to the radio operators' table. Not much was going on there at the moment. The Yard wasn't keeping in constant radio contact with the raiding parties. On Gideon's orders, it was letting them all get on with their jobs in their own way, under instructions to report as soon as an arrest had been made, but otherwise only to call if they hit trouble. "And it had better be serious trouble," Gideon had said. "Remember just how easily police wavelengths can be tuned into – and God knows, we've had leaks enough already tonight."

The result of these orders had been a tense, twenty-minute silence, so complete that it was as if Lemaitre, Honiwell, Riddell, Barnaby and all their men were in a spacecraft on the far side of the moon.

Gideon wasn't too happy about breaking it; but if he was guarded, and just asked to speak to Lemaitre, without giving any eavesdropper a hint that Lem was conducting a major raid –

That proved to be impossible, though.

"You can't speak to him now, sir," came the voice of a young constable in one of the police cars. "We're outside Longford Terrace, and – "

That, Gideon remembered with a groan, was the apparently run-down tenement block in Lambeth that actually housed the headquarters of the Barry Mayne mob. This young constable had just announced that crucial part of the night's operations to the world! Not that it mattered, he supposed, if the arrests were now imminent – and imminent they seemed to be.

"Mr. Lemaitre has just got out of the car, sir, and although it's hard to be certain – we're parked in an alley on the far side of the road, and visibility isn't too good – I think he is proceeding up the steps to the front door. Do you want me to signal him to come back?"

"No, no," grunted Gideon. "Just tell him that I must speak to him – as soon as he's through."

If, he told himself, Lem would be in a fit state to talk to

anybody once he was through with that dangerous face-to-face session with Barry Mayne . . .

★ ★ ★

For a number of people all over London, that black, drenching October evening had turned into a dark and bitter night of fear.

Fear was even being felt, for example, by the jaunty Lemaitre as he walked up the last few steps to that front door in Lambeth. Over in the Riddells' semi-detached house in Wimbledon, Vi was lying, wide-awake and fully dressed on her bed, wondering if at any moment the phone would ring with the news that Tom had fainted – or worse, suddenly lost control and panicked during his part of the raid.

Riddell himself at that moment was arriving in a large police area car outside the flat in Bayswater where the drugs king Jeremy Kemp had been seen a few hours before.

The car had just drawn to a halt by the kerb, but to Riddell it felt as though it was still moving. Worse – the pavement, too, seemed to be moving as he stepped out on to it, first heaving and rolling like a stormy sea, and then rushing towards him as he stumbled, swayed and fell into the darkness.

The darkness of the night of fear.

★ ★ ★

In the A4 Ward of St. Giles Hospital, Hammersmith, the darkness was kept partially at bay by the cold, blue-shaded light of the bulbs hanging low over the night nurses' table in the centre of the room. But over the beds and in all the corners, it lingered, that darkness, precisely mirroring the sense of dread that lingered in all the corners of Maggie Fullerton's mind.

She wasn't sitting in the ward proper, but in a little partitioned-off room at one end of it – the nearest that the hospital, hard-pressed by the government's economy drive, could manage to a private ward. It had no doors, this room, only curtains covering the entrance, which Maggie had drawn back, fearful of a surprise attack. She felt safer, being able to see all the way down the ward, although the sister on night duty wouldn't have approved: it was a men's ward, and the patients could be embarrassed sleeping under the eye of a female visitor. Not that anyone noticed the open curtain. That end of the ward was very dark.

The panic, amounting to near-hysteria, that had come over Maggie when she had found Brian lying in the study had died down now. She was past sobbing at the sight of his unconscious body: it was too familiar, she had been beside it now for hour after hour. She was past screaming at the two policemen standing stolidly in the gloom on the other side of the bed: hospital regulations forbade talking above a whisper, and she was calm enough to realise that she'd simply be flung out if she made a scene.

All she could do was squeeze Brian's hand in the darkness, reassure herself by listening to his loud breathing, and try to believe what the night sister had told her.

"There's nothing to worry about at all, dear. The doctors think your husband could be coming out of the coma at any time. That's why they've agreed to your staying by his side. And with these two policemen here, I am sure Mr. Fullerton is as safe as anyone could be – even if there is an attack, which I do feel is most unlikely. In all my years in nursing, I've never heard of a hospital patient being murdered by a criminal gang. It's just something that criminals don't do. So just forget about it, once and for all. Here, take this tablet – it'll soothe your nerves . . ."

Maggie had refused the tablet. Something – in fact, everything in her mind – told her that she must keep alert. And keep alert she had, every minute, every second, until now.

By now it was getting difficult. It was 2.42 a.m. by her watch, and the dead weight of all those hours of grief and terror were piling up on her. She felt hollow, drained, exhausted, beyond feeling anything except an overwhelming desire to sleep.

Would it matter so desperately if she dozed off, she asked herself. Perhaps the sister was right – there was no danger. Perhaps she'd been silly, schoolgirlish to build up this monster in her imagination this menacing, all-powerful Someone Big . . .

Perhaps . . . Perhaps . . .

The blue lights above the nurses' table began to blur as she looked at them, and Maggie Fullerton was on the point of drifting off to sleep when it happened.

The big swing doors at the far end of the ward crashed open, and someone threw something into the room. Something that fizzed and then exploded with a brilliant purple flash, pouring smoke everywhere.

By that time, the two policemen were across the ward. They'd moved so fast that both were near the explosion when it happened. One of them reeled back, momentarily blinded. The other jumped on the object and stamped it out.

Patients were waking up in the nearby beds, some gasping and choking, one swearing. Just for a second, the nurses were too scared to go and see to them. One nurse sprang on to the table, just as though terrified by a mouse.

The policeman finished jumping on the object, then held it up, laughing, to show the room.

"No need to get your knickers in a twist, girls. It's only a firework. Not a big one, either. What we used to call a penny banger when I was a boy. Excuse me," he added, hearing scuffling feet and drunken laughter outside the door. "I've got work to do."

He and his colleague dashed out into the corridor, and returned dragging two yobbos, obviously very much the worse for drink and probably returning home from some early Hallowe'en party.

There was a lot of fuss and bother while the culprits' names and addresses were taken, and they were forcibly ejected from the hospital.

By this time, the night sister had been fetched from her room. Under her watchful eye, the nurses calmed down, but were still a little giggly. The moment of false alarm over, A4 Ward became quiet again. The nurses settled the patients, giving sedatives to one or two of them, and then returned to writing notes (or doing crosswords) under the sombre lights. The constables resumed their positions by the bedside of Brian Fullerton, who seemed to be breathing rather harder than before.

There was only one real difference to the scene.

Maggie Fullerton was no longer there.

"Wonder where she's gone to," one of the constables murmured.

"The loo, most probably," the other replied. "We were lucky that didn't start her hysterics again."

But Maggie Fullerton had not gone to the loo. She had slipped out into the corridor where she had noticed there was a public telephone.

That explosion had settled it, as far as she was concerned. The thing had only been a penny banger – but it could have been a bomb, and if it had been, they would all have been blown to pieces and that Someone Big would have won.

It had obviously been sent as a warning from Heaven, she thought – sent to show her how right she'd been, and how vulnerable Brian was . . . to the big attack she was more certain than ever was coming.

But she wasn't panicking now. She knew just what to do. It had been no use calling Matt Honiwell. He was only a chief detective superintendent, not high enough up to understand top-level crime. She had to aim at the top, the very top. And in her handbag she'd found a dusty old card that had been lying about in there for years, ever since that time she'd volunteered to help run an auction sale for the wives of injured policemen. The card had been given to her by the head of the sale's organising committee, and there was a scrawled telephone number on the back, with a note: "If you need any help, call me – K. G."

"I've never needed help more than now," Maggie Fullerton told herself as she calmly started to dial the number. But her dialling grew more and more frenzied as she remembered who she was dialling: Kate Gideon, the wife of the Commander of the whole C.I.D.

# 10 "Leaking Like a Sieve"

Lemaitre's fears subsided as he finally reached the battered door of Mayne's HQ, to be replaced by a sudden spasm of bewilderment. The moment he started to knock – or rather, to rattle the letter-slit, because nothing resembling a knocker was in sight – the door swung slowly open.

It had obviously been left on the latch, an odd thing for anyone to do in a dubious part of Lambeth in the middle of the small hours. His East End upbringing had given Lem a very suspicious nature, and never had it been more strongly aroused.

Half of Barry's cronies could be hiding behind that door, he thought, armed with anything from knives to sawn-off shot guns, and he wouldn't be surprised if the other half were waiting for him somewhere in the darkness of that hall.

He took a step backwards, far enough to give him room to raise a foot, and delivered a hefty kick to the door, crashing it right back on its hinges. That should give any mobster hiding behind it a bloody nose to remember him by, he thought, and hurriedly ducked sideways, expecting a fusillade of shots to come out of the blackness ahead.

But there was nothing to be heard – not a grunt, not a groan, not a breath, let alone a shot.

"Blimey!" said Lem. "Don't tell me there's nobody home . . ."

Still moving cautiously, he stepped into the hall. The

place smelt dank and decaying, as if it hadn't been occupied for years. But that was all part of Barry's cunning window-dressing. He intended this to seem like the entrance to a slum. The luxury started upstairs, on the first floor, which linked up with the first floors of all the other houses in the terrace to create a bizarre hidden flat so enormous that it rivalled any Park Lane penthouse, and provided ample accommodation for Barry and all his innumerable hangers-on.

Lem knew all this because he had been here before. But never before had he met a situation as curious as this. What the hell was going on? Had Barry retreated into his luxury suite, leaving the rest of the place unguarded – and if so, why?

Strongly tempted to go back and whistle up some men to accompany him, but nevertheless determined to see his "heart-to-heart-with-the-boss" ploy through if he possibly could, Lemaitre started up the bare, creaking stairs to the first floor. He found a light switch at the foot of the stairs and switched it on. He was rewarded by a sombre gleam of light from a bare twenty watt bulb above his head.

Humming under his breath to keep his spirits up, Lem strode briskly to the top of the stairs – and immediately found himself almost ankle-deep in luxury. At the moment when the first floor was reached, the threadbare carpet, looking as though it dated from about 1948, gave way to a thick scarlet pile that looked as though it cost all of £100 a square yard. There was another light switch here – a circular "dimmer" one. Operating it, he found himself bathed in a golden glow reminiscent of the foyer of the Covent Garden Opera House.

And that was just the start of it, Lem knew. He'd never been a guest here long enough to confirm the rumour himself, but the story went that Mayne had a genuine Picasso hanging in the toilet.

He walked forward softly – it was difficult to do anything else across that luxuriant pile – and then suddenly stopped dead in front of the rich mahogany door of the Barry Mayne holy of holies itself.

The door was open, just as the front door downstairs had been, and swinging gently on its hinges, to and fro.

"Oh, leave it out, Barry, this is ridiculous," said Lem, under his breath. It hadn't made sense for the door in the street to be unlocked, unbolted and ajar. It was totally insane for this one to be, with all the valuables in the flat beyond it.

And yet the fact had to be faced that that was precisely what had happened. Pushing the door wide – not kicking it this time; if there'd been an ambush, it would have been downstairs, not up here amongst Barry's treasures – Lem strode dazedly into the flat, and was soon going through the whole place, turning the lights up in room after room. There was evidence of hurried packing in some of the bedrooms; drawers pulled out, coathangers lying on the floor. A few bare patches on the walls, pointlessly spotlit by carefully positioned lamps, suggested that priceless paintings had been taken down and stashed away. But there were no signs that a struggle or a shoot out had taken place, or anything else that might have driven the Mayne mob away. The entire flat had been left almost exactly as it always was – with the difference, of course, that it was wide open for any passing yobbos to vandalise, any passing thief to burgle, any enemy gang to wreck or set ablaze.

"Well, Barry boy, you've certainly foxed me this time," Lemaitre muttered – and then suddenly whistled. He had thought of a possible reason for Barry Mayne's strange behaviour – and could only hope that once again he'd jumped to a wrong conclusion.

As he put it over the police radio to Gideon, a moment after he'd returned to the police car:

"I'll tell you how it looks to me, Gee Gee – and take a deep breath and a couple of Aspros, because you're not going to like it at all. The way I see it, Barry could only have cleared out and left his place wide open like that if *he knew for certain there was going to be a police raid at any minute.* It'd be logical to leave the doors open then. He'd know that otherwise, we'd only smash them down – and it probably nearly broke his heart to think of axes busting into all that posh mahogany on the first floor."

★ ★ ★

Lemaitre was right. Gideon didn't like hearing that at all. A sense of impending disaster, cold and dark and dank as the night outside, swept through him. If Barry Mayne had had such precise knowledge of the coming raid, it looked as though, despite all his precautions, despite bringing in only men he had known for years and would literally trust with his life, the leaking was still going on.

He forced the thought of that out of his mind as violently as a goalkeeper slamming a menacing ball clear of the net.

"Leave me to worry about that, Lem. The important thing is you've finished your part of the job, and are free to go back to Warnham Green. And you've got to get there straight away."

Lem was about to groan "Oh, no. Not the Strangler case again!" But something in Gideon's tone told him the situation was too serious for grumbles. For once, he kept quiet and listened – his sharp, thin features becoming sharper and thinner by the second as he was brought up to date on everything that had happened.

"Hell!" he muttered. "Nothing's certain in this game, is it? If ever a case looked as though it was sewn up for good – still, I should have known it wasn't. The very sight of Exton gave me the shivers, and when that girl started ogling him – blimey, I could have cheerfully strangled her myself for being such a stupid little nit!"

"Never mind all that," Gideon barked. "Get moving, for God's sake. You've very little time left if you're going to save her. Maybe – " he fought hard against that chilly disaster feeling – "maybe you've no time at all."

Lem remained his irrepressible self.

"Thanks for those cheery words of hope and comfort, Gee Gee. They warmed the cockles of my heart. I'll be in touch – when I can. I'm obviously in for a big night."

"Join the club," Gideon grunted – and had just taken off the headphones when he was obliged to put them on again, to take a radio call from Tom Riddell.

Riddell sounded very strained. He had recovered from his sudden blackout of a few minutes before, to find his second-in-command had taken over the raid on the flat of the drugs king, Jeremy Kemp. They had already knocked, got no reply, then smashed down the door and gone in.

"No joy, though, I'm afraid," Riddell reported. "The place is deserted – just like everywhere else we've raided."

Gideon nodded. The Kemp raid – yes, of course: it had been a three-pronged attack, hadn't it, on the back of the Playhouse Theatre in the Strand, the Theatre Museum in Wardour Street, and the Bayswater flat. Riddell, in charge of all three raids, would have had radio reports on what had happened at the other centres.

"You mean – nothing's been found anywhere? No drugs – no men – "

"'Fraid not," Tom replied, sounding more strained than ever. "Nothing – except signs of hurried getaways, everywhere. Anyone would think there'd been a tip-off – not just that there was going to be a raid, but that it was going to happen – tonight."

Gideon said nothing, for the simplest of reasons. He suddenly had nothing he trusted himself to say.

Riddell went babbling on. He seemed less strained suddenly, and was attempting that bright eagerness he had shown earlier that night. An eagerness that was somehow frightening –

"Not that I'm beaten yet, George. There's still that secret flat in Pimlico I told you about. I'm going there now."

It was on the tip of Gideon's tongue to shout: "For Pete's sake, don't. Pack it in and go home!"

He remembered just in time that this was supposed to be Riddell's big night; that his idea that Kemp might use that Pimlico flat as a bolt-hole was sound and shrewd, and that if he let him go there, he *might* pull off the coup of a lifetime. And break the night's chain of disasters . . .

So he just said: "Right, then, Tom. Good luck – and take care."

This time he made no attempt to take off the headphones – which was just as well. Matt Honiwell was waiting to be switched through. Like Lemaitre and Riddell, he had nothing but negatives to report. The elusive Arturo Salvados had excelled himself, and failed to put in an appearance at any of his innumerable known haunts.

"The annoying thing is," Matt added, "that he obviously was at his Esher place, less than an hour before we broke in. He smokes herbal cigarettes, and I could smell them everywhere. Anyone would think – "

"There'd been a tip-off," Gideon finished for him, wearily. "Yes, Matt. I'm beginning to think that too. And not just one tip-off either. Lem and Tom Riddell have had the same experience as you."

Matt immediately raised the obvious question; the one that Gideon had been dreading.

"You mean – it looks as if Gideon's raid has been leaked just like the other one?"

"It's a possibility," Gideon admitted. "Look, Matt: pack things up at Esher and come back here as quick as you can, will you? Saving the raid is going to call for a crisis conference – and I'd like you there."

"Right, then, I will be," said Matt, his voice cheerful and friendly as ever, giving no sign of the tiredness and frustration he must be feeling.

Gideon hoped he could say the same about his own voice, but doubted it. In fact, he could hear the hoarse gruffness in it as Hobbs came up, and he found himself snapping:

"What the hell is it now?"

Alec also looked desperately tired, although he managed a wan smile.

"I've just had Paul Barnaby on the line, reporting on the results of six subsidiary raids to round up henchmen and sidekicks – known accomplices."

"You needn't go on," groaned Gideon. "I can see from your face, there were none of them home."

Alec added to his wry smile an equally wry, helpless shrug.

"He netted a few sprats, but there were no mackerels in sight," he agreed. "What do we do now, George? I've got men on watch at all the airports and docks, of course. None of these villains will be leaving the country tonight, that's for sure. And if you want roadblocks – "

"Roadblocks!" Gideon exploded. "Talk about locking the stable door after the horse has bolted! Mayne, Kemp and Salvados could be practically anywhere in Britain by now – and wherever they are, one thing's certain: they'll be laughing themselves sick at the thought of the fast one they've pulled on us."

Suddenly he was pacing up and down the room, ignoring the startled glances of the radio operators and the staff answering the phones. Not that any of them glanced up for long. Gideon's face had that ferocious look which, at one time or another, had made almost everyone in the Yard building shake in his (or her) shoes.

"But they won't be laughing for long. I promise you. This operation is only just beginning. Somehow – *somehow* – we'll get them yet."

Even Alec, who knew Gideon better than almost anyone else in the force, was surprised at the stubborn defiance in his tone. It was like George, of course, not to admit defeat even when it was staring him in the face, but not at all like him to lose touch completely with reality. And surely, the reality of the present situation was that the raid had proved totally abortive, and was now over, done with, dead.

Aloud, he said, as mildly as possible (he didn't want that famous Gideon glare to be turned on *him*):

"Frankly, I don't see that there's much point in going on with *any* operation until we've tackled the security question. We took every conceivable precaution tonight – abandoned the old raid, sent everyone connected with it home, brought in you and all your most trusted men – and yet still every move we were going to make was known." Suddenly Hobbs's weariness was taking over; the mask of coolness was cracking, and he was almost gabbling again, the way he had done on the telephone at the very beginning of this long, long night. "We've got to face it, George: Mayne, Kemp, Salvados – they all knew just when we were coming. Every hour, every minute, it seems, the whole of Scotland Yard is leaking like a bloody sieve."

It was Alec who was getting the odd glances from the operations staff now. Gideon frowned. If word got round that the Assistant Commissioner (Crime) was close to panic –

"Let's go somewhere where we can't be overheard, shall we?" he suggested quietly.

"If there's any such place in the building," said Alec bitterly – but he obviously saw the sense in what Gideon said, and led the way into a small inner office. The place was surrounded by glass, and looked to Gideon about as private as the aquarium tank it so closely resembled, but at least it seemed to be soundproof. He just hoped that no one outside could lip-read.

Once in there, Gideon resumed his restless pacing. He slid a hand into his jacket pocket, where it started fumbling with an old briar pipe. He never smoked it now, but always kept it on him; the feel of it somehow steadied his nerves and helped him think.

"Now, listen," he began as calmly as he could. "There hasn't necessarily been a leak since I took over. The first leak told the Big Three all they needed to know. Scott-Marle gambled on the fact that, because the original raid was scheduled for a week away, they wouldn't run for cover too fast – and *my* raid would be able to catch them, so to speak, with their bags half-packed. Well – the gamble failed, that's all. The boys were smarter than we thought. One whiff of danger and they were off like a shot. That would explain why we drew blanks everywhere . . ."

Gideon stopped there, suddenly – aware that he had been almost gabbling himself, talking so fast that he was out of breath. Why, he wondered. Was it because he was secretly far from convinced by his own theory, and was trying to bluster?

The cigarette smoke left by Arturo Salvados . . . the fact that Barry Mayne had been reckless enough to leave his front door open – things like that did suggest that they had suddenly received positive information that a raid was coming tonight – and had got themselves out just in time . . .

The goldfish tank office might be soundproof, but it wasn't insulated from the outside world. There was a telephone on one of the desks inside it, and it suddenly rang.

Swearing under his breath – he had had enough calls of one kind and another for one night – Gideon picked up the receiver.

"G-g-good evening, sir," said a stammering voice. "Price here."

Derek Price was one of the youngest chief detective superintendents under Gideon's command, a bulldog-like young man with a bulldog-like determination, handicapped by a curious inability to communicate anything clearly or concisely. Gideon had learned from experience that it paid to be patient with Price, and he struggled desperately to be patient now. He had sent the young Superintendent down to the home of the supergrass, Rene Renalto, as soon as he'd learnt of his murder. That had been well before one, and it was now nearly three. It seemed as though Price, determined as ever, had remained at the scene of the crime half the night, investigating what had happened.

"I – I've just come across s-something I think will interest you, sir," he said, in his usual barely audible manner.

"Right," said Gideon. "What is it? Speak up, for Heaven's sake. It's a terrible line."

It always sounded like a terrible line when Price was on the phone. It took Gideon all of five minutes to get him to half-stutter, half-mutter out the facts.

Renalto had been found, as Gideon already knew, stabbed in the back at the wheel of his car, outside his own garage. Price had brought a scene-of-the-crime team with him, who had taken photographs, dusted everywhere for fingerprints, and removed the body, once the police doctor had looked at it. Then Price had sent the team home, except for a constable stationed outside the house for the night. He himself had remained on the premises, sifting through the contents of cupboards and drawers.

"I thought the home of a supergrass ought to provide valuable leads of one s-sort or another," he said.

"Quite right," said Gideon, wondering just how longer Price would take in coming to the point. "And did you find any?"

"No, sir – but while I was searching, I suddenly realised that there was an – an answering machine connected to one of Renalto's phones. Renalto had obviously switched the machine on before leaving the house, and I noticed a bulb winking on the machine to show that an incoming message had been received sometime during the night."

Gideon tensed.

"From some contact who didn't realise Renalto was dead, I suppose."

"Yes, sir. I've listened to the message, and I think it could be important. Shall – shall I play it over the phone?"

With consummate patience, Gideon managed a mild: "Yes, Price. Please do."

He held the receiver so that Hobbs could listen too, with the result that both men received the shock together: the shock of the night so far.

A thick Cockney voice, hoarse with excitement, was yelling:

*"Here's the latest, Rene, mate, straight off the grapevine. After you spilled the beans about the raid being leaked, Scott-Marle's changed all his plans, and brought the whole operation forward to tonight. And you know who's in charge now? The Old Man of the C.I.D. himself, George Gideon – under orders to bring in his pet cronies to take over where Warburton & Co. left off.*

*"I'll ring again as soon as there's more news, but the reckoning at the moment is that Gideon's raid will be between 1 and 2 a.m., and that the command line-up will be Lemaitre (dragged off the Strangler case which he's making such a shambles of), 'Cuddles' Honiwell, always an old mate of Gideon's, and maybe Riddell – though there's a big 'if' attached to him, because some say he's been half off his rocker since the Stannet business. Probably Gideon will set Lemaitre on to Barry Mayne. It's a toss-up who'll be going for Kemp and Salvados."*

The voice changed its tone from hoarse excitement to equally hoarse alarm.

*"A word of warning, tosher. As you'll realise, the Big Three*

*know now that the leak was leaked back to the police. They're working on who did it, and the story goes that they may be having none too kind thoughts about you. If I was you, I'd do what everybody else seems to be doing tonight – getting out for the sake of their health. Believe me, Rene. You're in serious trouble or my name ain't Fingers –"*

The speaker had reached the end of the time allowed for a message on the machine, and a shrill whine cut off his scared voice. "Fingers," thought Gideon. Once, years ago, the underworld slang for pickpockets. It suggested a small-time crook – or someone who had started life as one.

"S-shall I play it over again, sir?" muttered Price.

"No," said Gideon. "We've heard all we need, I think. Good night and thanks, Price. You've been a very great help."

He hung up, surprised at the shakiness of his own hand as he did so. He suddenly realised that he had not eaten or drunk anything since Kate's toddy, and that seemed a millennium ago. He shouted out for someone to bring coffee, in a roar that effortlessly penetrated the "soundproof" glass surrounding him. "And a sandwich," he added. "Ham with plenty of mustard."

"And the same for me," said Alec, in a fair imitation of the Gideon roar.

Neither spoke again until the coffee and sandwiches had been brought, and they were drinking and munching. Though Gideon's sandwich proved difficult to get down; his mouth and throat felt as dry as a bone, and the coffee didn't do much to help.

"Well," he said at last. "That settles it, doesn't it? This place *is* leaking like a sieve. And there's only one way in which it could be doing that. It must be riddled with informants – so many of them that no matter how we change the personnel involved, every detail of what we plan gets out."

It was left to Alec to raise the question he dreaded.

"Which, then, of the raid personnel do you reckon could be informants?" he asked quietly.

Gideon gulped some more coffee, half-choking as it went down the wrong way.

"It could have been any of the two thousand in that hall," he spluttered, when he could find his voice.

Alec shook his head.

"I'm afraid it couldn't, George. How long does it take information to filter through an underground grapevine, and then get back to a supergrass? An hour, surely, at the very least. Which means that those facts we just heard must have been leaked pretty early in the night, certainly before one. Now who at that time knew that you were taking over, and planning to carry out the raid? Scott-Marle obviously. You, yourself. Me – and the people you rang up about it: Lemaitre, Honiwell, Riddell . . ."

"But there were others," Gideon protested. "You and your team started calling men from all over London."

"Ah, but we were careful," Alec said. "We just told them to get here fast, and let them assume it was a major operation. We never mentioned a raid on the Big Three. *Or* that you were in command. *Or* when the raid would be . . ."

Hobbs broke off at the sight of Gideon's face. He looked not like a haunted man so much as a *hunted* one – and Alec realised he had forced him into a terrible corner, confronting the most appalling task of his career: the task of deciding which of his oldest colleagues, his most trusted friends, could have turned traitor.

It was a job which Gideon's mind simply refused to face at first. It went blank on him, like the screen of a TV set that had blown a fuse. Then it started rebelling, insisting that there had to be a fault in Alec's reasoning somewhere. Could anyone imagine Lem passing facts over to the Big Three? Or Matt Honiwell? Or Tom –

At the thought of Tom Riddell, Gideon paused, so tense that he was hardly breathing. Riddell had been acting strangely for months, even years. This very night, he had been showing constant signs of some deep inner tension. Was it possible that all that was due to – guilt?

Gideon wasn't proud of having entertained that thought. Every instinct told him to forget it – except one. That basic copper's instinct to get at the truth, no matter what it cost. If, of course, that *was* the truth –

The telephone rang at that moment, for what seemed the millionth time that night. For once, Gideon was relieved to hear it. Anything to get away from those suspicions.

He snatched up the receiver as eagerly as a starving dog grabbing a bone, and then felt almost like dropping it again. It was a Detective Inspector Notley reporting from Jeremy Kemp's secret flat in Pimlico, where Riddell had led his team in that last desperate bid to catch the drugs king.

"I'm afraid we've drawn a blank here, sir," he said. "We've broken in, but the whole place is deserted."

"Don't worry, Notley. That's par for the course tonight," Gideon told him, adding tensely: "But where is Mr. Riddell?"

There was a long pause. Then Notley said:

"I'm really not sure, sir. While we were going through the flat, searching for possible hiding places and so on, he suddenly said he'd leave us to get on with it, and disappeared."

"Disappeared?"

"He just went out through the front door, slamming it behind him, and strode off somewhere on his own. I wouldn't ordinarily question the actions of a superior officer, sir, but – frankly, we're all very worried about him. He had a blackout earlier tonight, when we were in Bayswater, and ever since, he's had a strange look, as though – as though he hardly knew what he was doing. Do you suppose he's all right?"

"How can I possibly tell without actually being there?" Gideon snapped, then pulled himself together sharply. He had no excuse for biting the unfortunate Notley's head off. The man was doing his best in a very difficult and embarrassing situation. Struggling to be calm and reasonable, he asked:

"I take it that Mr. Riddell didn't say anything to anyone about where he was going?"

Notley's reply gave him one of the nastiest moments of his life.

"Detective Sergeant Greaves here, sir, says he heard Mr. Riddell mutter something under his breath – to himself, not to any of us – just as he was going out of the door. Greaves wouldn't swear that he had heard it right, but it sounded like: 'I've got to see Fingers'," he said. "The name doesn't mean anything to us here, sir. Does it by any chance mean anything to you?"

# 11 Danger Zone

Notley had been right in saying that Riddell was in such a state he hardly knew what he was doing.

He had known clearly enough when he had gone striding out of the front door of the Kemp flat. He remembered that there had been a very precise intention in his mind, and a very urgent purpose behind it.

But now that he was out in the damp, black night, amongst the maze of streets leading off the Pimlico Road alongside the tracks of Victoria Station, he was suddenly as lost and confused as he had been earlier, when driving from his home to Scotland Yard.

Then the trouble had been that he had kept taking wrong turnings. Now he was in a still worse position. He couldn't remember if there *was* a right turning to take.

Pimlico wasn't exactly unknown territory to Riddell. As a young constable, he had pounded a beat round here, in strange, distant days when there had still been bombed sites everywhere, masses of uncleared rubble with weeds growing all over them. Now the picture was different, but equally gloomy. Recession and so many residents moving out of the area had created street after street of boarded-up houses, closed businesses, empty shops. They all looked the same in the harsh light of the orange street lamps – or was it that they *were* the same, that he was just walking round and round in circles, getting nowhere because there was nowhere to get, the victim of just a crazy impulse from an overstrained brain?

He'd do better to stop, and try and make his way back, Riddell told himself – but his feet didn't seem to be listening. As far as they were concerned, it was just as though he was pounding the beat again: not just walking, but "proceeding", in good old police fashion, solidly, implacably plodding on and on . . . And suddenly the odd realisation came to him that his feet now seemed to know where they were going. It was though they were in touch with a deeper, still rational part of his brain.

Almost as if he was sleepwalking, though no sleepwalker ever strode so heavily and purposefully as he was doing now, Riddell found himself turning right and then left, and then right again, to halt finally at the mouth of a dark alley. A battered street sign was just legible in the light from a nearby lamp.

Vincent Lane, S.W.1

He stood, staring at it for just a second, and then suddenly a number came into his head. Nine. He had to go down the alley and find No. 9.

Why? he wondered almost rebelliously. Why the hell should he? What was all this about? What – why – what – why –

The whats and whys became a whirling maelstrom into which he suddenly felt himself sinking. He swayed, stumbled, nearly fell – and then a miracle happened. His brain abruptly cleared – and clear, Tom Riddell's brain had few equals for sharpness.

Of course. He had come to look up "Fingers" Kelsey, who lived at 9 Vincent Lane. All the time that he had been building up evidence against Jeremy Kemp, Fingers had been an enormous help. He was a shifty little character, once a run-of-the-mill pickpocket, who had got involved with the Big Three set-up many years before, and had done all manner of small jobs for them ever since. He'd always been a small-time villain, as his name implied; but he'd kept his eyes open, knew how to put two and two together and make four, and also knew how to keep his ear to the grapevine. He was the first to catch any whisper that was going round, and probably knew as much about the doings of the Big Three as almost anyone. Then, the previous year, he'd had a heartbreaking personal shock: his daughter had committed suicide after getting hooked on heroin. That had turned Fingers against Kemp and all he stood for, which was why he had passed on useful tips to Riddell again and again. Riddell suspected that he sometimes passed tips elsewhere as well – he was a close crony of Rene Renalto, the biggest supergrass in London . . .

It was through Fingers that Riddell had known about Kemp's secret Pimlico flat, and tonight, when he had found it deserted, it had occurred to him that the most sensible thing to do was to walk the short distance over to Fingers's place, and see if he had any suggestions to make about where the drugs king might be hiding now.

He hadn't wanted any of the men to come with him, of course. Riddell's relationship with Fingers had been a delicate and deeply secret one. It would be as much as the little crook's life was worth if the slightest whisper got out that he had a police connection. Which was why Riddell had simply left his team to get on with it, and gone striding out into the night. With Vincent Lane only a short walk away, he hadn't bothered about a car. How was he to know that his brain would seize up on him, and turn all Pimlico into an endless maze –

That was enough of that, Riddell told himself severely. Thinking about the nightmare experience might bring it back, might start him swaying and stumbling again. He'd better get himself to No. 9 quick.

Moving at such a pace now that he was almost running, Riddell turned into the alley, which was almost pitch black once he was a couple of yards down it. He wished to God he'd brought a torch, but he seemed to remember that Kelsey's place – a brightly painted little house, with a front door giving on to the street – was about four along on the left.

It was so dark now that he had to slow his steps and start to grope his way forward. But he was still moving too fast not to trip and fall headlong over something soft and yielding that lay across his path.

Something that groaned, softly, hollowly. Something that seemed to be lying half-way in and half-way out of Fingers Kelsey's front door.

Gasping, Riddell picked himself up, blinked round him, and then reached into the doorway, found a light switch, and clicked it on.

Light from the hall poured out on to the pavement – and on to the prostrate body of Kelsey himself, lying face downwards, with a knife in his back.

★ ★ ★

Riddell was shaken – but into action, not another bout of nerves. He stooped to pick Fingers up, to get the front part of his body off the pavement – but then he remembered that any movement could be fatal, with a knife in that position. It was terrible to leave the little man even for a second the way he was now – his face pressed hard against dust and concrete, the blood pouring surrealistically into a gutter. But what choice had he?

He was stepping carefully over the body, to get to the telephone he could see fixed to the wall a yard inside the front door, when Fingers whispered sharply:

"It's Tom Riddell, isn't it?"

"That's right, Fingers, it's me."

Riddell's own voice sounded as breathless as Kelsey's.

"Well, listen, Tom. Leave it out, going to the phone. It's too late to help me now, and I'd rather you hung about to hear what I've got to say. It's something you won't hear from nobody else, because hardly anybody knows it except me."

Riddell knelt down by Fingers's side, and almost had to put his ear to the ground to hear what Kelsey was saying. The little crook's voice was becoming fainter and fainter, like a radio whose batteries were very, very low.

"First, get this. The Big Three aren't really the Big Three. They're the Big Four. Mayne, Kemp, Salvados and one other. I don't know who the fourth man is, except that he's rich, owns a big house – and I *mean* a big one – and has kept his nose so clean that there's never been a whisper against him.

"So if you want to know where the Big Three have scarpered to tonight, the answer's that they're all round at No. 4's place, where they reckon they can lie low for ever, if need be. And if you want to know where No. 4's place is . . ."

The faint voice began, infuriatingly, to ramble.

"Christ, tosher, what a way to go. Face down in the gutter. And there was I, not two hours ago, warning Renalto *he* was in serious trouble! Never thought the Big Three would get around to bothering about me. But they're bothering about everyone tonight – closing every mouth, you might say, that might give away their big secret."

Riddell, hating himself for his heartlessness, struggled to bring Kelsey back to what he had been on the point of giving away earlier.

"But they haven't closed *your* mouth, Fingers. So tell me the secret. No. 4's place – where do we look for it?"

"Can't tell you for sure, Tom. But the word goes it's round – round Hammersmith way. And it ain't the Hammersmith Palais, I'll tell you that for free."

He started laughing shortly. The laugh turned into a choke, then a gurgle, then (most terrible of all) a rattle – and Fingers Kelsey was dead.

* * *

*Hammersmith . . .*

It was a long time before the full significance of that word sank in on Gideon.

Riddell rang him straight away from the phone in Fingers Kelsey's hall, and gave him an on-the-spot report on the situation and all that had led up to it, including a verbatim recapitulation of Fingers's dramatic final speech.

Gideon's reaction was first and foremost, a sense of overwhelming relief, tinged with shame that he had secretly allowed Tom's name to soar to the top of his list of suspects. He should have known that Riddell, no matter what his state of mind, would never be anything less than a loyal colleague. But there was far more than that to be relieved about. The longer he listened to Tom's clear, concise résumé of the facts, the more obvious it became that Riddell's nervous troubles had not impaired his basic shrewdness in the smallest degree. He still had that sharp police brain – and tonight it wasn't merely functioning; it had brought off a brilliant coup, providing the first spark of hope that Gideon had glimpsed in a night of disaster, débâcle, despair . . .

"Congratulations, Tom," he said, and felt so strongly about it that he said it again. "Congratulations from us all!"

"On what?" said Riddell, rather bitterly. "I was too late to catch Kemp, too late to save Fingers, and – and – " He broke off there. He had been on the point of confiding that he'd spent half the night wandering around in a daze, but that was hardly a sensible thing to confess to the Commander of the C.I.D., however old a friend he might be. He just said, lamely: "Too late for just about everything."

Gideon's tone remained congratulatory.

"But not too late to save the whole of tonight's operation – the whole of Gideon's raid!" he said. "Don't you realise, Tom? Your Fingers has given the Big Three's game away completely. All we have to do is work on the clue he's given us, and we can still net all three of them before dawn."

"All four of them, if Fingers got his arithmetic right," said Riddell.

"True enough. All four of 'em," Gideon laughed. The relief, combined with the sudden possibility of victory after so many numbing defeats, was affecting him like alcohol on an empty stomach. He was feeling so light-headed that he had to remind himself severely that although the breaks might be coming at last, he was still very far from being out of trouble.

He was no nearer to solving the mystery of the information disclosures – and for all he knew, the Yard might still be "leaking like a sieve". The Big Three, the unfortunate Fingers had claimed, had been busy "closing all the mouths" who could betray where they were hiding, so it might prove impossible to track them down, after all.

This gloomy thought, though, Gideon felt he had a right to reject. Surely to Heaven it shouldn't be difficult to locate a big house – a very big house – in Hammersmith, even if the mysterious No. 4 who owned it *had* kept his nose clean?

"Tom," said Gideon. "Once you've taken care of the situation at Fingers's, I want you to get yourself down to Hammersmith police station. Get a scale map of the area. Get whoever's on night duty to help you. I want you to pinpoint all the houses with, say, a value of £500,000 upwards throughout the area – and ring me back as soon as you can with a list of them. Okay?"

Riddell promised to get on to it right away, and rang off before Gideon remembered he'd been talking to a sick man; that Tom had had a hell of a night, and ought not to be put under any more strain. Still – who could say whether or not it would do him good to be made to keep that shrewd brain working?

Comforting himself with that thought, Gideon looked up, and saw that Alec Hobbs was still standing beside him, and had obviously somehow been following the whole conversation. All trace of tiredness had left his face; his man-of-the-world air had slid off him, too, and he was rubbing his hands like an excited schoolboy.

"So the Big Three have all gone to ground in the same place," he said, "and we can soon sort out the exact location of their hole! This is looking good, George. Very good indeed. I should have remembered Tom's trick of turning up trumps at the crucial moment – and this time, he's not just turned up trumps. He's handed us all the aces, from the sound of it. I'd better rally all the troops we've got left and pass the word that from now on, all roads lead to Hammersmith."

"To – *Hammersmith?*"

The sharp, startled question was barked across the "goldfish-tank" office by someone who had just put his head round the door.

It was Matt Honiwell, coming for that crisis conference – and the moment Gideon glanced up and saw him, crisis was what was in the air.

At the sight of Matt's face, the floodgates opened in Gideon's mind, and one dazed realisation followed another.

He remembered suddenly about Brian Fullerton and his Maggie . . . and that Fullerton was a detective constable in Hammersmith.

That put an entirely different complexion on their whole story. The super-criminal that Fullerton had been keeping a file on – someone so big, and yet so far above suspicion, that he hadn't dared breathe the name even to his wife – wasn't it possible that he was the silent partner of the Big Three?

The very fact that his home had been raided tonight, of all nights, seemed to suggest it. The Big Three had been frantically covering their tracks and wiping out all dangerous informers – as Rene Renalto and Fingers Kelsey had discovered to their cost . . .

Gideon started, as another realisation dawned – one so chilling that it wiped out his earlier elation, and left him momentarily stunned.

If Fingers Kelsey was right, and the Big Three had gone to eatth with their mysterious No. 4, where they believed they could lie low "for ever", then one thing was as certain as tomorrow's dawn. They could not afford to let anyone live who could give their hiding place away. Which meant that Maggie Fullerton had not been exaggerating when she'd said her husband was poorly guarded. Indeed, she'd been understating the danger! If the men behind eighty per cent of London's organised crimes were after Fullerton, and had to silence him if they were to have any hope of survival themselves, then they'd do *anything* to get him –

Matt Honiwell was still only just inside the doorway, and was still asking, dazedly "Hammersmith? What about Hammersmith?" when Gideon came storming across to him, grim and glowering.

"I'll tell you what about Hammersmith, Matt. You've got to get over there – and surround St. Giles Hospital with as big a guard as if it were Fort Knox and Buckingham Palace rolled into one."

Matt grasped the situation in a flash.

"So Fullerton's Someone Big really is – someone big."

Gideon nodded.

"Big enough," he said, more grimly than ever, "to make whatever ward he's in the deadliest danger zone in London. God help anyone who's in it if you're not there in time."

* * *

At that moment, the plight of Brian Fullerton was just as much in Kate Gideon's mind as it was in George's.

Kate had not been able to follow all of what Maggie had said on the phone, but from her chaotically blurted out story, one thing had come through very clearly.

The wife of a sick C.I.D. man was in desperate trouble, and was calling from a hospital only a couple of miles away.

That had been enough for Kate. She had quietly dressed; gone downstairs; got out the small red Volkswagen Polo which she always used for shopping and personal trips, and shot off down the deserted roads from Fulham to Hammersmith at nearly 70 m.p.h.

It wasn't that Kate was given to speeding. As a matter of fact, there were few things she hated more than driving – or being driven – fast. But that note of electric urgency in Maggie Fullerton's voice was still in her brain, and seemed to be charging the wet, dark night all round her, dragging her like a powerful magnet towards (where was it? Oh, yes, she had it written down in her diary) – Ward A4, St. Giles's Hospital, Hammersmith.

Kate drew up outside the hospital, parked her Polo in an empty space marked "DOCTORS ONLY" – for the wife of a C.I.D. Commander, she had scant regard for red tape – and walked briskly through the main entrance. There was nobody about, but signs along the walls of the hospital corridors guided her swiftly in the direction of A4.

It is doubtful if she would have turned back or even walked a shade less briskly if she'd known she was heading straight for the deadliest danger zone in London . . .

# 12 Hit Men

A minute later, Kate reached Ward A4. She remembered Maggie had said her husband was in a private room at the far end of it, and was tiptoeing quietly across when suddenly she found her way barred by two bewildered nurses, and what was worse, an outraged night sister.

"The visiting hours at this hospital are three to six p.m., not a.m.!" she began, loudly enough to wake half the patients in the ward. "We have made an exception in the case of Mrs. Fullerton, but – "

Kate had a genius for calming people, but it was taxed to the utmost now.

"I am here at the request of Mrs. Fullerton," she began, and then broke off, realising that was quite the wrong approach to take.

"Are you indeed?" the night sister barked. "And just who is Mrs. Fullerton to request any such thing?"

Kate tried a more tactful line.

"She sounded so distressed I came to relieve her, if necessary. It sounded to me as though she desperately needed sleep. But if you don't agree – well, obviously, I'm in your hands, sister."

The sister began to be mollified.

"In my opinion, that woman needs all the rest she can get," she said, and dropped her voice to a confidential whisper. "We have had a terrible night here, with drunken vandals invading this very room – quite apart from two policemen being here all the time."

"It sounds as though it was a good job they were," said Kate, mildly.

"Well, yes," the sister admitted grudgingly. "But their presence is very unsettling for everybody – patients and nurses alike. Particularly the nurses."

"Why? Are they all that handsome?" asked Kate, with a mischievous twinkle in her eyes.

The sister was not amused.

"The girls reckon they were heroes," she said. "Though what's heroic about stamping out a stupid firework beats me. Well, it's no use standing here talking, Mrs. – er – "

"Gideon," said Kate, and could hear, right across the ward, a startled muttering from the policemen in the private room. They obviously had sharp ears, and were listening to the whole thing.

Suddenly Maggie Fullerton herself appeared. Even in the gloom, she looked as white as a sheet, and was trembling so much that she could hardly speak.

"You came!" she said dazedly. "You came yourself!"

"I just thought I'd pop along and see what I could do," Kate murmured.

She expected Maggie Fullerton to start mumbling thanks. Instead, she found herself being stared at reproachfully.

"But – but where's the Commander?" she demanded.

Kate was so taken aback that she found herself, for once, stumbling over words.

"George is at the Yard tonight," she said. "Urgent business."

Maggie's stare was suddenly more than reproachful. It was openly accusing.

"Haven't you even *rung* him?" she said.

When Kate admitted that she hadn't, it started a near-hysterical outburst.

"Weren't you listening? I thought I'd explained so clearly. Brian's in great danger – the very greatest. And so is everyone here in this room. Don't tell me even *you* can't understand – "

She was almost screaming. Patients were waking up and nurses bustling about all over the ward.

The night sister had heard enough.

"Will you please pull yourself together, Mrs. Fullerton, and for Heaven's sake, keep your voice down. Your husband already has two policeman looking after him. What more do you want – an army?"

Maggie Fullerton, though, was unstoppable.

"They couldn't prevent even a gang of drunken yobbos walking in here," she screamed. "How do you imagine they can stop hit men?"

"Hit men?" gasped the sister, as if she had never heard the word.

"Hired gunmen," explained Kate. "Professional assassins. Mrs. Fullerton believes that a dangerous gang is after her husband, headed by one of the biggest criminals in London."

Maggie's eyes widened, and she looked more accusingly than ever at Kate.

"Then you did understand what I was saying on the phone," she breathed.

"I got the gist of what you were saying, yes," Kate replied. "But – "

"But you didn't really believe me? You thought I was just some silly, hysterical wife, who would calm down and see reason once the wife of the great George Gideon had come and held her hand?"

There was a long, embarrassed silence.

Anybody except "the wife of the great George Gideon" would probably have lost her temper at that point, turned and walked away, and driven straight home.

Kate didn't, because the sheer intensity of Maggie's fears was communicating itself to her more painfully than ever. The magnet that had drawn her here was holding her rooted to the spot.

Suddenly she was behaving almost like George – reproaching, blaming herself.

Maggie was right. She *had* behaved patronisingly. She *had* treated her more like a pathetic nut case than a woman with a rational anxiety.

The night sister was doing the same, at this very moment.

"Now listen to me, Mrs. Fullerton," she said. "I know you are distressed about your husband, but you must stop all this screaming and fussing. Unless you agree to take a sedative, and undertake to cause no more disturbance in this ward tonight, I am afraid I shall have no choice but to order you off the premises until the morning."

Both the night sister and Kate would remember Maggie Fullerton's reply for as long as they lived.

They were standing with their backs to the far end of the ward, but Maggie was facing it and suddenly pointed towards it dramatically.

Not with terror now, but with bitter, hopeless resignation, she said:

"Will you be ordering *them* off the premises too?"

Kate and the sister whirled round – just as the swing doors slammed with an ominous thud behind a group of six men who had just walked in.

None of them wore masks, but nobody was looking at their faces. All eyes were on the revolvers they were holding in their hands.

One of the nurses screamed. The one who had jumped on the table at the sight of the firework now leapt underneath it, as though that would protect her. One or two patients gasped. Others placidly slept on, some noisily, grotesquely snoring.

The constables came out of Fullerton's private room. The armed one raised his own gun.

"Don't," said Kate. Her years with Gideon had taught her the trick of speaking commandingly. The constable instantly let the gun fall to his side.

The night sister made a desperate bid to be commanding herself.

"Who are you? What do you want?" she shouted, her voice not up to the task she demanded of it. It rang out across the ward cracked, strident, desperate and shrill.

One of the intruders spoke at last. Just four words.

"Fullerton. Where is he?" he said.

"Don't answer," said Kate quickly.

Nobody needed to.

"You won't get him. You'll *never* get him!" Maggie Fullerton screamed, and running across the ward, disappeared into the little room. Kate imagined her throwing herself on top of Brian, protecting her body with his, and suddenly felt like sobbing herself.

The two constables took up positions in front of the private room, one of them defiantly drawing the curtains across the entrance behind him, the other raising his gun again.

A single shot rang out: not a deafening roar, but a sound like a wheezing cough. The men were obviously using silencers, thought Kate. The armed constable collapsed groaning, clutching his shoulder. The other, red-faced, sweating, stood aside.

The six men advanced down the centre of the ward, straight towards the curtained entrance to the little room, through which Maggie's sobbing could still be heard.

Straight towards it – until Kate, coolly and without the slightest fuss, stepped forward and barred their way.

★ ★ ★

It is doubtful if even Kate could have barred it for long, by herself. But the night sister joined her, and as the leading gunman ordered the two women to step aside, his voice was drowned by the most welcome sound that anyone in that ward had ever heard: the jarring, jerky wail of a police-car siren outside. Not just one siren. Within seconds, there was a jangling cacophony of competing sirens, clearly coming from all round the building.

"Just in case there's anybody in there trying anything already," were Matt Honiwell's first words as he arrived outside the hospital, "it'll do no harm to let 'em know we've got the place surrounded."

He had, in fact, eight police cars with him, and a contingent of some thirty men. While Matt barked radio orders, they spilled out of the cars and in seconds did, in fact, have the hospital surrounded, with four or five men at every exit, and a dozen left to follow Matt as he went charging up the steps to the main entrance.

This time there *was* somebody about: a jittery security man dithering around in the entrance hall, who had been simply brushed aside by the intruders less than three minutes before, and had only just got through ringing the police station.

"They told me not to worry, a lot of you were on your way," he said. "But you'd be worried, Superintendent, if you'd seen those men. Six of them there were and every one of them had a gun – *and* wasn't afraid to let me see it. I could have sworn my last hour had come – "

The quaint old expression didn't amuse Matt. It could so easily have been literally correct. Men who stalked into public places coolly showing guns, and brushing aside security men as though they were flies, sounded like everything that Maggie Fullerton had been warning him about: a top criminal's killer elite. God, why hadn't he listened to her?

If he didn't act fast now – faster, maybe, than ever before in his life – then one thing was certain: Detective Constable Fullerton's last hour *would* have –

"Ward A4. Which way?" he barked. He had learned from ringing the hospital that Fullerton was in a room adjoining that ward. Stopping only a split-second to hear the security man's instructions, he flung himself towards the staircase.

He had a revolver in his pocket, but kept it there as he arrived outside the ward (which turned out to be on the first floor), with a party of breathless men behind him. A shoot out in a hospital was something to be avoided at any cost.

Well . . . almost any cost.

Running a hand through his mop of curly hair, and finding it, to his surprise, already sticky with sweat, Matt walked slowly up to the large, grey-black swing doors of the ward, and pushed one of them open.

The next moment, he was staggering backwards, bruised and shaken.

Someone the other side had been waiting for him, and had kicked the door viciously back in his face.

"Listen, copper," a voice said.

It wasn't a sneering or jeering voice; just a very calm one, stating facts.

"It was lucky for you you never made it through that swing door. Because the first copper who comes through it won't have time to blink before he gets it between the eyes. Okay?"

Matt didn't trust himself to say anything for a moment. The door had caught him right across the cheek, and felt as though it had half-cracked his jaw. It was as agonising as though every tooth in his head had started aching at once – and yet somehow he had to stay cool. There were nurses in there and a good two dozen patients, in addition to the helpless Maggie and her Brian. The last thing he wanted to do was say anything which made these gunmen trigger-happy.

Finally he managed to say, soothingly:

"Keep your hair on, boys. Nobody's coming in through this flaming door."

He hated giving that assurance. He knew it wouldn't be exactly good news for all the people on the other side. For their sake, he hastily added:

"Not for the moment, anyway."

"It had better be a long moment, copper," the voice replied. "Just about the longest in history."

"We'll see about that," said Matt, as genially as possible. "We'll see . . ."

The pain was lessening a little and he could think clearly again. His first thought was this man might be deliberately keeping him busy, while the other five got out of the ward through another door. He looked round and saw that a young man in a white uniform – a male nurse or house surgeon, he wasn't sure which – was at his side. From him he learned that there was another door, and also an emergency exit leading to a fire escape. Hurried whispered orders sent men scuttling away to cover both.

The spokesman for the hit men was talking again now.

"Just in case you're not bothered about a bullet between the eyes, Inspector – or whatever you are – "

"Honiwell," said Matt. "And the rank's Chief Detective Superintendent, if you want to know."

"I don't," said the other. "It'd be all the same to me if

you were the almighty Gideon himself. If any of your men takes one step through that door, then not only *he* gets it – but the sister here and half of her nurses too."

"Charming," said Matt. "Why not make it half the patients as well, while you're about it? They should be helpless enough to make suitable victims for you cowardly, murdering bastards."

But he said it under his breath, far too softly to be heard through the door. There was a terrible chance that they might think it smart to take him literally. With so many lives at stake, he couldn't risk saying anything that might upset them, anything at all. He remembered suddenly his reputation for being amiable, cuddly Matt. He ought to be able to say something soothing and placating now. But when he tried, the words stuck in his throat, and all that happened was that he started to sweat again from his forehead, armpits – it seemed from every pore.

"And talking about hostages," the spokesman went on, "we've got a lady visitor here – I don't know who she is, but she acts like a cross between Lady Diana and the Queen Mum. She's got to be someone important to carry on like that. Tell us your name, ducks . . ."

There was an odd pause. It was obvious that whoever the woman in question was, the man had seized her and was holding her roughly.

"I said tell us your name!" he said again.

The silence continued. Matt suddenly couldn't stand it.

"Leave her alone, or it'll be the worse for you!" he shouted.

It was an empty threat, and he knew it, even as he said it; but it seemed to work.

A low gasp of relief indicated that the woman had been released on the other side. She said something, for the first time: a soft, icily polite "Thank you."

Matt started slightly. He must be going crazy, but the voice sounded familiar. Where the hell had he heard it –

"We'll get her name from somebody later," the spokesman said. "Meanwhile, I'll tell you this, Mr. Chief Detective Superintendent. She's our No. 1 hostage. And by No. 1 I mean she'll be the first to get it if anyone comes through that door. Understand?"

"I understand perfectly," said Matt grimly – although there was in fact a lot he *didn't* grasp about what was going on behind that door. Why should the unknown hostage have so stubbornly refused to give her name? It was as though she thought that knowing who she was would hinder the police in some way; but why should it? If only she'd said more than just those two cold words –

Matt decided to thrust the problem out of his mind. He had too much to do to start puzzling out minor mysteries at the moment. He only hoped it *was* minor . . .

His next task was obviously to contact Gideon. He had a police walkie-talkie on him, which could be connected via the police car radio outside to the Yard – but it needed to be bellowed into, and he didn't want everything he said to be heard through the door. He turned and walked about half-way down the stairs to the ground floor before he started using it. Then, the switch-through to the Yard having been accomplished, he found himself shakily, reporting to Gideon:

"We came here just too late. The hit men – six of them, obviously a crack killer team – have taken over the whole ward adjoining Fullerton's room. I've got thirty men with me, and have surrounded the hospital and covered all the ward exits. But the men are threatening to shoot the night sister, half the nurses and a mysterious lady visitor if we attempt to move in. In other words, George, I've a classic siege situation on my hands, in the worst of all places: a hospital. If only I'd listened to Maggie Fullerton – "

Gideon's voice cut in roughly.

"Don't start blaming yourself, Matt – this has been a night for mistakes, and we've all made our share of 'em," he said. "The question is, how to get out of this mess – quick."

"Is there a quick way?" said Matt. "Siege situations can drag on for days."

"Yes, but this one's different – very different," Gideon snapped back. "We're not dealing with crazy hi-jackers using hostages to make political demands. We're up against a gang of professionals who are basically after one man's blood, and one man's only. Fullerton is the person in that hospital who's in real, imminent danger. The hostages will only be at risk if they try to intervene."

"Or if *we* try to intervene," said Matt.

"Maybe," said Gideon. "But we might have to take a chance on that."

Matt's mouth, and even his lips and tongue, went dry. It was as though all the water in his mouth had poured out in the sweat that was still making his hair a sticky, syrupy morass between his fingers.

"You're – you're not telling me to just forget about the hostages, and go in?"

"All I'm telling you to do," Gideon replied, "is get back outside that ward and keep them talking. Do anything, say anything to prevent them shooting Fullerton until – "

"Until what?" said Matt.

It was just as well, he thought, that he had gone half-way down the stairs. Gideon's roar, even weakened and distorted by the walkie-talkie, sounded loud enough to wake the whole of St. Giles.

"Until I get there," he shouted. "I'm coming over right away!"

# 13 Hobbs

Alec Hobbs was, as usual, by Gideon's side, and overheard all his bellowed interchange with Matt Honiwell.

By the time it had finished, he was looking dazed and incredulous.

"Did I hear right?" he said. "You're going to smash your way in there, regardless of what happens to – to anyone?"

Gideon stood up, glowering.

"Frankly, I don't know what the bloody hell I'm going to do," he said. "But if I don't do something, Maggie Fullerton is going to see her husband shot dead right in front of her – by a hit gang that imagines it can get away with murder, simply by making a few wild threats at nurses and some odd woman who's strayed in from the night."

"From a callous gang loaded down with weapons – are *any* threats wild?" asked Alec.

As Gideon significantly said nothing, he went on:

"Look, George. Hadn't I better get the terrorist boys on to this? They've had experience both of hi-jackings and sieges galore. They've got special electronic equipment, trained psychiatrists on call to chat up the criminals – "

"And a machine which will save Brian Fullerton?" Gideon snapped drily. "No, Alec: there's only one hope for him, and that's if I can play it my way. As for the hostages, don't worry. I won't put their lives at risk – more than I have to, anyway."

He added the last bit after the door of the operations

room had slammed behind him, and he was on his way to the lift. It wasn't the thought of the hostages that haunted him as the lift swept him downstairs; it was still the plight of Brian Fullerton, lying unconscious, with Maggie pleading for his life – as passionately as she'd been warning everyone, all night, that he was ridiculously poorly guarded. How right that poor woman had been. And what idiots he and Matt Honiwell had been to think that she was out of her mind –

He rushed out of the Yard's back entrance and reached his parked Rover in seconds. Settling heavily behind the wheel, he saw something in a cubby-hole under the dashboard which he hadn't noticed before: a thermos flask, with a note nestling beside it.

*Extra Toddy ration – in case you need it.*
*You never know, love – you might!*
*KATE*

Gideon smiled to himself, and realised with a pang that he'd hardly thought of Kate once, during this long nightmare of a night. He wondered if she was fast asleep – or would she be lying awake, anxiously, knowing he was facing one of the biggest challenges of his life?

He hoped, devoutly, that she was asleep. After all, she did have heart trouble, and strain of any kind wasn't good . . .

Just for a moment, he allowed himself to think about her, and to wish that he was away from all this, lying sleeping beside her.

Then he was roaring at a reckless 80 m.p.h. – faster even than she had gone in her Polo – through the night.

It wasn't a magnetic impulse that was drawing *him* towards St. Giles Hospital. It was the cold certainty that only he could stop that constable being murdered. And not all the threats to all the hostages in the world was going to stop him.

* * *

The moment Gideon had left the Yard, urgent telephone calls for him began to pour in, which Alec Hobbs had to handle as best he could.

The first was from Lemaitre, who was now back at Warnham Green police station, and had had new thoughts about the Stocking Strangler case.

"Sounds like Gee Gee's having a night to end all nights," he said. "Not that I feel much like singing 'This is a Lovely Way to Spend an Evening' myself."

"Never mind all that," said Alec sharply. "Just tell me how I can help you, and if I can't, for God's sake get off the line."

"Fair enough," said Lem. "Though I don't know if you *can* help me, really. I just wanted to try out an idea on Gee Gee, and if it didn't grab him, well, okay, I'd think again."

"An idea about what?" said Alec. "For Heaven's sake, man, you're supposed to be in the middle of organising the biggest manhunt London's ever seen."

"Well, it so happens that I'm not," said Lem. "And I'll tell you why. If Exton's strangled Judy Moss, and dumped her body somewhere, he'll have left the area hours ago, and could be anywhere from Ipswich to Inverness by now. We've got details of his car, and I've already circulated them to all areas in any case. Okay?"

"So far as it goes," said Alec doubtfully. "But what if he hasn't done it yet? What if he's still with her somewhere?"

"Ah," said Lemaitre. "That's the big question, as far as I'm concerned. Because that's what I reckon is the most likely thing. I've been studying a lot of case histories of mass murderers these last few weeks. They all have one thing in common. They lead double lives – "

"You amaze me," said Alec heavily.

"Yes, but hang about, I haven't finished yet. Each of their lives is in a watertight compartment. You might think that a man who Jack-the-Rippers girls every other week couldn't meet *any* girl without wanting to Jack-the-Ripper her. But no. It usually turns out that in his other life, the man has a wife and kids or maybe a girl friend just like anybody else. You get the point? These men only kill when they are in a certain situation. Exton, for example, kills when he sees a girl, a stranger, walking along a street at night. Even then, it isn't any girl. It has to be one he can creep up behind, pounce on, half-strangle, then rape and finish strangling in a dark street or alley. He might be quite safe in any other situation – say, with a girl whom he knows admires him, and who wants to go to bed with him."

"You're really telling me you don't think Judy Moss is in any danger?"

"I'm saying there's a good chance that she's not, that's all. I watched the two of them down at the police station earlier tonight. Judy was obviously knocked out by Exton. I got the impression he was enjoying being so obviously her flavour of the month, as you might say. It was probably a big kick for him to be looked on as a rescuing hero. You see what I'm getting at? It's miles away from the type of situation in which he normally strangles. Apart from that, our Clive's a bright lad, and believes he's sitting very pretty. Now that he's got poor Jones apparently caught red-handed as the Strangler, he must reckon on Jones being sent to Broadmoor for life and himself being free of all suspicion for good! Is it likely that he'd chuck away all that by strangling a girl tonight? Or if he did still feel the urge, would he be stupid enough to choose his original victim, the girl he's been seen leaving the police station with? Not on your life – if he's the shrewd cookie I take him for."

"Just a minute," Hobbs began, but Lemaitre, in full spate, never waited a second, let alone a minute, for anybody.

"So here's my suggestion, Alec boy," he went on, hardly aware that that was an odd way to address the Assistant Commissioner (Crime). "I propose to kill the whole idea of a manhunt tonight. The less cause we give Exton to think we suspect him at the moment, the better. It's any odds that he and Judy are spending the night together somewhere – "

Alec finally managed to break in on the flow of words.

"Are they?" he said tensely. "Then where? Exton's flat's empty, remember – Dexter went there and found the stockings – "

"It's obviously a case of 'your place or mine', isn't it?" Lemaitre said. "She took him somewhere."

"But she's living at home, with her parents – "

"A couple of religious nuts, I gather, who keep reading the riot act to her, and weren't expecting her home anyway," Lem said. "I reckon she's been out all night before – a good few times. Which means she's got places she can go – friends who'll put her up and let her and her boy friend have the spare room or a couch in the corner. You don't know what they're like, the young generation. My daughter Linda – just turned eighteen, she has – "

"Never mind about your daughter!" Alec shouted. "Just finish what you're trying to tell me. You reckon that – "

"I reckon that Clive will be a good boy tonight," Lem said. "And he believes that where the police are concerned, he's got a beautiful star billing as the Have a Go Hero of the Year. So come the morning, he'll kiss Judy goodbye and come sailing back to his flat as happy as a sandboy – where Dexter and me and half the Strangler unit will be in hiding, waiting for him. And maybe I'll get one of his stockings out from under the floorboards to fasten round his wrists in lieu of handcuffs. Be the right sort of gesture to end this ruddy case . . ."

Lem was talking wildly now, thought Alec, not a hard thing to do at half past three in the morning after the sort of night they'd all had. The question was: was he *thinking* wildly, too? That was what he had to decide. There was a lot of sense in what Lem had said; shrewd Cockney common sense, at that. But they weren't up against a common-sense criminal. A cunning one – yes. A *brilliantly* cunning one . . . but –

"Lem," said Alec suddenly. "I'd like to give my official blessing, so to speak, to your approach. But I'm afraid I can't. You could be right about everything – but you could be totally, dangerously wrong."

He expected Lemaitre to start arguing, perhaps even swearing. Instead, there was a moment's silence on the line. Then, very mildly for him, Lem said:

"You're going to tell me, aren't you, that Clive boy's a

raving psycho, and can't be counted on to be logical, in anything he says or does. I know. That thought worries me too. In fact, it's been giving me shivers down my spine all night – shivers that started at the very sight of him, before I knew he was the Strangler."

"Then listen," said Alec, talking softly now, but with great urgency. "I'll tell you what sends shivers down *my* spine about your plan. You're assuming that Clive Exton is in complete control of his own actions – that he decides just when he will and when he won't become the Stocking Strangler."

"Well, surely if he didn't," said Lem, "we'd have caught him weeks ago."

"In the ordinary way, he *may* be able to restrain himself – to some degree," said Alec. "But there's nothing ordinary about the situation he's in tonight. If you're right, and he's spending the night with Judy Moss, don't forget what's happening. He'll be lying there, for hour after hour, beside the girl *that the dark part of his mind once chose as a victim – and whom he's already half-strangled, this very night.* I don't know much about weirdos, Lem, but I can hear a voice whispering inside that lunatic's head: 'Go on. Finish the job.'"

Lem took the point immediately.

"And no matter how much he gets a kick out of being thought a hero, and wants to keep his nose clean and his halo bright," he said, "that urge could get the better of him. Yes, you're right. This calls for action. I'd better get round to Mr. and Mrs. Moss for a start. They've got to know *some* of their daughter's friends. Know any texts from the Bible that might help me?"

"I can tell you what I'm thinking," said Alec grimly. "Whether it's a text or not – let's hope to God you're there in time."

"Amen to that," said Lem – and added one odd thing before he rang off.

"Thanks, Gee Gee. That was just the straightening out my addled brain needed."

Alec started – and felt a warm glow flooding through him. That "Gee Gee" had been only a slip of the tongue, of course – but if it meant he had given Gideon-standard help to Gideon's oldest colleague, then this was one of the proudest moments of his life . . .

Not that it lasted long. Within seconds, the telephone was ringing again with another urgent call for Gideon.

This time it was Riddell, ringing up from Hammersmith police station. He had been consulting the records there, with the help of the night staff, and had come up with a list of the owners of the six largest houses in the Hammersmith area. Tom sounded bright and breezy – too bright and breezy, Alec thought; but then, he'd been like that all night.

"By the way," he said, "this place is going crazy, because of a hold-up or something at St. Giles Hospital. Every available man is being rushed down there. You know about it, I suppose."

"I have heard the odd whisper," drawled Alec, with something approaching his old urbanity. More grimly, he added: "Give me the list of names and I'll see George gets it as soon as he comes in. He's out just at the moment."

"Gone to St. Giles like everybody else?" said Riddell, jokingly.

Before he realised what he was saying, Alec found himself replying: "Yes, he has, as a matter of fact."

"Right. Thanks," said Riddell. "Then I can go there, and give him the list myself."

"Hey. Wait!" said Alec, but it was too late. Riddell had already rung off, and was presumably on his way – a man sick with nervous tension heading for the most nerve-racking scene in London.

But before Hobbs could even begin to worry about that, the telephone rang again, and he found himself coping with the trickiest call of the night.

It was Scott-Marle, ringing up for his hourly progress report on events.

Hobbs did not see how he could avoid giving a full account of the happenings at St. Giles, even though he knew it would produce an immediate remonstrance.

"Gunmen taking a hospital ward hostage? Good God, Gideon shouldn't try and handle a thing like that by himself!

I gave strict orders that all siege situations should automatically be passed to the Terrorist Squad. I'm surprised you didn't remind George about that."

"As a matter of fact, sir, I *did* mention it – "

"And he ignored you? But you shouldn't have stood for that, Hobbs. Why on earth didn't you *order* him to bring them in?"

Alec took a deep breath, and then realised that he had the perfect answer.

Very urbane now – in fact, almost purring – he murmured:

"Because, sir, you requested me to *take* orders from Commander Gideon, all through tonight."

That, at least, settled Scott-Marle.

With a grunted command to keep him posted every *half* hour from now on, he rang off, and at last the telephones on the desk in front of Alec became quiet.

Hobbs was grateful for the silence – but not for long. It gave him too much time to think about what might be happening at St. Giles – and, most worrying of all, what Gideon might be doing there.

Because, although he would have bitten his tongue off rather than say so aloud, there was one thing about which he privately agreed with Scott-Marle.

At least in his present, recklessly determined mood, Gideon should *not* "try and handle a thing like that by himself".

# 14 Hostage

On arrival at St. Giles, Gideon immediately found himself surrounded by a crowd of C.I.D. men, some asking for instructions, some wanting to tell him the latest news. There were even a few bleary-eyed reporters already on the scene: local boys, probably, dragged out of bed and rushed to the spot by their night editors, in case something big broke before the top pros from Fleet Street could make it out to Hammersmith. From their expressions, it was obvious that something big *had* broken as far as they were concerned. Gideon had arrived in person to take over!

"What are you going to do, George?" said one.

"Is it true you're sending for the S.A.S.?" asked another.

"Probably," roared Gideon. "To clear *you* out of my way!"

They stood back at that, and let him go through to the hospital's main entrance.

One of them, though – a girl in T-shirt and jeans who only looked about seventeen – tried one more question.

"They say the police are going to let them massacre all the nurses and the patients to save the life of one bleeding copper. Is that true?"

Gideon turned for just one moment to snap: "The bleeding copper, as you call him, happens to *be* a patient!"

That was the wrong answer, he knew. It would start rumours that he was utterly ruthless. But at that moment, he felt utterly ruthless: too angry, at all events, to care what anyone thought or felt. Of one thing he was certain. Men who threatened nurses and the sick to get their way could never, in a hundred thousand years, be allowed to win . . .

One thing at least cheered him as he strode up the stairs to the corridor outside Ward A4. One of the C.I.D. men, obviously a colleague of Brian Fullerton's from Hammersmith police station, had reported: "It's all right so far, sir. They've not shot Dreamboat yet."

This news was confirmed by Matt Honiwell, whom he found standing right outside the ward's big swing doors, who turned and grinned with relief when Gideon appeared beside him. He looked as though he had never been so pleased to see anyone in his life.

"Thank God you're here, George," he whispered. "I've kept the chat going as best I can, but Christ, it's not been easy. They've threatened to shoot Fullerton half a dozen times, but something's stopped them. Partly my threats, I think – I've sworn we'll go in and take them, the second I hear a shot, no matter what happens or who gets killed. And it could be that I ended up by convincing them."

Gideon nodded.

"There's no 'could be' about it," Matt, he whispered back. "You've put the fear of God into the toughest hit men in London. Not bad going." And that, he told himself, was an understatement. For the mild, "cuddly" Matt, it was very good going indeed.

Not that his victory had been without cost. Honiwell was as covered with sweat as though he had been in a steam bath, and he kept mopping his face with a handkerchief as wet as a bathroom flannel.

"The most puzzling thing," he said, "is this woman they've got in there. She's their No. 1 hostage, they keep saying – the person who'll get it first if we attack. But they can't make her give her name. It can't be Maggie Fullerton – she's been sobbing non-stop in the background. It can't be the night sister or anyone on the hospital staff – or they'd know who she was from her uniform; her rank anyway. So, she must be some kind of a visitor. But who'd be visiting a hospital at past three in the morning? One thing's obvious.

She's got a hell of a personality. Just by her manner, she's convinced them she's important. One of them even called her a cross between another Princess Diana and the Queen Mum!"

Gideon nodded.

"Obviously, quite a lady," he murmured. "But it bothers me why she's so insistent on staying anonymous. What harm can it possibly do anyone to know her name?"

In his bewilderment, he forgot to whisper – a mistake for someone who had appeared so often on TV as spokesman for the police that his was one of the best-known voices in Britain.

There were startled whispers suddenly on the far side of the swing doors – and then came the voice of the chief hit man.

"Well, well, well. So the great Gideon himself is here! We're honoured, Commander. In case our dear friend Superintendent Honiwell hasn't made our position clear, I'll just repeat the main facts. Whatever we do, and whatever you hear out there – and I'll tell you frankly, that in a moment it will be a shot – it won't pay you to come in. We've got guns levelled at two nurses, the night sister, and most important of all, this lady I'm holding now. She hasn't told us her name yet, but I'm sure she'll tell *you* if you ask her nicely, Commander – as you must if you don't want me to break her wrist – "

Before Gideon could reply, or even think of what to say, a lot of things happened in very quick succession, although to him they seemed to be happening with all the slow-motion timelessness of a nightmare, the worst nightmare of his career, perhaps of his whole life.

First came a calm, authoritative voice – obviously that of the night sister.

"I can't stand this any longer. The woman he's holding is Mrs. Gideon, Commander – *your wife!*"

Then there was a choking cry – in the most familiar voice in the world.

"Yes, George, it's – it's me. I didn't want you to – to be worried – "

Finally came the most terrible sound of all: the thud of a falling body.

"She's fainted, Commander," came the night sister's voice. "And I don't think it's just a faint – her lips have turned blue. Has your wife a weak heart, by any chance?"

Gideon's own voice sounded as distant to him as a faint mountain echo as he said: "Yes. For God's sake, be careful with her . . ."

And then came the nightmare climax, which brought him as close as he had ever come in his life to losing control.

"She'll be careful with her – if I let her," the No. 1 hit man said, his voice triumphant, openly sneering. "And I just may decide not to, Commander – if you don't play ball."

Suddenly it was Matt Honiwell who was having the nightmare feeling. Gideon suddenly threw himself at the swing doors, and Matt found himself seizing him, and struggling to drag him back; the most hated task he had ever undertaken.

It wasn't a struggle he could have won if Gideon hadn't, almost instantly, recovered himself and stopped dead in his tracks, his head bent, his huge frame trembling.

"Bless you, Matt," he breathed, very softly.

Scott-Marle's standing instruction that all siege situations should be handled by the terrorist branch and their specialists – and no one else – flashed through his brain.

And for just one ghastly moment of near-panic and near-desperation, it also flashed through his brain that for once, Scott-Marle was right.

* * *

The desperate moment didn't last. One deep breath, and Gideon was himself again – or as nearly himself as he could be with Kate lying just the other side of that door, in God knew what condition, getting God knew what help and attention, and probably none at all.

Somehow managing to sound cold and rational, as though he was talking about anyone in the world but Kate, he said:

"I think I should warn you that if a person dies through being deliberately denied medical treatment, it will obviously count as murder. Which could – and almost certainly would – mean a thirty-year rap for all of you, even if you spare Fullerton."

The chief hit man laughed, savagely.

"Spare Fullerton? You're crazy if you think we'd do that," he said. "He's just had a little stay of execution while we worked things out. And now that we have, Commander, I've news for you. None of us is going to prison – not for a single day."

Gideon frowned. The man didn't sound as though he was bluffing, but rather as though something was making him supremely confident. He was at a loss to think what it could be, but his first job was to shake that confidence – at any cost.

Aloud, he began, scornfully:

"Look. I don't know what your name is – "

"Straker," the man said. "Ben Straker, in full. We're not all as shy as Mrs. Gideon."

"Right. Then look, Straker." Gideon's tone remained scornful. "Do you really think that after you've murdered a policeman in cold blood, I'm going to tell my men to stand back and let the six of you walk out of here?"

Straker's strange confidence wasn't even dented.

"I think you will, Commander. Because you haven't any choice. We'll be taking your good lady with us – maybe a couple of nurses too – in case you try to follow our car."

Gideon swallowed hard.

"And just how far do you think you'd get?"

"That's our business," Straker sneered. "But it could be, Commander, that you'll be surprised."

One of the other hit men realised their leader had given too much away, and whispered a warning. But it was too late. The whole situation had suddenly dawned on Gideon – the reason for Straker's confidence, the wild scheme that was forming in the hit men's minds.

They must be in on the big secret that Fingers Kelsey had leaked to Riddell: the fact that the Big Three was really the Big Four – and that No. 4 was a millionaire, living above suspicion, in a big house right here in Hammersmith. If they could force Gideon to let them get to a car, dragging hostages with them, they must reckon they could easily drive it, unseen, to No. 4's – and then disappear off the face of the earth as far as the police were concerned.

It was a crazy idea, of course; but it wouldn't have been so crazy if he had had no inkling of No. 4's existence. He would have expected the car to streak right through and out of Hammersmith, and would have set up roadblocks a mile or a mile and a half away. It might have taken the police hours, days, maybe a week, to work out where the car had vanished to – if it had doubled back and slipped into a house in the local Millionaire's Row. And by that time, the Big Three – or Four – and their choice sextet of killer henchmen would have long been out of the country. And Kate and the other hostages they'd dragged to the car? It was easy – all too easy – to imagine them reappearing in a couple of days as bodies floating under Hammersmith Bridge, with no clue to where they'd come from at all.

The theory not only made sense. It made it very clear why "topping Fullerton" was an essential part of the hit men's plans. He only had to recover consciousness, and say one word, for their whole scheme to be wrecked. He had been in deadly danger from the outset. But it would take nothing short of a miracle to save him now.

Unless he could somehow convince them that it was too late – that the scheme was already wrecked –

At that point, Gideon's thoughts were interrupted by a chilling thought. Time was running out.

He heard Straker whispering, presumably to one of his companions. He caught the words: "Take over, I've that little job to do."

Footsteps sounded – faint, clacking ones on the plastic-coated floor of the ward. They were receding, so Straker was heading away from this end of the ward, towards Fullerton's private room.

As if that didn't tell him enough about the job that Straker had in mind, the next second he heard a woman screaming. Obviously Maggie Fullerton, who was *in* that private room.

"No – no, keep away, don't – "

Her screams were joined by another voice, much nearer to the swing doors. A fainter voice, but a very firm one.

"George – George, you've got to stop him."

Gideon's heart gave a great leap. It was Kate, fully conscious again.

He could hear the night sister now.

"Lie still, Mrs. Gideon, I'm sure the Commander is doing everything he can."

Gideon strode towards the swing doors. Matt tensed, but made no attempt to stop him; there was, in any case, no need. All Gideon did was push the left door forward a tenth of an inch, and put his eye to the chink thus created. It gave him a very limited view of the ward, with more to be guessed at than glimpsed, but he could make out a few things – some of them vitally important. Kate was lying on a bed, not on the floor, as he'd imagined; the night sister was bending over her, and a hit man was standing over *them*, a revolver in his hand. Two other hit men were over by the nurses' table; they also had guns, and the expression of terror on the nurses' faces intensified Gideon's feelings of despair. A fourth gunman was keeping an eye on the patients, and the two constables, both of whom had been made to stand against a wall, although one had an injured shoulder and seemed in agony. At the very end of the ward, Gideon could just see a tall, tough-looking man whom he took to be Straker. He was standing with his back to Gideon, at the curtained entrance to what was obviously Fullerton's room. Gideon guessed that he had a gun in his hand, and was taking aim at Fullerton. But something was stopping him firing; probably Maggie was in the way. He was saying something that didn't carry over his shoulder. He could be telling Maggie that if she didn't get out of the way, she'd be blasted too.

"Straker," said Gideon, and although he wasn't even shouting, his voice cut effortlessly through the distance between them. "If you're determined to earn that thirty-year stretch for murder, there's nothing I can do to stop you. But I can tell you this. It won't do you a bit of good, topping Detective Constable Fullerton. Because there isn't a thing he can tell us that I don't already know."

That shook Straker – slightly, at any rate. He spun round and was suddenly facing the swing doors. His features weren't clear at this distance. They looked sharp and rat-like, but that might, Gideon thought, be his imagination projecting an expected image on to a faraway blur. His voice, now that he was a shade uncertain of himself, was hoarser, higher-pitched, although still thick and sneering.

"Nice try, Commander, but you're dreaming if you think that kind of talk is going to cut any ice with me. If you know that much about the Big Three, how come they've been making f—g wallies of the Fuzz all night long?"

There was a long silence, made worse by the fact that it wasn't really a silence at all. Faint, echoing noises of every description, from Maggie's distant screams to a nurse's hysterical sobbing, from a bed creaking to a patient's heavy breathing, came through the chink in the swing doors in front of him; while sundry other noises, of the coughing, clothes-rustling, foot-shuffling variety, reminded him of the throng of waiting men who packed the corridor behind him.

Gideon ignored them all, but instinctively raised his voice to make sure it carried above them.

"How do you know we haven't been setting a trap for your precious Big Three all night?" he said steadily. "Making sure that they lead us to their celebrated associate – No. 4?"

That shot went home all right. The faint figure of Straker started so violently that it was visible right across the ward. His body spun in a half-circle as though he'd been slammed in the stomach by an invisible man.

"No. 4. What No. 4?"

"The one that's loaded," said Gideon. "And lives in a very large house right here in Hammersmith. Which you boys would be pretty stupid to head for, even if you got out of here – because for all you know, we've already got it surrounded and could be raiding it at this very minute. Do you still think we're wallies, Straker?"

He stopped, breathless, realising that he hadn't just been talking – he'd been roaring at the top of his voice.

And it had worked, almost beyond his dreams.

Fullerton was no longer in immediate danger. Straker had come away from the private room and was striding towards Gideon, across the ward.

As he came nearer, Gideon realised that his mental picture had been right. Straker's face was like a rat's – and at the moment, like a cornered one's. But his eyes were gleaming: he was shrewd, and had seen a way out of the trap.

"You're bluffing, Gideon – and I can prove it. If you hadn't, you'd have told us the name of No. 4. But you don't know it, do you? No one knows it – except the Big Three – and us – and Fullerton." He was suddenly smiling. "Looks like I've still got that job to do, doesn't it, Commander?"

He turned and was suddenly walking back to the private room.

It was all Gideon could do not to groan aloud.

He had heard that siege situations were always like this, ending in an endless, nerve-grinding ding-dong battle between the spokesman for the police and the leader of the other side. It often – in fact, as far as he could remember, it *always* – went on for days.

Well, it couldn't, this time. There was no way he could save Fullerton if it went on for even another minute. And Kate – every second of this could be putting an unthinkable strain on her heart . . .

His fury rose as his spirits sank. If only he hadn't lacked that one vital bit of information – the identity of No. 4 – he was sure he could have ended this thing there and then. Instead of that, the worst had happened: it wasn't just that his hopes had been torpedoed, his credibility had been blasted. Nothing he said would be believed from now on –

He had been staring too long through that knife-edge of a slit in the door. Suddenly his eyes started streaming; the whole scene misted over. He drew back from the door, blinking and wiping his eyes, and couldn't see who it was who was suddenly standing beside him, thrusting a piece of paper into his hand.

It was one of the surprises of his life when he heard the voice of Tom Riddell, bright, breezy and breathless from taking the stairs up to this corridor three at a time.

"That's the list you asked for, George – the six top millionaire householders in Hammersmith. Thought I'd bring it over to you personally when I heard you were here. I – er – I gather things aren't going too well. Is there anything I can do?"

"You've very probably done it, Tom," said Gideon gratefully – and turned back to the door.

It wasn't going to be easy, but he ought to be able to swing something now, he thought. After all, somewhere amongst those six names in his hand, the chances were he *did* have the real identity of No. 4.

"Straker!" he roared. "Straker, list – "

A faint sound from the other side of the door stopped him dead: the subdued, sneeze-like snort of a professional killer's silenced revolver.

# 15 The Name in Black

Almost immediately – faint, distant, echoing, but all too audible to Gideon – came the sound of a woman moaning: a continuous moan, half-sobbing, half-shivering.

For a terrible moment, Gideon was forced to the obvious conclusion: he was listening to Maggie mourning her dead husband, killed without even returning to consciousness, killed despite all her frantic efforts, killed because of police blindness and stupidity.

But then he heard Straker shouting: "That served you right, you bloody cow. How many times have I told you tonight to get away from that bed?"

So it was Maggie who had been hit, probably not fatally: hit men were usually careful only to kill those whom they'd been specifically ordered to.

The next bullet would be for Fullerton. It would be fired any second – and no amount of calling out to Straker could stop him now.

Only one thing would, Gideon told himself.

If he could shout the identity of No. 4 across that ward – positively proving that the death of Fullerton would achieve nothing, change nothing – it might, just might, stop Straker dead.

He glanced down at the sheet Riddell had given him, and swore. His vision was still blurry, and made worse by the sweat running into his eyes from his forehead. The typing was almost impossible to see.

He wiped his eyes so fiercely that he might have been trying to wrench them out of their sockets. The trick worked. Suddenly his sight was clear – and so were the names on the sheet.

Six names, and he had less than a second to pick one. This was like Russian roulette played a terrible new way, he thought, with five chambers of the revolver loaded, and the weapon pointed at somebody else's temple.

Then he noticed that the choice had, in fact, been made for him.

One of the names stood out from the sheet in darkest black, while the others swam before his eyes. It was exactly as if there was only one name his brain was *allowing* him to read.

*Monty Marlowe, River Manor, Hammersmith, W.6*
*(£10,000,000 property at least)*

Monty Marlowe . . . Gideon had heard of him. Marlowe had been a popular rock star in the early 1960s, although he'd faded from the limelight soon after. It certainly made sense to pick him. Success a quarter of a century ago hardly explained how the man could run to a £10,000,000 mansion now.

But even if there was a copper's shrewdness somewhere behind the strange behaviour of his brain, did he dare to trust it – with so much at stake, so many lives at risk?

Not that there was any more time to think. Maggie's distant sobbing was rising to a scream, a sure sign that there was no time for anything except –

"*Marlowe*," roared Gideon, not through a chink in the doors, but recklessly swinging them wide, his stentorian bellow shaking everyone and everything in the ward. "*Monty Marlowe, Straker. He's your No. 4.*"

He stopped there, his whole throat throbbing from the effort of shouting when it had, in fact, gone bone-dry.

The ward was very silent now. Not a bed creaked, not a sheet rustled, not a soul moved – or even seemed to breathe. Only the echoes of Gideon's voice could be heard, booming dully round the dark perimeter of the place – and the pool of darkness at the end which concealed Brian Fullerton's private room.

Peering hard into that blackness, Gideon could just make out the room's entrance. The curtains across it had been drawn, presumably by Straker when he had stalked through, intent on finishing his victim this time once and for all.

If he'd failed, thought Gideon, that sneeze-like shot would be coming from there . . . any second – any split-second – now . . .

But the silence went on, and suddenly a new realisation dawned.

*If he'd failed, the shot would have come before now.*

He'd won.

It wasn't only that Straker was obviously too shaken to come back through the curtain. The other hit men scattered round the ward all had the same stunned look: the look of deep-sea divers who have suddenly learned that their parent ship is sinking. None of their guns were pointing anywhere but at the floor . . .

"Right," said Gideon and led the way across the ward, Honiwell, Riddell and the other men trooping behind him. "Cheer up," he added to the white-faced nurses as he passed them. "The cavalry has arrived at last."

To Kate he didn't have to say anything. Before he knew it, she was up from her bed, had coolly sidestepped past the man who was standing over her, and was walking along beside him.

"Do you think Mrs. Fullerton's all right?" she whispered to him anxiously, and seemed astounded at the fierce intensity with which he gripped and squeezed her hand, and at something which looked very much like tears of relief in his eyes.

* * *

Maggie Fullerton was all right. Strangely enough, she was very much all right, even though there was a gaping bullet wound in her shoulder which was bleeding profusely.

Seemingly completely unaware of the pain, she was smiling all over her face – because Brian Fullerton had at last returned to consciousness and was sitting up and blinking round him.

Gideon was soon giving him plenty to blink at.

He strode across to Straker, who was standing, silent, sullen and motionless by the bed, and grabbed his gun. Straker let him take it without a word, and had nothing to say, either, when Gideon formally arrested him and called out to the men behind to take him away.

Handcuffed, and about to be led out through the curtained doorway, he did finally find his tongue, and snarled at Gideon:

"You think you've won, don't you? All you've got to do is go round to Monty Marlowe's and nab the Big Three."

"Four," Gideon corrected him gently. "I think we might take your Mr. Marlowe too, while we're there, don't you?"

Straker looked exactly as though he was about to spit in his face, and probably would have done, if the men holding him hadn't dragged him back half-way through the curtaining. The material momentarily covered his face and muffled his voice; but it didn't blunt the razor-sharp edge of hatred in his tone.

"You'll never take them, Gideon. They're not called 'Big' for nothing. Any one of them's worth ten – no, a bloody hundred of you."

"Then I'll just have to hope your arithmetic's a bit shaky, won't I?" said Gideon mildly. "I know mine is, at this time of the morning."

Straker was suddenly shrieking.

"You'll be the one who's shaky before they've finished with you, Gideon. I tell you, you won't be taking the Big Four, not in a million years. *They'll be taking you.*"

The threat was so strange that it made Gideon stare, although there was nothing to stare at now but the sagging curtain. Straker had been dragged away across the ward on the other side, and as Gideon went to the curtain and parted it, he could see that all six of the hit men had now been gathered together into a bunch, just by the swing doors, ready for marching away. There were so many policemen now milling round the ward – some C.I.D., but most in uniform – that it was difficult to see anything except men in blue.

The sight gave Maggie Fullerton great satisfaction.

She was lying beside Brian now, but on top of the bed. Kate was fussing over her until the night sister could be called, holding a sheet tight against her shoulder as a very temporary measure to stop the flow of blood.

Maggie still hardly seemed to notice her wound. Her good arm was round her beloved Brian. He was alive, he was conscious, and that was enough to make this a moment of triumph for her; a triumph that the sight of all those blue uniforms made complete.

"I kept *telling* them that it would take a lot of men to protect you," she whispered to Brian. "Now they're here – and you're safe at last. Thanks to Mr. and Mrs. Gideon."

The speech exhausted her, and she hardly seemed to hear Gideon grunting:

"It's really thanks to one of the bravest policeman's wives it's ever been my privilege to know, Mrs. Fullerton. You!"

★ ★ ★

A minute later, the night sister and a nurse, visibly shaken, arrived on the scene, and Maggie Fullerton was being rushed away to receive the urgent attention she needed. An officious-looking doctor appeared, who ordered Gideon and Kate out of the private room.

They turned to go, but Fullerton himself stopped them.

"There's – there's just one thing I must ask you, sir, if you can spare a moment. How – how did you know that Monty Marlowe was No. 4?" His large, dreamy eyes – so incongruous in the face of a detective constable – looked almost hurt. "I thought that no one was on to him except me."

Gideon hastened to reassure him.

"Nobody was, Fullerton – and that's something that's going to be remembered, I can promise you, at the highest level. What puzzles me is how you came to suspect him yourself."

Fullerton's face seemed to glow with pleasure at this praise.

He explained that he had been driving past Marlowe's place in a police Panda one night when he had noticed two suspicious-looking figures in the back seat of a car which was turning in to Marlowe's drive. A shaft of light from a street lamp had happened to catch their faces, and he had recognised them as Jeremy Kemp and Barry Mayne.

Gideon was even more impressed. The names of the Big Three were known to just about every man in the force, but only the sharpest of detective constables would have taken the trouble to memorise their faces.

"I reported the incident at the station, but was told I'd probably imagined it," Fullerton went on. "I was sure I hadn't, and started keeping watch on the premises when I was off duty. I soon realised I hadn't made any mistake. Kemp and Mayne – and Salvados too – were frequent callers, usually in the small hours. That was when I decided to start taking notes and building up a file." At the thought of his beloved file, Fullerton's eyes gleamed with excitement – but a moment later, they were dulled by exhaustion. "Knew . . . knew it would be risky, of course . . ." His voice began to trail away. "Thought it . . . thought it a risk worth taking . . ."

The doctor was now almost literally trying to drag Gideon away. But still Fullerton wouldn't let him go.

"Just one more thing, sir. You still haven't told me who *did* tip you off about Marlowe . . ."

Gideon hastily explained about Fingers Kelsey, and the list he had been handed with the names of the six millionaire householders.

"And you just picked Marlowe's name at random, sir?"

Gideon hesitated for a moment, and then found himself telling the plain and simple truth.

"Well, not exactly," he said. "From that short list, it *had* to be Marlowe – as far as I could see . . ."

* * *

Assuring Fullerton once again that his contribution would not be forgotten, Gideon walked out of the private room – to face one of the biggest challenges of that nerve-racking night.

If ever there had been a time in his career which called for immediate, concerted, all-out action, it was now.

He made a quick calculation. The hit men had arrived at the hospital half an hour before. The Big Three (whom he must henceforth think of as the Big Four) would be expecting a report from them at any moment. When they didn't get one, they would scent danger – and bolt.

It was even likely, supremely clever at intelligence work as they were, that they had had someone watching the hospital, maybe standing amongst the crowd of reporters outside. Someone who was even now rushing to some telephone to report the rumours that the siege was over, that Gideon had won.

Of course, they couldn't know that the big secret of Marlowe's involvement with them was out. It was true that everyone in the ward, and all the policemen standing behind him, had heard him shout the name; but it wasn't likely that any of them could have slipped out to telephone without being noticed. Still, that wouldn't stop whispers, and with a famous name like Marlowe's, the news would soon be spreading like a forest fire all round the hospital – and the crowd outside.

There was no doubt about it, Gideon thought. His only common-sense course was to get round to Marlowe's River Manor place with the least possible delay. It shouldn't be difficult. It was only round the corner. All the men he needed were here, including two of his hand-picked leaders: Honiwell and Riddell. And a lot of the men had been issued with revolvers. Right from the beginning, this had been a night with a big risk of shoot outs, as the heads of London's organised crime found themselves finally cornered and at bay.

That risk had now become a virtual certainty. It wasn't hard to guess that the Big Four, whether they got wind of other rumours or not, would be speedily alerted as police car after police car went roaring out of the hospital grounds in the direction of the river. They wouldn't be able to bolt at that stage – the first car should be outside the manor within minutes, perhaps in under one minute – but they could be prepared for a last-ditch battle.

And a consortium of criminals of the calibre of Barry Mayne, Jeremy Kemp and Salvados – backed by the millions of Monty Marlowe, and all the resources that they could buy – could put up a very deadly fight. Gideon disliked the thought of leading his men into a thing like that, so badly-briefed that they hadn't even a plan of River Manor, or any idea what sort of place it was.

It had cost £10,000,000. They knew that. But millions more could have been spent on all kinds of protective devices inside –

Once again, Gideon realised, his brain was wandering, running riot amongst wild possibilities. It was the time of night, he supposed. The early hours weren't ideal for clear thinking.

Yet lives depended on him thinking as calmly and clearly as ever in his career.

He walked out into the main ward, into the stream of milling policemen, and started barking orders – which abruptly changed that stream into channels of men filing out through the swing doors, heading downstairs for the main entrance and out towards the fleet of Pandas and area cars outside.

One private arrangement he had to stop and make: a police car that would take Kate round to their daughter Penny, Mrs. Alec Hobbs. He couldn't bear to think of her being on her own for a second for the rest of the night, even though she was looking much better now, with her lips showing no traces of that tell-tale blue. Her grey-blue eyes were as calm as ever, and even twinkled as he told her: "I've got to take care of you now. There can't be many men who suddenly find themselves married to a combination of Princess Di and the Queen Mum."

"Suddenly?" she murmured. "Do you mean you'd never noticed it before?"

Gideon grinned.

"No. But from the way you order me about, I should have suspected a drop of royal blood."

Kate laughed outright – but then just a hint of anxiety appeared on her upturned face.

"Take care, love," she whispered.

Then, giving him a light peck on the cheek, she whisked herself away. An awed-looking nurse appeared in her stead.

"You're wanted on the phone, Commander. A Mr. Hobbs from Scotland Yard."

Gideon was about to follow her, but changed his mind. He didn't suspect Alec, of course, but he couldn't report to him without mentioning the raid – and the less anyone at Scotland Yard knew about that the better.

"Tell Mr. Hobbs I'll ring him later," he said, and went out through the swing doors of the ward. In the corridor, he found Honiwell and Riddell waiting for him.

Both men were flushed with excitement over the recent triumph, but in Riddell's case the flush didn't look a healthy one. His eyes had a feverish gleam, suggesting he was close to nervous exhaustion. Matt was probably living on his nerves too, Gideon thought, but with him, things like that rarely showed. His smile was warm, confident, assured.

"So this is *it*, now," he said. "Where the Big Three – or rather Four – get their final comeuppance."

"*If* we're lucky," Riddell said.

"Whether we're lucky or not, Tom," Gideon corrected him grimly, and led the way downstairs, and across to his car, with a speed and fury that made even the waiting reporters scuttle out of his way.

Only in the furthermost corner of his mind was he remembering Straker's last mysterious threat.

"I tell you, you won't be taking the Big Four, not in a million years. *They'll be taking you . . .*"

# 16 Strangler

Halfway across London, and about half an hour earlier, another policeman had gone charging out to his car with almost equal speed and fury – Chief Detective Superintendent Lemaitre, on his way to tackle Judy's parents, Mr. and Mrs. Moss.

The ever-impulsive Lem had been galvanised by Alec Hobbs's warning about Clive Exton. His previous certainty that Judy Moss was in no danger – that Exton was far too slick an operator to jeopardise everything by murdering a bird he'd practically picked up in the presence of the police – had now been blown to atoms.

The trouble was, he supposed, that all through his career, he'd been dealing with East End villains – heartless and callous as they came, some of them, but all with their heads screwed on the right way. In this case, for the first time, he was up against someone whose head was screwed on the wrong way; who not only committed crimes so heinous they were beyond all reason, but would commit another even if he had every logical reason in the world not to.

The more he thought about it, the more he realised that Hobbs was bound to be right, and that odd shiver down his spine had spread right up to the nape of his neck, and past it to start a cold tingling under his scalp, as though phantom fingers were scratching at his very brain.

Served him right, he told himself. He'd been smug and

stupid and at any moment, unless he looked very lively indeed, Judy Moss would be paying for it with her life.

Less than three minutes after leaving Warnham Green police station, he had arrived at Rushmore Gardens, where Judy's parents lived. In another minute, he was on their doorstep, ringing the bell with one hand and hammering on the knocker with the other.

Judy's father opened the door: a bald-headed, bespectacled little man in a dusty-looking dressing-gown, who was literally twitching with anger – an anger that was no whit abated when Lemaitre revealed his identity.

"Oh, so you're from the police, are you? Isn't it enough that you should ring us up at half past two, without practically knocking down our front door at after four? Is it suddenly against the law to sleep?"

This was an incredibly cruel reaction from a father whose daughter had had such a narrow escape that very night. But Lem remembered that no one had told Mr. Moss exactly what had happened. He had just been rung up and asked whether his daughter had come home from the police station.

Lem tried desperately to remedy the defect.

"Mr. Moss," he said. "You obviously don't realise that your daughter Judy – "

Moss's twitching became more pronounced than ever.

"I'll thank you not to mention that name in my hearing, or my wife's," he almost spat. "That shameless, scarlet girl has lost all right to call herself a daughter of ours. I'm not surprised she's been in trouble with the police. I hope you catch her, and lock her up for years. I only wish you could flog her, horsewhip her – "

Mrs. Moss appeared now, at the top of the stairs behind him. She was a severe-looking lady who reminded Lem of the wicked housekeepers portrayed on the screen in the old days by actresses like Flora Robson.

"Not that God Himself won't be punishing her, one of these days," she called out. "Living with men, walking the streets like a common prostitute – how many times have we warned her that the wages of sin is death – "

Lemaitre decided that the best course was to be brutally blunt.

"Are they, madam? Well, she very nearly bloody paid them tonight – and for all I know, may be paying them right now."

This dramatic announcement didn't register with Judy's father.

"I'll thank you not to use foul language here," he began.

But Mrs. Moss did look shaken.

"Quiet, Maurice." She came further down the stairs, her eyes suddenly staring. "What is it you are trying to tell us, Inspector or whoever you are? That Judy's in some sort of danger?"

"You could put it like that," said Lem drily. "She's nearly had the life choked out of her once tonight by the Stocking Strangler. And I've – I've reason to believe she may be with him now."

The moment he'd said that, he regretted it. Mrs. Moss was suddenly swaying, and holding hard on to the banisters.

"The Stocking Strangler! Did you hear that, Maurice? We warned her time and time again – "

"It's God's judgement on her, that's what it is," her husband shouted back. "And on us, for not bringing her up to fear Him."

They didn't seem to want to hear the details of what had happened, and Lem did not enjoy forcing them to. The tale of police ineptitude he had to tell was difficult enough; but getting across to these "religious nuts," as he thought of them, the horrendous truth that their daughter might have invited the Stocking Strangler to spend the night with her was one of the most difficult jobs he'd ever tackled. By the end of it, he was hoarse – and the Mosses were so shocked that they looked as if they'd neither of them ever speak again.

But Lem kept relentlessly on.

"All right, all right," he said. "It's a wicked world, and your daughter may not have turned out to be God's answer to it. But please forget all that. If you ever want to see her again, you've got to help me."

Mr. Moss recovered his voice – but only to utter the most terrible words Lem had ever heard from a father about his own daughter.

"We do *not* ever want to see her again, I assure you. And from what you've just told us, it would be better if this monster *did* strangle her, the – despicable slut that – that she is – "

Evidently a part of Maurice Moss found the words terrible too. His twitches became a continuous spasm, and he leant back against the wall, his whole body writhing as though he was already in the Hell he envisaged for his daughter.

The sight shook Mrs. Moss into being almost motherly. She came the rest of the way down the stairs and put an arm round her shaken husband.

To Lemaitre, she said:

"Don't mind him, Superintendent. He worshipped the ground Judy walked on – until she left home to live with a man a year ago."

Mr. Moss was now barely coherent.

"Serves me – serves me right," he was babbling. "'The Lord – the Lord only shalt thou worship . . .' This is the wrath of Jehovah on her – on me – on us all!"

Lemaitre ignored this and concentrated on Mrs. Moss.

"A man?" he said. "Could you give me his name and address?"

"Stan Leavis. He's a commercial traveller – lives in a maisonette, 10 Marslake Road," said Mrs. Moss, and was suddenly almost chatty. "Judy lived there too – "

"To her eternal shame and damnation," muttered her husband.

" – until just a fortnight ago," Mrs. Moss went on. "Then they had a row, and she came back to us."

"More's the pity!" muttered Mr. Moss.

Mrs. Moss once again ignored him.

"I think, though, that Judy never gave up hoping they could make it up," she said. "I believe she was going round to that flat tonight. She went out about eleven, and, as you know, told us not to expect her back."

Lem's eyes narrowed.

So if this Stan *had* refused to take her back, that explained why Judy had been walking the streets. Afraid to go back home and face a lot of "wrath of God" stuff from her parents, yet barred from her boy friend's flat, there had been nowhere for her to go – but right into the clutches of the Stocking Strangler.

Just for a moment, Lem thought he had a bright idea.

"That boy friend's flat," he said. "Does your daughter still have a key to it?"

Mrs. Moss said that it was possible that she had one, but she didn't know.

Lemaitre nodded absently. He was no longer interested. What was he thinking about? he asked himself. The last place in London where Judy would take her new conquest would be anywhere near the flat of her old flame!

So the bright idea died – and he spent a fruitless ten minutes trying to get the Mosses to give him the names of Judy's other friends. They didn't seem to know any of them. In fact, apart from the details about her living with Stan Leavis and being turned out by him, they didn't seem to know anything much about their daughter at all.

Except, of course, that she was a slut and a scarlet woman upon whom the wrath of God was now descending.

Mr. Moss was still insisting on that, and his wife was – now rather tearfully – agreeing with him, as they finally closed the door; although almost immediately, a burst of sobbing came from behind it, which followed Lemaitre all the way to his car.

As he drove away back to the station, Lem felt like sobbing too.

Time was running out, and all he'd got to go on was a single name – Stan Leavis – and a single address, 10 Marslake Road . . . which were both utterly useless, because if anything in life was certain, it was that Judy and Exton *wouldn't* be there!

⋆ ⋆ ⋆

At that very moment, in the bedroom of Stan Leavis's maisonette at 10 Marslake Road, not more than four hundred yards away from Rushmore Gardens and almost within earshot of Lemaitre's speedily departing car, Judy Moss turned over in her sleep and snuggled up to her handsome "rescuer".

Clive Exton, who was wide awake, smiled down at her in the near-darkness. He even allowed himself to stroke her hair. There wasn't any danger now that he'd have any uncontrollable impulses where she was concerned; he was sure of that.

After all, they'd made love, three times over, and each time, he'd felt warmer towards her. It was so sweet and trusting, the way she kept looking at him, her eyes telling him all the time how much she loved him, how grateful to him she was for saving her.

"For saving her," he told himself, smiling in the darkness and savouring the exquisiteness of the irony for about the thousandth time, "from that nasty, naughty old Stocking Strangler."

He felt like giggling again, but didn't. That was another thing he'd somehow managed to bring under control, since that final outburst in the car outside Judy's parents' house. He hadn't liked the way she'd looked at him *then*. Puzzled. Frightened. Almost suspicious . . . Fortunately, the moment had passed; his need to giggle had passed, and gradually, as the hours wore on, other irritating little peculiarities of his had gone too. He hadn't had any sudden urges even to *touch* her neck . . .

Of course, he hadn't dared to let himself fall asleep. Once you handed over to your subconscious mind, anything could happen. Just one of those blissful dreams in which he saw an endless succession of naked, goddess-like beauties, and ended by sacrificing one of them on a crimson altar under a blood-red sun . . . just one of those dreams, and he would wake up utterly powerless to prevent himself doing anything. The very thought of them started strange adrenal juices churning in his stomach, and the blood rushing –

He hurriedly turned over on to the other side, so that he had his back to Judy. She didn't find it so easy to snuggle up to that, and made a faint, half-snoring protest, almost like a kitten's purr. That was the thing about Judy, he told himself. She was so very much like a helpless kitten. No one but a brute would think of hurting her.

It was strange. He had never felt protective about a girl before – but now he felt it so passionately that at that moment, he could cheerfully have killed anyone or anything that menaced her.

In fact, he actually began imagining himself beside her in a dark alley, engaged in a life-and-death battle with some sex fiend who was –

Then the dread thing happened. He fell asleep.

His subconscious took over, and the fantasy rapidly changed into a familiar form. *He* became the attacker, a black excitement rising inside him as he twisted a stocking round the neck of the girl he had just been fighting for.

"No," he found himself groaning. "*No* . . ."

With a great effort, he forced himself back to wakefulness. Only now things were different. He was sweating all over. And he couldn't bear the feel of Judy's body against his.

He stumbled out of the bed and stood beside it, stark naked and shivering, blinking around him in the unfamiliar bedroom, looking for the door that led to the combined bathroom and loo.

Perhaps, if he sluiced his face with cold water –

The next second, though, he had forgotten all about the bathroom.

He'd seen something that fascinated, mesmerised him.

The curtains over the window were parted slightly in the centre, and let in a sliver of light from a lamp-standard in the street below. The sliver was slanting right across the room and spotlighting the back of a chair on the far side of the bed.

Judy had done her undressing there, and had left – lying over that chairback – a pair of tights.

Clive Exton was across the room in a flash.

The feelings that no one but a brute could harm her, that

he could kill anyone who tried, were swept aside in a torrent of excitement that mounted to a frenzy.

The place didn't feel like a room any more; more like a black, black alley. He picked up the tights, and felt them slowly and lovingly as he turned back towards the bed, and the softly snoring – or was it purring? – Judy.

# 17 Rescuer

When Lemaitre arrived back at the station, the first thing Inspector Dexter did was to remind him about Henry Jones, who was still locked up in the cells.

"Should've let him go a long while back, sir," he said. "But I thought I'd better get your authority, since you signed the charge-sheet."

"Ah, yes, I officially arrested him, didn't I?" Lem remarked. "And tore the poor devil off quite a strip for having the cheek to say he wasn't the Stocking Strangler. It's a hard life, isn't it? What a reward he collected for trying to be a hero."

"No more than he deserved, if you ask me," Dexter said darkly. "As far as I can make out, the man spends every night deliberately hanging about round dark alleys, hoping to save girls from fates worse than death. Something creepy about that, in my book."

Lemaitre wasn't sure.

"If every dark alley had a Henry Jones hiding in it, it'd be a much safer country," he pointed out.

"Not for the Henry Joneses," Dexter replied. "We'd be bringing in their mangled bodies in lorry loads."

Lemaitre shuddered. He knew what was wrong with Dexter. He was still smarting from having been so completely hoodwinked. But it wasn't all that fair to take it out on Jones – who seemed to be one of the most unfortunate individuals alive: a natural innocent whom everyone naturally assumed to be guilty . . .

Lem walked down to the cells and had a look at him. He was lying on a bed at the back of his cell, sleeping the sleep of the just – which, Lem supposed, he had a pretty good right to do.

He woke him up in the nicest way he could think of – by noisily unlocking the cell door, and clanging it wide open.

"Okay, Jones," he said. "I've a bit of good news for you. You're not under arrest any longer, and are quite free to go. Good luck. And don't forget to give the next girl you rescue a smacking great kiss from me."

Henry woke up with a start, and it was a while before he could take the situation in. He stared at the open door suspiciously, and the last thing he seemed to want to do was use it.

"But the – the *real* Stocking Strangler," he said. "Where is he?"

"That's something I'd give a great deal to be able to tell you, laddie," Lemaitre said. "The plain truth is, we were so sure you were the Strangler that we let the real one walk out of here scot free."

Jones suddenly showed that he wasn't by any means as dim as he had appeared. The effects of that blow on the head were finally wearing off.

"With the girl?" he said sharply. "The girl that I – "

"With the girl that you tried to rescue, yes," said Lemaitre – and was startled at the speed with which Jones was bounding up from the bed. "What's all that about, son?" he asked. "You're not thinking you might be able to go out and rescue her all over again?"

Henry Jones had never met anyone, least of all a policeman, who seemed able to see right into his head. He stared blankly, incredulously. Then, quite simply:

"Why not?" he said.

Lemaitre burst out laughing. It felt like the first time he'd laughed all night.

"You're a glutton for punishment, aren't you? But you're out of luck, I'm afraid. This time the Strangler won't be operating in any dark alley. He'll be doing it in comfort and style – in some bedroom which the poor benighted girl has taken him to herself! And if you can figure out where that might be, you'll have earned yourself not just your freedom, but the undying gratitude of the whole of the Metropolitan Police."

"Bedroom?" said Henry dazedly. It was almost as if he'd never heard of such a place. Of course, Lem remembered, he rarely used one himself, at all events during the night. "Have you tried the girl's own home? And – and the Strangler's?"

Lemaitre grimaced.

"I wasn't born yesterday, Henry my boy, even if you were. Of course we've tried 'em – and drawn blanks in both cases, I'm afraid." Something – probably a combination of weariness and frustration – made him unusually communicative. "And the only address that I got out of the girl's parents was the flat of her old boy friend – which she left a fortnight ago after a flaming row. I don't think it's too likely she'd be there, do you?"

Jones once again showed that the label "mental defective" couldn't fairly be applied to him at all.

"She might be," he said. "Anything's worth a try, I'd have thought."

Lemaitre snorted.

"Don't be more stupid than you can help. The boy friend is still there, at this moment. They had *another* flaming row, only tonight – "

He stopped there, abruptly, remembering that there was no proof of any of that. All that was known was that Judy had left her parents, bound for Stanley's flat, at eleven o'clock, and had been walking the streets, lost and miserable, half an hour later. She *could* have found that Stan had gone away, scarpered. *Maybe with someone else* –

Lem suddenly found himself eying Jones with a new respect. It dawned on him that he wasn't a thick, or a crazy young man: just a lost one. With no friends, no family, no roots, no job, no prospects, he was retaliating on reality by living out, at the age of twenty-four, the ludicrous day-dreams of a fourteen-year-old. But what did those fantasies really amount to? Boiled down, they reminded Lem of feelings he himself had had in the very distant past: the basic urges of every raw recruit to every police force in the world – to save life, to smash villains, to fight crime.

"I've got a bit more news for you, sunshine," he said abruptly. "Unless I'm much mistaken, you've got the makings of a bloody good copper."

Before the stunned Jones could reply, he added:

"And you can start your new career right now – by coming with me."

Lem in a hurry never took the slightest notice of formalities. He should have signed Jones out, cancelling the charges; he should have collected men to accompany him. He did neither of these things, but, after giving Dexter the briefest of accounts of where he was going, and allowing Jones the shortest of moments to collect his belt, tie and other belongings, simply charged out of the main entrance and headed for his car, with Jones staggering and blinking along behind him, his brain ablaze with a brand-new vision: himself as a champion of the Law.

Lem's brain was far from bright with visions as they turned into Marslake Road. He knew very well that he was clutching at a straw. And even if he wasn't – even if he *had* stumbled on the place where Judy and Exton had gone, the odds were a million to one that it was too late now to save her.

No. 10 didn't prove hard to find. It was a maisonette occupying the upper floors of a rambling Victorian house, two along from the end of the road. Lemaitre stopped the car and got out, fighting against a heavy sense of dread.

"Well, here we are, Jones lad," he said. "And don't be too hopeful. In this game, believe you me, it doesn't pay."

Jones proved again that he was sharper by far than he appeared.

"Someone's here, anyway," he said. "See that light?"

Lemaitre had, in fact, just spotted it: a window lit up at the side of the house. A small, square window, of frosted glass – almost certainly a bathroom or toilet.

"Doesn't signify much," he muttered. "It could be just that the boy friend is home after all, can't sleep and is visiting the loo."

They made their way up a flight of outside steps leading up to the first floor, and the front door of No. 10. For the second time that night, Lem found himself simultaneously banging a knocker and pressing a bellpush. The strident results resounded all through the building, and started dogs barking half-way down the street. But no other lights sprang on and when Lem stopped for sheer shortage of breath, there was nothing but an ominous silence from beyond the door.

"Shall I break the door down?" asked Jones, as though it was something he did every day of the week.

Lem was about to make a sour, crude joke – something about giving whoever was in the loo a chance to pull the chain – when he heard an odd creaking, from quite close at hand. He didn't like that creaking. It started those shivers going again, and they were running through him like an electric current all the way from his scalp to his toes.

"Stand back, son. I'll do the breaking," he said – and delivered three mighty kicks at the door. It resisted all of them, but the glass in the top half was smashed to smithereens, so that Lemaitre could lean through and turn the handle inside. The door hadn't been bolted, and opened without a sound – except for the sinister tinkling made by odd slivers of broken glass falling on to the carpeting behind it.

The next moment, Lemaitre and Jones were standing inside a dark hall, listening intently.

The creaking was still going on, but suddenly ended in two far more terrifying sounds: a slithering followed by a thud which shook the floor of the whole maisonette.

Jones was suddenly a rescuer with a capital R again.

He rushed headlong in the general direction of the sounds – a door leading off on the right, the handle of which could just be glimpsed through the darkness. Lemaitre called after him, aware that anyone could lie in wait, behind a closed door. But Jones grabbed the handle, turned it, sent the door crashing back on its hinges, and went storming through into the blackness of the bedroom.

It wasn't completely dark in there. The rays of a street lamp were coming through a gap in the window curtains; and there was a gleam of light from under a door on the far side, leading probably to a bathroom. These two light sources were just enough to reveal that there was someone on the bed. Someone who did not move.

Jones stopped dead, becoming as motionless as the figure on the bed.

Lemaitre, behind him in the doorway, muttered: "Brace yourself, lad. You're not seen as much of this sort of thing as I have."

And he clicked on the light-switch.

It was just as well that he had warned Jones, he told himself. The light for a second was so dazzling that he could see nothing except that it was a naked girl, obviously Judy. Then, slowly, the other details of the scene of horror sank in.

She was lying half on the bed and half on the floor, in a grotesquely twisted position, her eyes wide and staring. There was a vicious, weal-like red blotch all round her throat, although there was no stocking to be seen. There didn't need to be, Lemaitre thought grimly. That weal was trade mark enough. He'd seen it on the throats of too many Stocking Strangler victims for there to be any doubt as to what – or who – had caused it.

He tried hard to be dispassionate, as he had been in all the other cases, but found it impossible. This time he had known the victim. Known her! Hell, he had watched her egging on the Strangler, and blindly, dumbly stood by while she had walked out of the police station practically in his arms!

There had been many times in his career when Lemaitre had felt like kicking himself. But now he felt like kicking himself right out of the force.

For a moment, he was plunged into such depths of guilt and shame that he hardly noticed what Jones was doing. Then it dawned on him that the stupid young goon was messing about with the evidence. He had pulled Judy's body fully up on to the bed, was patting her cheeks, and desperately trying to apply a fumbling, amateurish kiss of life.

"For Chrissake," said Lem. "Don't you know that the first rule is never to touch a body?"

The "stupid young goon's" reply almost literally sent him reeling.

"Even," he stammered, "even, even . . . if she's still breathing?"

* * *

For a long moment, Lem's brain refused totally to accept that she could be.

He had seen too many Strangler victims not to know that the man always finished the job. And that tell-tale mark on Judy's throat, her staring, sightless eyes, the way she was lying –

It was only gradually, as he saw the colour beginning to return to Judy's cheeks, and heard her breath come first faintly, then strongly, that he was forced to admit that he had fallen victim to his old fatal habit of jumping to conclusions.

And it really could have been fatal this time . . .

"You're doing well, sunshine," he managed to get out at last. "In your first ten minutes as a deputy policeman, you've saved a life, and shown me up as the criminally careless old fool I'm getting to be."

Jones didn't say anything. Rather to Lemaitre's relief – the admission had caused Lem a lot – he hardly seemed to have heard a word. All his attention was focussed on the girl, whose eyelids were flickering, and who would obviously be conscious soon.

Lemaitre suddenly tensed. Those noises they had heard: the creaking, the slithering, the thump that had shaken the floor. Were they explained now? Had they been made as the girl struggled with the Strangler, the slithering and the thump being caused by her half-falling on the floor? If so, the Strangler must be here, now. Probably hiding in the bathroom –

In two seconds, Lemaitre was across to the other side of the bedroom, and trying the bathroom door.

"All right, Exton. I know you're in there – " he began. But the words died in his throat as a flood of second thoughts poured into his brain.

That creaking hadn't sounded remotely like bedsprings. And a girl slithering half off a bed wouldn't cause a thud that had shaken the floor, even out in the hall . . .

Expecting anything now, from a gruesome spectacle to a cunning trap, Lemaitre flung open the door.

What he saw was not only gruesome, but at first glance, totally unbelievable.

The naked body of Clive Exton was lying half in, half out of the bath, in a twisted and ungainly heap. Its face, turned towards the ceiling, was twisted too – and for the second time, Lemaitre found himself looking at staring yet unseeing eyes.

There was no possibility, though, that Exton was still breathing. His face was greeny-grey, already wax-like; and round his throat, tightly knotted and biting into his flesh like a garrotte, was a stocking – or, to be exact, two stockings, that looked as though they were actually the ripped remnants of a pair of tights.

The impression that the impossible had happened – that the Stocking Strangler had somehow come out here and strangled himself – was so strong that Lemaitre had to lean back against the door, close his eyes and collect himself before his mind stopped boggling, and the common-sense solution occurred to him.

When he opened his eyes, he looked up at the bathroom ceiling – and there, tightly bound round the metal top of a globe-shaped light fitting, was more nylon material, obviously the rest of the same pair of tights.

It was clear enough what had happened now.

On the point of strangling the very last breath of life out of Judy Moss – perhaps sensing that if he went on a second longer, she would be beyond hope – Exton had whipped the tights from round her neck, and dashed into the bathroom. In what must have been a mad, suicidal frenzy, he had tied her tights to the top of the light fitting, just where it jutted out from the ceiling, in such a way that they formed a noose. Then, standing on the edge of the bath, he had inserted his head into the noose, tightened it round his neck – and jumped.

Death was unlikely to have been instantaneous, to put it mildly, Lem thought with a shudder. The nylon wouldn't have been strong enough to break his neck. He must have swung for minutes in helpless, writhing agony; the agony of all his five victims rolled into one.

His lifeless body must still have been hanging there when, with Jones, he had come through the front door. The creaking had obviously come from the light fitting, which had been pulled half-way out of its socket by the strain. A few seconds later – when they were crossing the hall – the nylon material had obviously given way beneath the body's weight, and the other noises they had heard had been made by its slithering fall down on to the bath below.

Lemaitre, taking no chances now, seized the body's wrist and felt for a pulse. There was none, and the fingers felt cold and clammy to the touch.

Feeling more than a little sick, he backed out of the bathroom and closed the door.

"Shouldn't go in there, son," he said over his shoulder to Jones. "It's the end of the story of the Stocking Strangler, and not what I'd call a happy ending – for *him*. Just when he was on the point of topping young Judy here, he went in to the bathroom and topped himself. And you'll be a ruddy genius if you can figure out why."

Jones said nothing. Lem looked round and wasn't surprised. Judy Moss had recovered consciousness, and was staring up at Henry – blankly, dazedly, but with just the beginning of a realisation of what he had just done for her.

At this of all moments, Henry didn't have to be "a ruddy genius" to work out why the Strangler had killed himself. Nothing in the world could be more obvious.

"Somewhere inside, *he* must have wanted to be Judy's rescuer," he told the startled Lem. "And for him, well, was there any other way?"

# 18 Darkness at Dawn

The very first signs of the sky lightening in the east, bringing to an end what felt like the longest, darkest night of his life, were visible as Gideon's car pulled up outside the gates of River Manor, and the whole motorcade which he was leading – eight police Pandas and two area cars, with more than thirty men in them all told – drew up behind him.

On Gideon's orders, the cars' sirens had been silent; but the revolving lights on their roofs had continued working, and now turned the road behind him into a bizarre fantasy of flashing, flickering blue. The lights had been necessary to help them scythe their way through the early-morning traffic, and had been effective: they had got here from St. Giles Hospital in eighty seconds flat.

Fast. But fast enough to beat the Big Four?

Gideon wasn't sure, and felt even more doubtful as he stepped out of the car, and stared up at the extraordinary building that towered over them, very slightly silhouetted against the faintly brightening sky.

"Good God," he growled. "It looks like a ruddy castle. A fairytale castle, at that."

"More like one out of a horror movie, if you ask me," said Riddell, stepping out of the car, with Matt Honiwell behind him. He sounded as though he was shivering, which might, or might not, be due to the cold of the early morning air.

"This place is known as Rock Castle around these parts,

sir," said the driver of the car, a young constable called Crowther, who obviously lived locally. "Monty Marlowe pulled down the old River Manor, and built it back in the 1960s. Remember seeing it go up when I was a boy. We used to take turns to shout out to the builders things like 'When does Count Dracula move in?'"

"Never mind about that," snapped Gideon. "Our problem is to stop anyone moving *out*. Matt, Tom – get men outside every visible exit. Fast."

Men were pouring out of all the cars, snaking back along the road.

Riddell and Honiwell shouted the necessary instructions, and small groups of men could be seen shooting off into the gloom.

"Rock Castle, eh?" Gideon muttered to himself, as he stared up at the fantastic pile. The place was beginning to look more and more like it now, except that it obviously wasn't made of rock, but of solid concrete, grey, cold, hugely forbidding in the slowly growing light.

It possessed a medieval style turret at each corner; a high wall surrounding it, interrupted by large wrought-iron gates, and just visible through the gates, a front door of iron-studded wood that looked as though it would take a hundred men and a battering-ram to break it down.

Now he came to think of it, it was just the sort of place that would be built by a rock star. That high wall would keep out an army of hysterical fans, and the rest would make an effective deterrent to any marauding criminals. Then, floodlit at night, with the river in the background, there couldn't be a better setting for lavish all-night parties. In fact, living himself in the neighbouring Fulham, Gideon seemed to remember reading accounts in the local papers about wild parties being staged here. But there had never been a hint of drugs being used or anything dubious; Monty Marlowe had been expert at keeping his nose clean, even then.

Which was why planning permission had been granted (probably eagerly, by a council anxious to oblige such a famous resident) and the Big Four had built themselves, in the heart of London and under the very noses of the Met, a headquarters where they could not only resist arrest, but withstand a siege for days on end!

Not that that *was* their plan, surely. It might take a long time, it might make criminal history, but such a siege could only end one way – and the Big Four must know it.

Which didn't alter the fact that if they were in a hysterically suicidal mood, and decided to make a fight of it, they were in a very strong position indeed.

Gideon glanced round. Riddell and Honiwell were just behind him, and so were all the remaining men – twenty-four or five of them at least.

"Right," he called out to them. "Follow me, all of you. And those that have guns, keep 'em ready." He suddenly grinned through the gloom. "Never thought you'd end the night by storming a castle, did you? But then, a copper's life is full of surprises. Watch out for bullets, all of you. Keep an eye on the windows – and the turrets. But even if you see a marksman, or catch sight of a gun barrel glinting, no shooting – unless I give the word. And when I say duck, *duck* – fast. Okay? Then we'll go."

He turned and led the way towards the wrought-iron gates. There was an electric bellpush by the side of them, which he pressed, expecting a deafening ringing. Instead, there was taped music through an amplifier: an electric guitar, playing the same five notes over and over again. The tune was vaguely familiar, even to Gideon; and then he remembered it was the opening bars of one of Marlowe's biggest hits, "Hey, Dilly Dolly Baby", sung or whistled by the whole nation somewhere around 1963. He could even recall his daughter Penny – now a distinguished soloist playing with national symphony orchestras – thumping it out on the piano when she was seven years old, and supposed to be practising the scales. He had once parted with all of five shillings, after extracting a promise from her that she'd never play the wretched thing again . . . No wonder Monty Marlowe had never come under police suspicion. His songs had played a part in everyone's life, even his own.

The jangling notes went on and on, then slowly faded.

There was no sign of anyone coming to answer. Gideon tried the gates. He expected to find them bolted on the inside, perhaps padlocked. In which case, the fun would begin in earnest.

To his relief and slight bewilderment, the gates were neither bolted nor padlocked. They swung open at his touch.

"Oh, Lord," he heard Matt Honiwell mutter. "Don't say it's here we go again."

He didn't need to ask what Matt meant. Gideon's men had experienced a night of doors opening unexpectedly easily – on to houses whose occupants had long since gone. Was this going to be another instance?

It was looking more and more like it, Gideon had to admit, as he flung open the gates and strode through them, in to a drive which seemed more like a courtyard in front of the mock castle.

Still walking very rapidly, half expecting a hail of bullets to come whipping down from one or all of the ominous turrets above, he went up the steps to the huge doors.

Ignoring the heavy iron bellpull hanging to one side – which looked as if it would produce "Hey, Dilly Dolly Baby" sung this time by a massed cathedral choir – Gideon strode up to the doors and tried them.

After a second –

"Yes, Matt," he said softly. "I'm afraid it is a case of here we go again."

The doors opened wide without a sound.

Instantly, as if by magic, lights sprang on in the hall beyond – luxurious, pink-tinged concealed lights revealing a stone-flagged chamber, with all the traditional items expected in a castle entrance hall: half a dozen gleaming shields on the walls, with swords hanging criss-crossed beneath them; ancient – or at least, ancient looking – suits of armour, as highly-polished as the shields; a huge chandelier and an enormous staircase leading to the floor above. There was even a massive stone fireplace, with a real coal fire – as real as any coal fire could be that was worked by electrically lit gas jets – springing to life before their eyes.

Gideon's heart sank as he watched the flames leap up.

It was almost exactly as if the Big Four had known they were coming, and were staging a mocking, ironic welcome.

But how could they have known – unless there had been another leak? And how could there have been another leak – when not even the Yard had been told about the raid?

It was Matt who mentioned the alternative possibility first.

"Maybe this is a trap," he said.

Gideon hardly heard him. He was so furious at the thought that the Big Four *still* seemed to have advance knowledge of their moves that, for once, he was completely reckless. Striding into the centre of the hall, he shouted to the others to follow him, and then started off in the direction of two large doors leading to the left, labelled, in Old English lettering, "YE MUSICKE ROOM".

By the time the men at the rear were filing through the main entrance he was already in Ye Musicke Room, and finding himself in the middle of a sound-and-vision nightmare, switched on the moment he'd opened the doors.

Rock music blared out of a battery of amplifiers ranged from floor to ceiling. Blinding, constantly changing lights – one second blue, the next green, the next crimson – flashed into his eyes from all directions, seeming to burn straight through his eyeballs and send their searing colours into the very centre of his skull. The thunder of the drum beats seemed to shake the floor.

Gideon blundered out backwards, clapping his hands to his ears and struggling desperately to make himself heard above the din.

"For God's sake somebody, get in there and shut that row off!" he bellowed.

He intended one of the young constables to go, somebody whose eyes and ears were attuned to disco effects.

Instead, of all people, Riddell went charging through the doors.

What happened to him inside nobody ever found out for sure. But probably the sudden assault of psychedelic sight and sound on his already shattered nerves was simply too much. Something in his brain snapped and he started firing in all directions. The crash of shots mingled with the tinkle of shattered glass as he hit first one of the coloured spotlights and then another. Finally he blasted away at the amplifiers. Fuses started blowing, making almost as loud reports as the shots – and when Gideon went charging back into the music room, the place was dark and silent and smelling of smoke.

As he groped about to find Riddell, suddenly the entrance hall behind him was plunged into darkness too. It was probably another fuse blowing somewhere, but for a moment, it seemed as though an unseen hand had turned off the switches.

Somebody somewhere panicked.

"A trap! We've walked into a f—g trap!" he yelled.

And suddenly more guns were being fired, by whom and at whom it was impossible to see.

* * *

Gideon's first thought was that a shoot out had started – the big shoot out that he had been expecting to happen somewhere all night.

"Down!" he shouted. "Down – everyone!"

Not that there was a lot of point in the command, he realised grimly. If his men back in the entrance hall were being fired on by gunmen on the staircase, or on the landing above, they would make easier targets crouching or lying flat than standing. The only factor in their favour was the near-darkness, and that could change at any second if those lights came on again.

His brain buzzing with as many alarm signals as the instrument panel of a plunging aircraft, Gideon started to grope his way back through the smoke-filled blackness of the music room towards the entrance hall.

He suddenly blundered into someone, and from his violent start and startled gasp, realised it was Riddell.

Tom was obviously still in a bad way. He was breathing heavily and struggling to speak.

"S-sorry about this, George, I – "

Gideon had no time to waste listening to apologies. He seized Riddell's arm, and virtually dragged him alongside him towards the double doors leading to the entrance hall.

The next moment, it was Gideon who was breathing heavily.

One of the doors was ajar, and suddenly let in a dazzling rectangular grid of light. The lights in the hall, including that great chandelier, had come back on, making his men sitting ducks for any gunmen on the landing.

Determined to intervene somehow, if only by roaring defiance, Gideon threw himself at the doors, and flung both of them wide open.

Then he began to breathe normally again. There was no sound of firing; no sign of anyone on the landing or stairs. The light failure in the hall had obviously been nothing but a prolonged dim-out caused by fuses blowing on an adjacent circuit. And the shots – to judge from the bemused, startled expressions on the faces of two of his men, the two with smoking guns in their hands – had been caused by nothing but the nervous fingers of strained and over-tired young coppers.

"False alarm," Gideon announced. Riddell, he realised, was standing beside him now, looking as shamefaced as the others, and pale and shaky too. If anyone needed a morale boost, it was Tom, he decided, and promptly thought of a way to give him one. "You were all taken aback, as I was, by Chief Detective Superintendent Riddell's extremely effective way of carrying out my orders. He did stop that deafening racket – damn quick." Grinning, he added: "Though I don't expect everyone to agree, I'd like to see him in action at a live pop concert sometime."

That brought a few laughs – nervous, awkward ones, but enough to relieve the tension a little. Those alarm signals, though, were still flashing all over Gideon's brain.

The Big Four didn't play games. They must have had a good reason for putting on that sound and vision show, and there was only one that he could think of: to delay the police search for as long as possible. Which could mean that they were still on the premises, and needed time to –

To do what?

To hide in some remote part of this crazy building, in all probability custom-built for such emergencies?

To make a dash through one of the side entrances, shooting the men he'd stationed outside it – the blaring music intended to drown the sound of screams and shots?

Or to –

Gideon decided not to consider other possibilities, though God knew, there was no shortage of them. Those two were enough to be getting on with, in all conscience. Stopping them would call for very quick action – on the part of every single man here.

"Right!" he shouted. "Matt, take your men upstairs. Tom – your lot can search the ground floor. And I *mean* search. A mad place like this could have dozens of hidden doors, sliding panels and all the rest of it – probably computer-operated! The rest of you, come with me into the grounds. Guns at the ready – and be careful. Duck if you see a shadow move . . ."

The men, all of them, he remembered, hand-picked by either Hobbs or himself, did move very fast indeed. Within split seconds, Honiwell and his party were up the stairs and out of sight. Riddell, after a moment's shock at finding himself still trusted to lead a major part of the operation, acted with speed and efficiency, hurrying with his men into the mangled chaos of Ye Musicke Room and beyond.

Gideon gave one more command before he headed for the grounds. He ordered a detective inspector to radio Hammersmith police station for reinforcements, to get here within minutes, if possible.

It was on the tip of his tongue to order roadblocks to be set up too, but he thought better of it. If the Big Four had already got away, he'd lost, and might as well admit it. He'd not even any car description to give.

The conviction was steadily growing on him, though, that they *hadn't* got away – not yet; that they were somewhere in – or maybe under – this ten million pound pop palace, and at any moment might –

He stopped thinking there. It was better to use his eyes and ears, and be ready to move at the slightest suspicious sight or sound.

He was in the grounds now, with an awed, tense group

of nine or ten men behind him, all of them peering round cautiously in the watery light of a very grey dawn. The castle backed on to a stone-flagged courtyard, filled with gimmicky statues of every kind, including a fake Venus de Milo, a giant, grimacing garden gnome, and an elaborate fountain with water gushing from the breasts of four nubile mermaids. The place looked as if it had been built to form a background for pop videos, and probably had been used many times for just that. In its weird way, it was not unpicturesque, with the mock castle wall rising all round it, and glimpses of the River Thames beyond.

There was only one thing that spoiled the view. Some building work seemed to be in progress over on the far side of the courtyard, near the wall dividing it from the river. Gideon could glimpse a pile of bricks and rubble, although it was hard to be sure of anything. A freezing early-morning river mist was rolling in, combining with the feebleness of the light to make every outline uncertain. Even the giant gnome seemed ghostly and ethereal, its grin appearing and disappearing like the Cheshire Cat's through the wreaths of mist.

"What the hell *is* all that?" Gideon wondered aloud, striding across the courtyard in the direction of the bricks.

Crowther – the young constable who had driven Gideon's car – was walking just behind him.

"I've read in the papers that Monty Marlowe was building himself a nuclear shelter, sir. I expect it's that."

"A nuclear shelter?"

"Yes, sir. The deepest and best-equipped in the world, the papers said, costing millions . . . It would be proof against almost any blast, and would be so well stocked it could be lived in for a year."

"This," said Gideon softly, "I've got to see."

A possibility as fantastic as the intermittently grinning gnome was beginning to take shape at the back of his mind: the thought of the Big Four burying themselves in the ultimate retreat for days, weeks, months – resisting the siege to end all sieges . . .

The moment he reached the actual building site, however,

the idea vanished as abruptly as a wreath of river mist. All he found himself staring down at was a ditch-like hole not more than fifteen foot deep, dug right up against the castle wall, with the pile of rubble just beside it. There were a few stone steps leading down, and a few signs of concrete foundations being laid at the bottom of the hole. But that was all.

"Huh," said Gideon. "If that's a million-pound effort, I'm the Venus de Milo! I saw bigger Anderson shelters than that being put up during the War."

Constable Crowther did not like to hear his suggestion being quashed, even by the great Gideon.

"Perhaps this is just some preliminary work, sir, and they are going to build the real shelter later."

"H'm. Perhaps."

Gideon was already climbing down the steps to take a closer look.

He did not get one.

In fact, it was a long time before he was to see anything again – except for a searing flash as a bomb went off, somewhere immediately above him to the right, followed by a terrifying glimpse of the whole stone wall toppling and tons of masonry falling from a great height, directly towards him.

Gideon didn't duck. He dived headlong down the steps into the hole ahead of him, landing just as the concrete foundation shook with what felt like the seismic force of a dozen earthquakes. A horrific hailstorm of bricks and rubble crashed around him, and every vestige of the dim dawn light vanished above him.

After that, there was only silence and darkness – a peculiar dank, stifling blackness that meant, Gideon knew, one thing and one thing only.

He had been buried alive.

## 19 Under the Rubble

For more than an hour, it was regarded as virtually certain that Gideon was dead; that no one could possibly have survived the formidable fall of bricks, concrete blocks and rubble that had occurred in that corner of the courtyard. When the fire brigade and the bomb experts arrived, they took one glance in that direction, and then automatically turned their attention to the casualties elsewhere in the yard.

Gideon himself had tried to attract notice by shouting; but the air was in such short supply that even the smallest intake of breath sucked earth and dust towards his mouth and nose, so that all he could produce was a series of half-choking wheezes, so weak that they sounded faint and distant to his own ears. His hands and arms seemed to be so weighed down by the rubble that he could not lift either of them, even half an inch. What had happened to his legs he wasn't sure, but there was no feeling in either of them – unless he made a desperate effort to move one, in which case his whole body was suddenly wracked with a blow torch-like flare of pain.

The only thing he was able to do was make a faint scratching with the fingers of one hand – but that had about as much chance of being heard, he told himself, as the scratching of a flea on the back of an elephant.

It wasn't much consolation, he knew, but to *him*, in that confined space, the sound was far from insignificant. It was as loud as thunder – almost as loud as the only other noises he could hear: the pounding of his heart and the roaring of the blood through his veins. The thickness of the rubble above him cut out everything else, trapping him in a tiny private world that was the closest thing to hell that he had ever known; perhaps that any man *could* know.

What made it worse was that he had agonising worries for company. The collapsing wall must have sent slabs of concrete across the whole courtyard. He had had this hole at his feet to dive into, and so (for the moment at least) had survived. But what about young Crowther, who had been behind him, too far away to jump? And all the others in the party, who had been standing in the middle of the yard? They could have been massacred, all of them.

If only he'd listened to Matt's warning that this whole set-up might have been a trap –

In a spasm of self-reproach, Gideon found himself sweating all over, and suddenly the pounding of his heart became so loud that it seemed to shake the earth all round him, and even rattle the rubble above his head. It took him a second to realise, dazedly, that a heart couldn't possibly do all that. Somebody must be knocking a heavy object – probably a spade – against a brick or a block of concrete immediately above his head.

The pounding stopped after about three strokes, as if it was a signal. Gideon intensified his frantic scratching, and shouted – or rather wheezed – "Hullo" as loudly as he could.

The next moment was one of the most unforgettable of his life.

There was a scraping, rattling sound as if something was being attached to one of the biggest pieces of concrete. Then came a crunching noise as it was lifted, probably by a crane. And finally, somewhere above him, a crack appeared in the stultifying wall of blackness that surrounded him. It was a small crack, not much bigger than a keyhole, but what did that matter?

It let in light, and air and – most wonderful of all – voices.

The first voice said: "I thought I heard a scratching. It's stopped now. Perhaps I was wrong."

Gideon realised that at the sight of that chink of light, relief had frozen him into immobility.

"No, you weren't!" he shouted – and could almost sense, down below, the waves of shock going through the rescue party above.

He heard a familiar voice now: that of Alec Hobbs, who had obviously rushed down from the Yard to take over. Alec, hoarse with excitement, was shouting:

"See? I *told* you to keep trying. I told you George – er, Commander Gideon wouldn't be – "

The rest of what he said was drowned by the noise of more lifting equipment being used; then another rock was raised, and the keyhole-sized chink became a one-foot square of grey October sky.

The square darkened as someone bent over it, peering in. Gideon glimpsed a bit of Hobbs's face – his nose and a part of the mouth.

"George – are you all right?"

His voice was so hoarse that he could hardly get out the words.

Gideon spat some earth out of his mouth, and found that he could manage, if not a roar, at least something approaching his old growl.

"All right – no," he called back. "Still alive – yes." Dust caused a spasm of coughing and choking, but the moment he could he continued, defiantly: "And probably kicking if someone could get this ton of phoney castle off – off me." His voice fell away at the end of the sentence, as though his lungs couldn't manage another word. He was surprised – and angry – at his own weakness, and struggled to speak again, although he was handicapped now by a sudden wave of pain. In spite of it, he managed to croak: "What about the others – Constable Crowther, Detective Inspect – Inspector Hamlin, Sergeant – "

Without missing one, he reeled off all the names of the men who had been just behind him.

Alec hesitated, obviously wishing he could give a different reply.

"Well – they've all survived, George, but some of them sustained pretty bad injuries. Young Crowther had a ton of concrete on his leg; they'll have a fight to save it, I think. Hamlin was half-buried, and still unconscious when they took him away. But most of the others only sustained cuts and bruises, through being knocked off their feet by the blast. Could have been worse, couldn't it?"

"A hell of a lot worse," said Gideon, very greatly relieved. Another spasm of pain gripped him and, as he fought it, sweat broke out all over his face, sweat which the cold draught of air flooding through the square above him seemed to turn to ice. Summoning up all his will power, he forced himself to think about what was happening above ground, not below it. "D-d-d-did – " he began, stuttering through his shivers, "did we g-get any of them? The Big Four, I mean?"

Again Alec hesitated before replying. Then:

"No," he said. "I'm afraid it's the old, old story, George. Nobody home."

"C-christ," said Gideon. "What a b-b-bloody disastrous night."

"Not so disastrous as we all feared until – until just a minute ago," said Alec, and suddenly, for a moment, was unable to speak at all. When he did find his voice again, the words came in a torrent.

"But forget about all that, George – you've got to relax, save your strength. Look: we've got an expert here on bomb rescue. And a doctor, both wanting to talk to you . . . I'll – I'll be back when they've finished."

Hobbs's head vanished, to be replaced by that of the expert – a grey-haired man with a gentle voice and a gentle smile, neither of which concealed the fact that he was very worried – and for some reason very scared.

"Good morning, Commander. Got some bad news for you, I'm afraid."

"Has anybody ever got anything else?" Gideon growled.

At least the shivering spasm was over, beaten, it almost

seemed, by his own will power. But even the slightest movement brought pain, and a sudden fit of coughing brought an explosion of it, as though a firecracker had gone off inside his chest.

"My news isn't all that bad," the expert replied, at length. "It's just that you're in an awkward position, technically. We shall have to go very carefully. Might be a good few hours before we've got you out."

It seemed to Gideon that a few more minutes of this, let alone a few hours, would finish him. He forced his brain to blot out the thought, reminding himself that after all, he had light now, and air, and people. If only there wasn't all this pain –

The doctor appeared next, and was hardly more cheerful than the bomb expert. A dour northern type, he fired off a lot of questions and responded to each of Gideon's replies with an ominous silence. He, too, gave the impression that he was secretly scared to death. Why? Gideon wondered. Was it him they were worried about? Surely whether he lived or died couldn't matter so much to these strangers.

"Just lie as still as you can, Commander," the doctor finished. "And don't move anything – anything at all – until I have had a chance to examine you. Right?"

"Right," agreed Gideon, not thinking it worth adding that his own body had given him the same instructions, and reinforced them with blistering agony every time he disobeyed. It was a relief when Alec's familiar features returned, although he was very tense now, too.

"George. I've just rung Kate, who's at Penny's, of course. She was determined to come straight over here, but I – I've ordered her to keep away."

Gideon grunted his approval. Kate's heart had had enough – more than enough – to stand up to already during the past night.

But apparently he had misunderstood Alec's reasons for giving that order. Hobbs was explaining them now, so simply and matter-of-factly that it was hard to grasp the full import of what he said.

"I may as well tell you, George. You aren't just in a

'technically awkward' position. They've detected another explosive device buried somewhere beneath you. That's why they don't want you to make the slightest move. And that's why I'm keeping everyone I can away."

* * *

There was a long pause. For a moment Hobbs wondered if Gideon had passed out, and swore at himself for being too frank too soon. The shock of this on top of everything else, even for someone with George's titanic strength and courage – He needn't have worried. Through the hole at his feet came the last sound he expected – a throaty chuckle.

"Well, I've spent half my career wishing I could put a bomb under somebody," Gideon said. "I suppose I can't complain when I finally find there's – there's one under me." Just a slight shakiness in his voice betrayed how greatly that courage was under strain.

Hobbs's own voice was shaking now – with anger.

"If it means a thousand nights like the last one, George, we're going to get these Big Four bastards. They're not fit to live, any of them. Not content with causing what, but for a miracle, would have been a massacre, they plant deeper bombs to booby-trap people trying to dig out the survivors. That's a trick even the sickest gang of terrorists on earth wouldn't sink to. You've always maintained that Mayne, Kemp and Salvados weren't vicious weirdos. They were just professional criminals, killing only when they had to. Well, they didn't have to kill this time, did they? They'd made their getaway. They'd made fools of us all – right through the night. But that wasn't enough for them. We'd dared to turn the heat on and tried to wipe out their whole sleazy organisation, so they were after punishing us for our impertinence. I've never come across such a display of sheer vindictive evil. The kindest thing to think is that they're psychos, the lot of them – though that's not exactly the word I'd choose."

Gideon did not reply. He had an obscure feeling that there was something wrong with Hobbs's theorising. All his long experience with the three super-criminals – the Capone-like Mayne, the smooth, sophisticated drugs king, Kemp, and the ever-elusive Salvados – suggested that they were cold and hard-headed, but vicious and vindictive, no. Of course, he didn't know about Monty Marlowe: behind his popular rock star front, *he* might have a twisted mind, capable of anything, and it was conceivable that he could have planted the bombs without the knowledge of the other three.

But it was far more likely that the Big Four had done all this, just as they did everything else, *for a coldly sane and logical reason.*

It was only a crazy hunch, he supposed, but the feeling grew that they might catch the Big Four yet if he could work out what that reason could possibly be.

All through the long hours of the day, when inch by painful inch, the rubble was cleared away above and around him, Gideon's mind kept coming back to the problem. He was grateful to have it to tackle. It kept him from brooding over what injuries he might have sustained; whether this might be the end of his career; if Kate's heart was okay, and all the other myriad anxieties that seemed to be piling up around him, behind the banks of searing pain. It also kept him from thinking too much about the fact that every single movement the rescuers made – every swing of the crane, every stroke of their spades, every raising of another bit of concrete, even every step they took – might result in him, and them, being blown sky-high. But it didn't keep him from remembering the courage they were displaying, and being both awed and grateful that so many unknown people were risking so much, solely on his behalf.

Gradually they no longer seemed to be unknown people at all. The face of the gentle-voiced bomb expert – who turned out to be one Sean McNally from Belfast, with a vast experience of such disasters – became as familiar as that of a close friend. And the ominous silences of the doctor, who, Gideon learned, was called Charles Quentin and came from Leeds, became fewer and fewer until he was positively chatty. Both men – and the whole rescue team – seemed to be losing their fear. Gideon could not understand why. After all, the cause for alarm was steadily growing, the further into the ground they reached. He didn't realise that the strange power he had always possessed – for reassuring people and making them give of their best – was functioning as forcefully as ever, even though he was flat on his back, scarcely able to move an inch, and still ninety per cent buried in the ground.

By the time the grey October light was fading, Gideon was only, in fact, about seventy per cent buried. The rocks above him had all gone. His head and chest were clear of the rubble, and so was his right arm, which Dr. Quentin pronounced undamaged apart from a few cuts and bruises. He could eat and drink now. Soup was brought, lashings of tea, and even a bacon and egg sandwich – and he felt much better for them. The condition of his hidden legs still remained doubtful. The violent pain in one of them had become more and more pronounced, and was by now almost continuous.

"Well, at least that means there's life in it," said Dr. Quentin, his accent now very northern. "A sure sign there's no paralysis, is that."

He started to cut away Gideon's tattered right sleeve, and was talking about a shot of morphine. But Gideon declined. His most priceless asset in this situation was his will power, he knew; that and his ability to control his brain, and force it to concentrate on some particular problem, regardless of all distractions. Morphine might well rob him of both – it could sap his will, cloud his thinking, leave him weak and helplessly fantasising. Anything was better than that. And, of course, there was still the question of the Big Four's motive to tackle.

He had no chance to tackle it just then. Hobbs finally allowed in a visitor: Matt Honiwell, who despite his tiredness, amounting to near-exhaustion, had been hanging about, waiting for a chance to see him, all day.

"If I'm blown up, George, I'll be in the best company I know," he said, running a hand through his mop of curly hair, and looking more like a benign teddy bear than ever.

He stayed, chatting, for all of half an hour.

Gideon learned that all Matt's men had escaped without a scratch, and that Riddell's had done the same: the thick walls of the mock castle had shielded them from the blast out in the courtyard. He also learned about Lemaitre's discovery of the hanging body of the Stocking Strangler. "It's the main news story in all the papers," Matt told him. "But on TV, I'm told, it's been replaced. They're giving constant news flashes about *you*."

TV cameras from both the BBC and ITV had apparently been set up outside the gates of River Manor, and only Alec Hobbs's stern insistence had prevented teams of cameramen descending on this very spot all day.

"I'm grateful for that," Gideon growled. "One thing I could definitely do without at the moment is having a mike shoved in my face and being asked how I feel." Talking of feelings made him suddenly think of Riddell. "How was Tom, the last time you saw him?" he asked, and knew immediately from Matt's expression that that was a question he would rather not answer.

Hesitantly, Matt told him that Riddell had suffered a nervous collapse, and had been taken, unconscious, to St. Giles Hospital.

"What caused it? The explosion?" Gideon asked.

"No. He got through that all right," said Matt. "But just afterwards, when he heard that you were almost certainly dead, he keeled over." Suddenly Matt's intense tiredness showed. He almost, in fact, behaved like Riddell, swaying on his feet.

"You'd better get home and get to bed," Gideon told him. "Or before you know it, you'll be keeling over too." He managed a weak grin. "I've enough to put up with without you landing on top of me."

As soon as Matt had gone, the grin became a grimace. The pain in that leg was suddenly so searing that his whole mind and body seemed to become a raging holocaust of agony. Very reluctantly, he allowed Dr. Quentin to come forward with the morphine. No thinking at all was now possible without it.

After that, the pain became remote and distant, but everything was now fuzzy and hazy, and the darkening sky a kaleidoscope of whirling grey. Then suddenly, surprisingly, he found his brain, far from escaping into woolly fantasies, taking a brilliant imaginative leap. It was as though the relative freedom from anguish and agony was enabling it to see clearly at last.

The problem that had been baffling him all day became abruptly absurdly simple. What had the Big Four been doing ever since he had arrived to raid their Rock Castle? *Trying one delaying tactic after another.* First they had attempted to delay the police with the blast of sound and vision effects in Ye Musick Room. Then they had used tricks with the lights to cause panic in the entrance hall. (If that hadn't been a side-effect of the blowing fuses.) Finally, just when he had been about to investigate their nuclear shelter, they had used the ultimate deterrent: a bomb, placed where it would be triggered off the second anyone set foot on the steps. And since then, it had been discovered that they had placed another bomb way underneath the first one. Why? It could only be – to stop anyone digging deeper.

*Digging deeper . . .*

Suddenly Gideon remembered what Crowther had said to him. He shuddered at the thought of how easily they could have been the last words the young constable ever said.

"Monty Marlowe was building himself a nuclear shelter, sir . . . The deepest and best-equipped in the world, the papers said, costing millions . . . proof against almost any blast . . . so well stocked it could be lived in for a year . . ."

Gideon started so violently that he made one of the rescuing team, who was gingerly shovelling some loose earth from around his chest, nearly drop his spade.

God, what an idiot he had been!

The half-built nuclear shelter which he had been investigating hadn't come within a mile of answering that description. He had realised it at the time – had said, in fact, "If that's a million-dollar effort, I'm the Venus de Milo!" But he hadn't drawn the obvious conclusion.

This building work was nothing but a fake, a blind. It was just to make people think that the nuclear shelter was still under construction. And there was only one reason, surely, why the Big Four should want such a thing to be believed.

It was to stop investigators looking any further . . . and *realising that the real nuclear shelter had already been completed, twenty, thirty, maybe fifty feet below!*

The more Gideon thought about it, the more certain he became that he had not only hit on the right solution, but knew for certain where the Big Four were now.

Clearly, there had not, after all, been any leak at the hospital. His arrival with his men at River Manor had taken the Big Four completely by surprise, although they had prepared plans for such an emergency, and put them into immediate effect. They had set up their delaying devices – subtle ones, not padlocked gates and locked doors, which would have advertised the fact they were still on the premises – and then rushed at all speed into the deep nuclear shelter, which was probably reached through a secret entrance somewhere in or near the courtyard. Probably the staff, if they had any, had all been sent away long before. No prying eyes would be welcome at a secret meeting of the Big Four.

They must have felt – indeed, they must be feeling – very safe down there, deep in the earth, surrounded by massive layers of ferro-concrete in a hideout that would withstand any amount of dynamiting, and with enough provisions to last them for a solid year! Not that they would have any need to stay there long. Almost certainly, the shelter had another entrance, leading out somewhere near the river – and as soon as the commotion had died down above them, all they had to do was wait for a dark night and arrange for a boat to complete their getaway.

It was a brilliant scheme, worthy of the four best criminal minds in London. But, of course, it all depended on no one suspecting for a moment that any such thing as the nuclear shelter existed. Probably it had originally been built under conditions of the greatest secrecy, but somehow the details had been leaked to the Press. That was why they had started the phoney building work as a cover-up. But they must have realised that anyone taking a close look at it would quickly size it up as a fake – and they had tried to make sure that no one who did take a close look lived to tell the tale.

The bomb, of course, wouldn't involve any risk to them. Literally a hundred bombs wouldn't make the faintest dent in a concrete shell designed to withstand a nuclear blast. They must have feared, though, that once the phoney shelter was blown up, someone might begin to suspect the truth, and had planted the second bomb to deter any deeper probing – or at least delay it until they had got clean away.

The whole thing added up and made such perfect sense that Gideon had no doubt it was right. The trouble was that the morphine which had sent his mind soaring would now not let it come back to earth – that terrible prison of earth and rubble which still trapped and half entombed him. The sky, darkening now to a deadly purple-grey, would not stop whirling round above him. The arc lamps which the rescuing party had suddenly switched on did not only dazzle him; they seemed to numb his brain, carrying all his thoughts away in a cold, white, brilliant torrent of light.

He felt suddenly light-headed, and as giddy as though he was being swirled along in the torrent too.

"Alec," he heard himself saying, as though from miles away. "Alec . . ."

Hobbs's face suddenly appeared in front of him, a dark silhouette against the blinding light.

"You all right, George?"

"No, I'm not all right," he heard himself reply. "I've just had a brainstorm, and can't bloody well remember . . . remember what caused it. Something . . . something about the Big Four – "

"Forget the Big Four now, George," Alec said, gently. "We'll catch up with them one of these days, I promise you, if it's the last thing I do."

"One of these days?" Gideon heard himself grunting stupidly. "Don't be silly. We can take them now. Tonight."

Alec was standing back now, talking to the doctor.

"Oh, Lord," thought Gideon bemusedly. "He thinks I've flipped – don't know what I'm saying . . ."

He closed his eyes against the arc lamps but that didn't

help. The insides of his eyelids became a searing red that reminded him of a blazing coal fire . . . the fire in the hearth which he had loved to poke as a child . . .

With a supreme effort, he somehow succeeded in pulling together his rambling, reeling thoughts.

"Listen, Alec," he suddenly roared. "There's a nuclear shelter underneath us . . . a multi-million pound one . . . and the Big Four are there . . . in it . . . *now* . . ."

Whether Alec had heard or not, he had no means of knowing.

At that point, he lost consciousness, becoming, for the second time in twelve hours, engulfed in darkness.

Only now it was the darkness of oblivion.

# 20 The Two Commanders

Suddenly faces replaced the darkness: lurid nightmare faces.

First there was Straker, shaking his handcuffed fists and screaming once again: "You'll never take the Big Four, Gideon. *They'll be taking you!*"

Then there was Constable Crowther, telling him: "Monty Marlowe's building himself a nuclear shelter. The deepest and best-equipped – "

He got no further before a big, Hiroshima-style mushroom cloud wiped out his young, eager, excited features. Through the cloud appeared Monty Marlowe, in black and white as on a 1960s television screen, singing "Hey, Dilly Dolly Baby". At least, that was the tune. But the words were different. They sounded like: *We're too big for you, Gideon, we're too big for you.*

Marlowe's face kept blurring and changing, first into the sharp features of Barry Mayne, then into the smooth ones of Jeremy Kemp, then to the shadowy, elusive ones of Arturo Salvados.

Finally, all four of them were on screen, so to speak, together, not singing at him but laughing. Just endlessly laughing . . .

He woke up, sweating, from the nightmare, and stupidly tried to turn over. A searing pain from the direction of his right leg reminded him that he was very far from being in bed; and other reminders followed in quick succession. The blinding arc lights when he opened his eyes. The hard cold touch of the concrete and rubble underneath and around him. The freezing night wind whipping across the courtyard . . .

Suddenly another face appeared, so welcome – yet so unexpected – that he thought at first he had stepped back into the dream.

It was Kate, bending over him, her grey eyes as serene as ever in the pitilessly fierce light.

"Take it easy, love. Look. They've almost dug you out now. Any minute, you'll be free . . . and coming home."

Gideon glanced down dazedly and saw that she was right. How long he had been unconscious he had no idea, but it must have been for an hour or more; it was now night, and miracles had been achieved by the rescue team in the meantime. Only his feet and ankles were now trapped, and men were at that very moment working to release them.

The doctor, who was still hovering over him, hastened to correct Kate.

"The Commander won't be coming home, Mrs. Gideon, not directly, I'm afraid. His right leg has been rather badly crushed. He'll have to go straight to St. Giles for an X-ray, perhaps an emergency operation . . . I've got an ambulance standing by."

Kate took the news as calmly as she took everything. Only Gideon noticed the flicker of anxiety crossing her face an instant before she smiled and joked:

"Ah, well. By now St. Giles is beginning to seem a home from home for both of us. I wonder if that sweet night sister will be on duty again."

Suddenly Gideon's mind cleared, and he was as anxious about her as she was about him.

"It's marvellous to see you, love, but what in God's name are you doing here? Don't you know there's a bomb – "

Alec Hobbs suddenly appeared, looking flustered and shamefaced.

"Sorry, George, but once she heard you'd passed out, nothing short of actually arresting her would keep her away." He smiled faintly. "And the prospect of carting my mother-in-law to the lock-up wasn't exactly appealing." The smile vanished as he turned, pleadingly, to Kate. "But you *are* in grave danger. And so am I – of never being spoken to by George again unless I get you out of here pronto, now that you've seen he's okay."

"I'll wait by the ambulance," she announced, and allowed absolutely nothing but calm confidence to show in her face as she blew Gideon a kiss, and said: "Don't be long, George, will you?"

Gideon managed a grin, if a wan one.

"I'll be there, I promise you," he said. "Just as soon as I can get away . . ."

Kate laughed. Then she was gone – having somehow succeeded in being there just when he needed her most: a miraculous trick she'd worked countless times during their years together. He wished he could say he'd always been there just when she needed him – but there had been times when police pressures had made that impossible. Once, in fact, they had nearly broken up because –

But he forced himself not to think about that.

Urgent things needed to be attended to – one very urgent indeed.

Alec had turned away, and was just going out of earshot. The rescuers were on the point of freeing his feet. In minutes, maybe seconds, stretcher-bearers would be here to whisk him off to that ambulance, and what chance would there be to talk after that? He had to get Alec back now. And somehow convince him that the Big Four could be here, on this spot or very near it, just twenty to thirty feet below.

"Alec," he called sharply.

To his great relief, Hobbs heard him, turned, and came back towards him.

"Yes, George?"

"Before I – passed out, I told you an idea which you may have thought crazy – "

Hobbs smiled.

"You mean about the Big Four being in a nuclear shelter underneath here? You're right, George. I did think you were being crazy – or, rather, delirious." The smile vanished, and his face became grim. "But then I started digging."

"Digging?"

"For facts, I mean. I rang Hammersmith station. Half the staff had heard stories about a million pound shelter being built. So I brought an expert contractor down here, who told me that a great deal of the concrete in this courtyard is fresh – laid within a couple of years at the most. Then I brought in a sonic detector – which picked up the sound of what could be air vents operating thirty to forty feet below us. On that evidence, I rang Scott-Marle – "

Alec broke off there, for a very obvious reason. Sir Reginald himself suddenly appeared on the scene, and took over, finishing Hobbs's sentence for him.

"And I was so impressed," he said, "that I've come straight down here. Rest assured, George, that if you're right, there's no fear that the Big Four will get away. I'm ordering every available man down here – a bigger operation even than last night's raid. I'm having them go over the castle and every inch of the grounds in search of a secret entrance. Not in this courtyard, of course, because of the bomb risk. I admit that's going to hamper things, but we're doing everything else we can. I'll soon be having such a big force surrounding the place that it will be like a besieging army. I only wish, George, that I could put one of your old and trusted hands in charge of the operation. But it might go on for days, with a bomb to be disposed of and tons of blast-proof ferro-concrete to blast through, and your men are already over-strained. Alec here's had no sleep for nearly forty-eight hours. Honiwell is in a state of near-exhaustion. Riddell – "

"Yes, Matt told me about Tom," Gideon said. "But there's my deputy, Paul Barnaby, and that new Chief Detective Superintendent, Price – "

Scott-Marle frowned.

"Barnaby's a good administrator, but a poor commander," he snapped. "Price has a brilliant brain, but is virtually inarticulate in a crisis. No, George. There's only one man I can see leading this operation as effectively as *you* would, if you were fit – and that's Commander Warburton."

Gideon could hardly believe his ears.

"Warburton?" he roared. "But – "

Sir Reginald folded his arms.

"I know what you're thinking, George – that I'm playing some kind of musical chairs with my commanders. Yes, of course Warburton was in charge last night when everything was disastrously leaked. But you've got to remember that, painful though it is to mention it, your raid also proved abortive because of leaks all the way. And you owe more to Wally than you know. When that call from the supergrass was received, and he realised that his Target Eighty operation was doomed, it was *he* who first suggested that you should be brought in to save the day."

"How very kind of him," said Gideon heavily, and forbore to point out that since the entire raid had been his idea in the first place, Scott-Marle should not have needed a parting prod from Warburton to call him in.

Scott-Marle could not have failed to notice the sarcasm in his tone, but brusquely ignored it.

"At all events, George, you can be sure you're leaving the business in the best possible hands," he said, adding, with one of his faint, cold smiles: "Even if they *are* Uniform and not C.I.D.!"

He walked away with Gideon glaring after him, a glare which rapidly became a grimace of pain as Dr. Quentin finished cutting away his right trouser leg, and started the painful process of cleaning and applying an emergency bandage to his crushed leg, which looked a mass of bleeding pulp from the thigh right down to the calf. What made the work extremely tricky was the fact that Gideon's left foot was still partially trapped, although at that very moment grappling hooks were being lowered around a final piece of concrete. Once that was pulled away, Gideon's whole body would at last be free.

"Right," said the doctor, stepping back to mop his face. Sweat was pouring down it, whether from the strain of working under these conditions or the fear of the bomb just below them, it was impossible to say. "Won't be long now, from the look of it, Commander. We'll soon have you on that stretcher and away to the ambulance. How are you feeling?"

"Bloody awful," Gideon was about to grunt. But he changed his mind.

Staring up at all the people who had been sweating and struggling since dawn to save him, with the ever-present threat of death hanging over them if they took a false step or made one clumsy move, he could only say, hoarsely:

"Bloody grateful – to you all."

* * *

It wasn't long before someone appeared to whom Gideon did *not* feel grateful, despite Scott-Marle's insistence on what he owed him: Commander Wally Warburton.

As usual when he sighted this man, whom some people said greatly resembled his own youthful self, Gideon had to fight hard to repress an instant feeling of irritation.

Warburton came striding up as if he owned the place, and lost no time in barking – or rather yapping – questions at all and sundry.

"How long will it be before we can move the Commander?" he asked McNally the bomb expert, in a way which suggested that he blamed him for having taken so long already. "We have an important operation to get under way here – and can't even begin it until your boys have dealt with that bomb."

The gentle-voiced McNally was too taken aback to reply. Dr. Quentin wasn't. His voice as northern as Yorkshire granite, he snapped:

"We're not exactly dragging our heels here, friend. Happen there could be another operation to be got under way – at St. Giles Hospital, on the Commander's leg. And I reckon it's a sight more important than anything you're doing, is that."

McNally found his voice at last – and it wasn't gentle now at all. He was apparently head of both the rescue and the bomb disposal work, and spoke in both capacities, very angrily.

"If you'd been working at high pressure for hour after hour, with a bomb liable to go off right under you, you wouldn't appreciate being asked tomfool questions," he yelled. "The Commander will be freed the second we can manage it – but defusing the bomb might take a good deal longer. In fact, since the damn thing appears to be buried in solid concrete, it might take the rest of the night. And if you dare to suggest I should try and hurry it up, risking lives just on account of a police raid – "

Even Warburton realised he had gone too far, and actually had the grace to apologise.

"All right, all right, everyone, keep your hair on. Didn't mean to give offence." He was right beside Gideon now, squatting on his haunches. "While we're waiting, Gideon, perhaps you'd like to hear my plans."

Surprised at this new politeness, Gideon said mildly:

"Very much indeed – Warburton."

The uniformed commander launched into a long description of how he proposed to carry out Scott-Marle's strategy of virtually "besieging" the castle, cordoning off a large area around it. "We'll be bringing in experts tomorrow to determine the precise location of the shelter," he continued. "And then we should be able to work out where the hidden entrance is. The air vents are important, too. Once we've found where they are, we should be able to use smoke-bombs or gas to knock the villains out."

"I shouldn't bet on it," said Gideon. "I don't know much about nuclear shelters, but any one that's worth its salt must be protected against contaminated air. At the slightest sign of smoke or gas, they'll switch off the vents and use compressed oxygen. And they may have a month's supply."

"Then we'll have to try blasting," said Warburton.

Gideon smiled faintly.

"With the amount of TNT you'd have to use, that could be dangerous," he said. "Especially near the river. We want the Big Four brought to trial, not drowned. No, you've got to face it, Warburton: you're in for a protracted and very messy siege. Unless – "

For once, he actually had the voluble Warburton hanging on *his* words.

"Unless what?" he yapped.

"Unless," said Gideon, "someone has a bit of common sense and puts himself in the Big Four's place. There they are, sitting in a glorified dugout, which for all its luxurious trappings can't be all that good a place to be in. If I were they, I'd want to get out of it at the earliest possible minute. *And as far as they're concerned, there's nothing to stop them doing just that.* After all, they haven't any reason to suppose that anyone up top dreams that their hideout exists. Unless whoever has leaked information before is still in contact with them, they must be telling themselves that the bomb stopped that fool Gideon from examining the place rather too closely – they probably imagine I'm past examining anything again! And that was their only danger.

"Do you see what I'm getting at? They almost certainly think that all they've got to do is wait until everything goes quiet above them, and then they'll slip out by a pre-arranged route – and for my money, that will be a secret exit somewhere by the river.

"Now, provided our security arrangements are watertight, I don't know how they'll tell when everything has gone quiet. It could be that they've got rooms bugged in the castle building, or perhaps they've some outside contact under orders to keep them informed by means of signals, or maybe a secret telephone line. But one thing's for certain. The more you follow Scott-Marle's idea, and have men scurrying about in, or keeping watch on, all parts of the building, the longer you'll be postponing the moment when the Big Four come out of their own accord."

Warburton wasn't just hanging on Gideon's words now. He appeared to be drinking every one of them in.

"What would you do, then? Evacuate the place completely? Send everybody home?"

"You've got it, Warburton," Gideon said. "Everybody, that is, except a small force keeping well out of sight down by the river – and a River Police launch keeping equally well out of sight by Hammersmith Bridge. The force and the launch to be in constant radio contact with each other, of course – with plenty of spotlights and marksmen on hand in case the Big Four decide to try and shoot it out or make a dash for it, or both. With an outfit like that, keeping as quiet as mice until the moment comes to strike, you could wind up this whole case tonight."

"But – but what if Sir Reginald doesn't agree?"

"He'll agree all right," said Gideon, momentarily wincing with pain. "Particularly if you tell him that this plan was discussed between us. That leaves only one snag that I can see. And how that can be overcome I'd give a lot to be able to tell you."

"What is it?"

"The question of the leaks. I've been assuming that the Big Four don't know that the police suspect anything. If someone on the inside leaks *that* information down to them – "

Warburton shuddered. He had, for the moment, quite lost his cocky air, and became almost confidential.

"I'd have said how could that possibly happen – but for last night," he murmured. "I don't think I shall ever forget that moment when a single call from that supergrass wrecked everything – everything I'd been planning and working on for months. And even bringing in you and your hand-picked men didn't change the situation, did it? All night long, I kept ringing Sir Reginald for the latest news – and every time, it was of another leak, another of the Big Four getting away. I don't know how I can prevent the same thing happening tonight – but I'll not just have hand-picked men, I'll have them where I can keep an eye on each and every one of them, all the time."

"You might find that just a little difficult," Gideon began, but then broke off, realising that the moment he had been waiting for all through this long, terrible day had arrived.

Slowly, infinitely slowly, the concrete trapping his left foot and ankle rose in the air – and he was free.

It was an irresistible temptation to move his legs – but after a split second, he realised he should have resisted it at all costs.

The most agonising spasm of pain he had yet experienced shot through him – and he could not help groaning as hollowly as a tormented ghost.

Warburton hurriedly stood up and stepped back.

"You don't want to waste any more of your strength talking to me," he said, solicitously. "Goodbye, Commander. Wish me luck. Because as far as I am concerned, this is still Gideon's, not Warburton's raid!"

He went off, waving. Gideon tried to wave back, telling himself that maybe he had misunderstood Warburton – when suddenly he was hit by a thought that shook him almost as much as that moment of agony.

Almost since the beginning of the case, one question had been at the back of his mind – a question that had proved totally unanswerable.

How could the leaks from the Yard to the Big Four have gone on continually all through the night when there had been a total change of personnel around midnight, and after that, the raid details had been known only to Scott-Marle, Alec Hobbs, himself and his most trusted men?

The question wasn't unanswerable now.

If Scott-Marle had been thoughtlessly confiding in Wally Warburton all through the small hours, giving him reports of the raid, then it was more than likely he had let slip a few raid plans too. Which meant that Warburton's name could be added to the list of people able to leak information to the Big Four after he, Gideon, had taken over. And before Target Eighty had closed down, Warburton had, of course, been ideally placed to pass on information – no one better, as he was Commander of the operation himself!

The more he thought about it, the more Gideon realised that Warburton not only *could* be the "mole" in the police camp: he *had* to be, unless he was prepared to suspect Alec Hobbs or Scott-Marle himself. Literally no one else had been in a position to pass over both the detailed plans of Target Eighty at the beginning of the night, and such vital particulars as the timing of Lem's raid on Barry Mayne's HQ in the middle of it.

Warburton had also, of course, been able to pass on the name of the supergrass – and was as responsible for the knife in Rene Renalto's back as if he had put it there himself.

"Right," muttered Gideon, staring after the departing Warburton, who was calmly crossing the courtyard to have a word with Scott-Marle. "Got you, my lad. Got you good and proper . . ."

He was about to call out to Sir Reginald when suddenly it was impossible to do or say anything, except grunt and groan with pain. He was being lifted on to a stretcher, and the stretcher-bearers were whisking him at top speed across the courtyard in the opposite direction, towards a side gate through which he could glimpse an ambulance and the waiting Kate.

A cheer went up from all around him, and he realised it was the rescue-workers rejoicing in the triumphant outcome of all their hours of struggle. He would have expected them to have run for their lives away from the area of that threatening bomb. Instead they were staying to see him off, and their cheers ended in a chorus of good wishes from them all.

"Good luck, Commander."

"We'll be thinking of you, mate."

"Get well quick."

Gideon grinned and waved back at them. It was a forced grin. They were standing between him and Warburton, him and Scott-Marle, him and every hope he had of stopping what was now beginning to seem like the inevitable triumph of the Big Four.

As his stretcher was carried more and more swiftly across the yard, swaying like a hammock as the bearers tried to negotiate the lumps of rubble under their feet, Gideon was able to visualise all too clearly what would happen next.

Such an important accomplice as Warburton was probably in the confidence of the Big Four. Certainly they would have contacted him and told him how to reach them in an emergency. So he would choose the first available opportunity to slip away, and would head for some spot in the grounds where there was a hidden mike or phone connecting him with the shelter below. After that, of course, he would see to it that his men were positioned exactly where the Big Four needed them to facilitate their escape.

In a matter of minutes from now, probably, they'd be away . . . unless he could work some kind of miracle, and get someone to listen to him before he was in that ambulance, and being hurtled to St. Giles, that emergency operation, and more unconsciousness, more oblivion, more nightmare visions of the Big Four laughing, laughing . . .

He was near the side gate now, and could see Kate running towards him.

Dr. Quentin, who was walking alongside the stretcher, noticed him struggling to sit up and start talking.

"No, no, Commander, that's a silly thing to do, is that. Just relax and lie quiet – quiet as we can while we get you inside. Then I've something here that will take away that pain . . ."

Pain . . . the wretched man was right, Gideon realised. The pain in his leg *was* starting up again – becoming unbearable, making it impossible to think . . .

Kate was suddenly bending over him, holding his hand. For once tears were glistening in her eyes.

"Thank God you're out of that, love. Thank – "

But she stopped there, puzzled at his expression. Pain was in his eyes, but also frustration, fury. Desperately sick, urgently in need of treatment he might be, but that couldn't alter the fact that basically he was once again a caged tiger. And as always, there was nothing she could do but try to set him free.

"Please stop," she told the stretcher man.

She said it quietly, but so firmly that a sergeant major in full voice could not have been more rapidly obeyed.

The stretcher was abruptly halted, less than a yard from the open doors of the ambulance.

The startled Dr. Quentin opened his mouth to protest, but then closed it again. There was no arguing with a Gideon roar – and that (to everyone's astonishment) was what was suddenly coming from the patient.

"There's something I've got to do before I'm carved up,

Doctor. So please get 'em to turn this contraption round – NOW!"

The stretcher men didn't wait for Quentin's okay. Before the doctor could open his mouth again, Gideon was already being carried – almost at the double – back into the rubble-strewn courtyard which had so nearly been his tomb.

# 21 The Big Four

Through the amplifier on the wall of the main room inside the nuclear shelter – a room slightly resembling a miniature airport lounge – Warburton's voice sounded hoarse and half-hysterical.

"Listen. We're in trouble, dead trouble. Gideon's twigged about the shelter. Scott-Marle's here and is talking about bringing men by the lorry load to surround the castle – 'besiege' it, he calls it . . ."

The four men sitting in armchairs around the room tensed and became motionless, except for one of them – the gangster-like Barry Mayne – who jumped to his feet and looked for a moment as though he was actually reaching for a gun.

A sardonic smile crossed the face of Arturo Salvados. The bank raid master-minder had nothing but contempt for the "tough-guy" tricks of his colleague.

"Save it, Barry, at least until you see the whites of Commander Gideon's eyes."

Neither Jeremy Kemp nor Monty Marlowe said anything. The ever-sophisticated Kemp appeared to be concentrating on biting the end off an expensive Panatella cigar. He was the only smoker in the room, Salvados having forgotten to bring a supply of his beloved herbal cigarettes. Marlowe, like the flamboyant "show-biz" personality he had always been, flung himself back in his chair and closed his eyes, as though in total despair.

At Warburton's next sentence, though, he sat up.

"Well, that's the bad news, now here's the good," the Commander's hoarse voice continued. "You'll never believe it, but guess who's been put in charge of the whole operation. Me!"

The Big Four clearly liked the sound of that. Mayne stopped groping for a real or imaginary gun. Kemp forgot his cigar. Salvados's quiet smile grew. Marlowe actually laughed aloud.

"Bless you, Wally, mate. Knew you'd swing it for us somehow," he said.

The amplifier on the wall had a microphone attachment, sensitive enough to pick up their voices from anywhere in the room. High above, in a disused part of the River Manor building, Warburton could hear Marlowe's comment coming through another amplifier, concealed at the back of a mock Tudor fireplace. The mike enabling him to speak to the Big Four was concealed there too: well-hidden, high above the reach of any casual searcher.

"Yes, I really think I *can* swing it for you – just," Warburton replied. He was talking very fast now, and sounding as near to hysteria as ever. "But only if you do exactly as I say." Without waiting to hear if they agreed or not, he rushed on: "Listen. That bomb under the courtyard. Are you able to trigger it off from down there?"

The Big Four glanced at a button, almost like a red bellpush, set in what looked like a control panel on the far side of their "lounge".

"No problem," said Barry Mayne shortly, and Marlowe added: "Up she goes, tosh, any time you say. I'd block up your ears and lie flat, but it shouldn't do more than shake the Manor. It won't be a bigger explosion than the last one – but the bomb lies deeper, so there'll be a bigger shower of rubble. And there won't be much left of the courtyard."

"Great," said Warburton, his voice low now, and trembling. "I can see the courtyard from here, as it happens – and what's going on there should interest you a lot. They've dug Gideon out now – I take it you know about what happened to him, from radio and TV – "

"Yes, of course we know," said Marlowe. "Serves the old bastard right. Wish we'd blown him sky high."

"Then get this," said Warburton. "Scott-Marle and Hobbs are standing right by the spot where Gideon was buried. That's where your bomb's located, isn't it?"

Salvados answered this time, quietly but clearly.

"Yes, yes. Under the concrete at the foot of the hole."

"Well, listen," Warburton went on. "Gideon himself is right over it now, too! They were taking him to an ambulance in a stretcher, but he's had them turn back, and they're carrying him across the courtyard right up to Scott-Marle. Obviously he's thought of something urgent to say to him – could be about you – could even be that he's on to *me*! Press that button now and you'll get him. You'll get all of them. For keeps."

The Big Four looked at each other.

Kemp slowly applied a light to his Panatella.

"It's quite a temptation, gentlemen," he said.

"To be resisted at all costs," said Salvados, with great intensity. All day the Big Four had been arguing about pressing that button, knowing that they had Gideon in their power; but Salvados had argued that the repercussions of killing such a popular national figure would be too serious. He repeated his argument now, with redoubled force. "If we destroy not only Gideon, but the Chief Commissioner of Scotland Yard, the hue and cry after us would be unimaginable. The police would never rest until they'd got us – no matter where we went."

"They'll never rest until they do that anyway," said Barry Mayne, "not while that f—g Gideon's alive. As I've been saying all day, let's top him while we can."

"I'm almost inclined to agree with you," Kemp was beginning when Warburton's voice interrupted.

He sounded wholly hysterical now.

"What's the matter with you all down there? Don't you realise that this is your big chance – your last chance? Press that button, and you'll cause the biggest diversion ever known – and leave every copper up here so stunned that there'll be complete anarchy for minutes, maybe an hour.

All you'll have to do is just stroll out through that river exit on to your boat. I'll make sure there are no look-outs, or anyone stationed near. You'll never have a better opportunity to get clean away."

Kemp was obviously even more strongly tempted.

"All that – for just the touch of a button," he said softly.

"Sounds like the bargain of the month to me," said Marlowe.

"Then what the hell are we waiting for? Have you all gone chicken, or something?" shouted Mayne.

As coolly as one of his own hit men, he crossed the room and raised a finger to press the button.

Arturo Salvados rose swiftly from his chair, and said: "No. Wait."

Mayne smiled nastily. He had as great a contempt for Salvados as Salvados had for him.

"No more waiting, pal. You've just been outvoted – three to one," he said.

And pressed the button.

* * *

The resultant explosion shook the room, but only about as much as a ten-ton lorry would have done, passing directly overhead.

Glasses rattled on the drinks cabinet, over by one wall. An inch of ash dropped off Kemp's Panatella on to the thick red fitted carpet. A burst of crackling came from the amplifier. But that was all until, some twenty seconds later, they heard the voice of Warburton, so shaky now that it was virtually a croak.

"You've done it, gentlemen, you've done it. The smoke's clearing out there, and there's nothing where Gideon, Scott-Marle and Hobbs were. Nothing . . . except a bloody great crater . . ."

For a moment, even the Big Four shuddered at the thought of the crime they'd committed.

"The repercussions," Salvados was saying softly. "My God – the repercussions – "

"Stuff all that," said Mayne. "Gideon's dead and in my book, that's worth three f—g cheers any day of the week."

"I'll drink to that," said Marlowe, and headed for the drinks cabinet, opening it with such an unsteady hand that he started the glasses rattling again.

Kemp strode across the room, and slammed the cabinet shut before Mayne could touch a bottle. He knew – they all knew – what the pop star was like when he'd had a few.

"Leave it till we're out of here," he said soothingly. "As we shall be, Monty – in less than a minute. Out of here, on that boat – and free . . ."

Turning towards the microphone on the wall, he called out:

"Okay, Warburton. We go on playing it your way. We're making for the river exit – now."

Pausing only to light a fresh cigar, Kemp led the way to the door, Marlowe following him eagerly, Mayne excitedly, and Salvados very reluctantly indeed.

* * *

Even Salvados began to feel a faint stirring of excitement as he and the others stepped out of a long, dark tunnel, and found themselves on a small quay about fifty yards up river from the Rock Castle building.

At first they thought that a fog, or heavy river mist, had come up, but then they realised it was smoke from the explosion, which even at that distance was so thick that visibility was down to around thirty feet.

That was more than enough, though, to show them that their getaway boat, a small craft that looked like a cross between an outsize motor boat and a miniature yacht, was moored by the quay, and ready and waiting for them to step aboard.

There was no crew on board her: the Big Four did not share their ultimate getaway secrets with one person more than they could help. But that didn't matter. Kemp was an accomplished amateur sailor, and Marlowe was rapidly becoming one under his tuition.

The four stood there, for a moment, looking around them, luxuriating in being outdoors after their hours within the confines of the shelter. The pall of smoke, so immense that it seemed to be hanging over half Hammersmith, didn't worry them. It was the ideal cover they needed for a quick escape.

"We could slip away in this even if every launch the River Police possessed was after us," said Kemp. "Not that, in fact, anything's going to be after us at all. From the sound of it, everyone's just a little too busy . . ."

From all around them, through the smoke, came sounds of people and organisations responding to the crisis: the shrieking sirens of fire engines, ambulances and police cars mingled with the mournful blasts from the foghorns of passing river craft into a continuous background cacophony. From nearer at hand, but surprisingly faint through the fifty yards of heavy smoke filling the intervening space, came the noises from the stricken courtyard: orders being barked, an urgent "look *out*!" being yelled, and a rumbling crunch as some last remaining bit of the wall fell in.

Only one of the four was unhaunted by the thought that it might be landing on someone who was maimed, dying or dead.

"Great, that noise. Sounds just like the very last nail being banged into Gideon's coffin," joked Barry Mayne.

Monty Marlowe laughed nervously. Salvados didn't even smile.

Jeremy Kemp drew hard on his cigar. The glowing tip seemed to go on and off like a winking emergency light.

"What the hell are we hanging about for?" he demanded. "Let's go while the going's good."

He jumped down on to the deck of the boat with the casual assurance of a seasoned yachtsman, and beckoned Marlowe to join him. Marlowe complied, and then both of them helped Mayne and Salvados aboard.

"I don't like this," Salvados was muttering. "It's too easy. Too easy by half."

Mayne spat over the side of the boat to show his contempt.

"Why shouldn't it be easy? It's headless chicken time back there. You can almost hear the bleeding coppers running round in circles – and even when they've stopped, we can trust Wally to start 'em off again. It's the perfect getaway set-up."

"Perhaps," said Salvados. "But I'll be happier when we get moving."

"Which should be in about ten seconds flat. Get ready to cast off when I signal, Monty," said Jeremy Kemp. He pushed past Salvados, crossed the tiny deck, and reached for the handle of the cabin door.

His fingers never touched it.

At that moment, the deck was suddenly a blaze of blinding light.

Kemp and the others swung round, to find themselves blinking in the glare from three powerful police spotlights, focussed on the boat from a point a few yards past their private quay. The quay itself didn't seem so private now. Shielding his eyes against the light, Salvados could make out a line of policemen standing on it, policemen who seemed to have sprung from nowhere. And they all seemed to be armed: he could see revolvers glinting everywhere. Mayne could obviously see them too. For once, he didn't even try reaching for his gun.

Kemp was the only one of the four who moved. He turned back in the direction of the cabin, and opened the door. He had a very desperate plan. If he could get the engine started, maybe somehow Mayne could shoot out the lights – and in the confusion Marlowe could cast off . . .

The plan collapsed as swiftly as the ash that fell from his cigar when suddenly, the cabin lights sprang on, and he realised that he was very far from being alone in there.

Two men were standing in the centre of the cabin, waiting for them, with a bevy of constables at the rear.

And as the Big Four saw who those two men were, their cheeks turned the colour of Jeremy Kemp's cigar ash.

"I'm afraid this is the end of your little voyage, gentlemen," said Sir Reginald Scott-Marle, at his smoothest and iciest. "Mr. Hobbs and I have other plans for you. You are all, I need hardly add, under arrest . . ."

The policemen moved forward. Kemp was marched out of the cabin, and lined up beside Mayne, Marlowe and Salvados on the deck. There they were briskly searched and handcuffed.

"And now," said Scott-Marle, "there is someone who is most anxious for a word with you, and I don't want him kept waiting. Take them on to the quay!"

It was difficult for the four to step off the boat in handcuffs, but Scott-Marle's men roughly speeded their progress. In seconds, they were all standing on the quay, which was still lined with policemen, although at one point the line was being broken. Two of the constables respectfully stood aside to allow a man on a stretcher to be brought forward; the last man on earth that the four ever expected to see confronting them again.

His face still covered with dirt and dust, his body – so large that the blue ambulance blanket hardly covered it – nearly doubled up with pain, Gideon nevertheless managed something approaching a grin.

"You've been highly honoured," he informed them. "Not many criminals get to be arrested personally by the Chief Commissioner and the Assistant Commissioner (Crime). But I'm afraid I was a bit beyond doing it myself. And after all, you are – "

His grin widening, he deliberately changed the tense.

"That is, you *were* – the Big Four . . ."

# 22 Jubilee

None of the four had anything to say as, under the direction of Scott-Marle and Hobbs, they were made to shuffle forward and stand in front of Gideon.

They didn't look so big now, he thought, lying back in his stretcher; more like a parade of Army defaulters. It was hard to believe that for a decade past, this quartet had been the brains and power behind so high a proportion of London crime – until he glanced up into their eyes, and saw the intensity of hate in Mayne's, the cool malignancy in Kemp's, the latent madness in Marlowe's and the quiet, brooding malice in those of Salvados.

No, he told himself. These were very far from being ordinary men. And if London was lucky, it might be generations before a rule of crime like theirs was inflicted on it again.

Salvados was the first of the four to speak. Although normally the quietest of them, curiosity simply wouldn't let him keep silent any longer.

Very formally – in fact, rather primly – he murmured:

"You've been very clever, Commander. I must confess to being completely bewildered."

Gideon laughed.

"That makes us even then. You've done your share of bewildering me these last forty-eight hours, I can tell you."

He was neither laughing nor grinning, but glowering angrily as he added:

"I suppose you're wondering why Sir Reginald, Mr. Hobbs and I weren't blown sky-high – as your crony Warburton assured you we'd be, once you pressed that button."

The expression of astonishment on their faces gave him such a sense of satisfaction that for a moment, the pain in his leg was dwarfed out of existence.

"I don't reckon I owe you anything, least of all an explanation," he snapped at them. "But if you want one, here it is. What Warburton told you was going on in the courtyard – me being carried across it in a stretcher to talk to Sir Reginald and Mr. Hobbs, who were standing by the hole – all that had actually happened *a quarter of an hour before*.

"And what I had wanted to talk to Sir Reginald and Mr. Hobbs about was the fact that I had identified Commander Warburton as your accomplice, and the source of all the leaks. I did, in fact, have myself carried across to them, and succeeded in convincing them that I was right. They immediately sent for Warburton, and the three of us confronted him."

Kemp suddenly interrupted.

"Whereupon he immediately broke down and confessed everything, Commander?" he asked sardonically. "In two minutes flat?"

"Who said anything about a confession?" Gideon retorted. "As far as I was concerned, there was no time for that. I simply put a proposition to Warburton. He could choose between being arrested and charged as an accomplice after the fact of all your crimes – which would mean a ten-year stretch at the very least. Or he could play ball with me, and get off with just a quiet little suspension from the force. He was so shaken that he decided to opt for the latter in two seconds, let alone two minutes, flat.

"The rest was simple," he went on. "I got Warburton to lead me to the place where he'd been told that, in emergencies, he could communicate with the four of you, down below. Fortunately, it turned out to be on the ground floor, so even on a stretcher I could follow him to the spot. And I was in the background, dictating virtually everything he said to you."

The astonishment on the faces of the four grew to something approaching stupefaction, which had such an analgesic effect on Gideon's leg that he was almost beginning to enjoy himself.

"*You* told us to – to trigger off that bomb?" said Monty Marlowe. "But what the hell for?"

"Primarily, to winkle the four of you out of your bowels-of-the-earth hideout," Gideon told him. "You'd come up like a shot, I reckoned, if you thought that Warburton was in total command, and there was nothing left of all the big brass of Scotland Yard except a crater. As for the risks involved in the explosion – they were pretty negligible. The courtyard had been cordoned off as a danger area all day. Nobody had been allowed in except the very brave and gallant people who had been working to free *me* . . . As long as the second bomb wasn't more powerful than the first one – and you, Mayne, were quick to inform me that it wasn't – letting it off would do no harm and perhaps a bit of good. The bomb expert, McNally, had told me that at its depth, it would prove a tricky challenge to the disposal boys. Detonating it did them quite a favour. Oh – and how did I know which was your getaway boat? Well, you didn't pick quite the most inconspicuous craft on the river . . ."

Suddenly Gideon wasn't enjoying himself quite so much. The pain was returning, sharp and blistering. It served him right, he knew. He had been crazy to insist on those stretcher-bearers lugging him down to the quay. But he hadn't been able to resist being in at the kill.

He turned back to the four, now in a smouldering fury.

"There was just one snag to my plan, as far as I could see," he told them. "I had cherished the mistaken belief that you were hard-headed criminals, but not vicious terrorists, and so I thought you might baulk at the prospect of pressing a button which would immediately end three lives, or five if you include my stretcher-bearers. How wrong I was. Except for you, Salvados – and you were only concerned about possible repercussions – none of you even hesitated. It's taught me an interesting lesson. There's nothing to choose between murderers. Terrorists, gang-leaders, stocking stranglers – you're all brothers under the skin. *Blood* brothers!"

His leg was now hurting so much that he hardly realised who he was talking to. He barked at Scott-Marle: "Get them out of here, for God's sake. I'm sick of the sight of them."

Later, when the four had gone and he was being carried towards the ambulance, with Scott-Marle and Hobbs walking beside him, he hastily apologised to the Chief Commissioner for ordering him about like that.

Never, in all his years as the C.I.D.'s Commander – twenty-five, in just six weeks' time – had he been so taken aback by a remark as he was by Scott-Marle's answer.

Curtly, jerkily, as though each word was costing him a fortune, Sir Reginald replied:

"The last thing you need to do is apologise, George. The more I think about my own sorry contribution to this business, the more I feel how much better it would have been if our positions were reversed – and, right from the beginning, *I'd* been taking orders from *you.*"

★ ★ ★

"I'm afraid this isn't much of a party," Alec Hobbs said. "But coming right after your first day back at the Yard, Sir Reginald reckoned it might overtire you if we staged too big an event. So at his suggestion, we've kept it secret from most of the staff, and just invited your closest colleagues."

"H'm. Very thoughtful," Gideon said – and did his best not to make it sound like a growl. It was true that he was still really convalescent, and not quite past the stage of hobbling painfully about; but he would have preferred to have seen just a few more faces around to celebrate his twenty-five years as head of what he liked to think of as the most effective crime-fighting department in the world.

The party that Scott-Marle and Hobbs had cooked up looked very select indeed. It was being held in a small partitioned-off area somewhere amidst the vast empty spaces of the seventh floor, which had reverted to being used for conferences and training courses now that Target Eighty was over. The area had been specially decorated, with silver "GGs" and "25s" lining the walls; a lot of sumptuous food was laid out on three buffet tables, and there were four girls from the canteen serving wine; but somehow it all had a lack-lustre air. And so far, it seemed, only twenty-five guests had arrived.

"One for each year," muttered Gideon glumly. Then, hurriedly grabbing himself a glass of wine (it was, at least, new-season Beaujolais), he made a determined effort to shake himself out of this sour mood.

This didn't prove difficult to do. After all, here was Kate beside him, her eyes twinkling as though this was one of the happiest occasions of her life, and here, around him, *were* the men who meant most to him, and who had done the most with him and for him, during all these years.

Here, for example, was dear old Lemaitre, spruced up to the nines, with his sparse hair dazzlingly Brylcreemed and rivalling the sparkle from his polished shoes. He had his faithful Fifi on his arm. Just one look at him took Gideon back far more than twenty-five years – right back to the days when they were detective sergeants together, and Lem had opened a book on which of them would make the highest number of arrests in a given month . . .

"How's the world treating you, Lem?" he asked.

"A lot better now I'm shot of the Stocking Strangler," Lemaitre replied. "And that Henry Jones – he's a boy, Gee Gee. I've fired him with the idea of joining the force. The trouble is, he hasn't a qualification to his name. But he's enlisted in more night schools than I ever knew existed, and I really think he'll be a Brain of Britain before long."

"Not if he spends the rest of every night haunting lovers' lanes," Gideon grunted.

"Oh, that's a thing of the past thanks to a certain Miss Judy Moss. It's an odd world, Gee Gee. I would have thought Jones's idea that being a rescuing hero was the way to fetch the birds was straight out of the ark. But after seeing Judy with Clive Exton, and now with *him* – well, I've got to admit it still makes the animals come in two by two. If you see what I mean . . ."

Before Gideon could be quite sure that he did, Fifi had whisked Lem away in the direction of the drinks, and he found himself talking to Tom Riddell, who was there with the ever-anxious Vi beside him. Not that Vi had anything to be anxious about tonight, Gideon thought. Riddell was showing no sign whatever of the nervous exhaustion that had put him in hospital three weeks before. The word had got round that he had played a major role in running the Big Four to earth, and that had evidently done wonders for his confidence. That gaunt look was beginning to disappear from his face, and with his big build, he suddenly seemed as immensely powerful a man as he had done years ago.

"No need to ask if you're okay, Tom," said Gideon. "You're looking what you always are and always have been, as far as I'm concerned: a tower of strength."

Riddell stared hard, as if wondering whether Gideon was joking. When he realised that he meant every word he'd said, the expression on his face made even Vi start smiling . . .

And now here was Matt Honiwell, good old "cuddly" Matt, with his mass of curly hair combed carefully back for once, and his wife Netta putting one stray curl back into place.

Always full of news about people, Matt was soon giving Gideon the latest about Detective Constable Brian Fullerton and the obstinate, courageous Maggie. Both were now well on their way to recovery, and Fullerton had compiled a new file on Monty Marlowe that would provide crucial evidence for the prosecution in the coming case against the Big Four.

"I'd like to have him working with me from now on," said Matt. "As a Detective Sergeant, or even Inspector, if that can be arranged."

"It certainly can be arranged," said Gideon, and then broke off, puzzled at the odd sound that seemed to be coming from the other side of one of the partitions that walled off the room.

It was hard to be certain above the chatter and the clinking of glasses all round him, but it sounded like a great crowd of people chanting.

He couldn't catch the words at first, but suddenly the

chanting became so loud that no one could miss a syllable of them.

"*Gideon . . . We want Gideon . . .*"

The next thing he knew, Alec, helped by Penny – a Penny resplendent in an off-the-shoulder organdie dress, looking radiant enough to take a bow at the Royal Festival Hall – was unlocking and sliding back the partition . . . to reveal an enormous conference hall, the very hall where he'd originally launched Gideon's raid.

It was as packed as it was then, but now with a hoard of laughing, cheering people – men and women both from C.I.D. and Uniform, of all ranks, all sizes and all ages, including veterans who must have retired many years ago – who came charging forward to surge round him with all the force of a tidal wave.

Just before the tide engulfed him, Gideon caught a glimpse of Kate's face, her eyes as mischievous as he'd ever known them.

"You've me to blame for this, love, I'm afraid," she said. "When Alec told me your party was going to be kept secret, I said that this was one time when the Yard *ought* to be leaking like a sieve . . ."

**JAMES McCLURE**

THE ARTFUL EGG

Someone out there is crazy. Crazy enough to kill a world-famous novelist and then strew her naked body with flower petals and herbs. Or is there method in this madness?

That's the question which tantalises Tromp Kramer and Mickey Zondi, his Zulu partner in the Trekkersburg Murder and Robbery Squad, as they begin an investigation that leads them into an alien world of painters and poets, sculptors and ballet dancers.

Then, to compound the pressure they're under, Kramer is ordered to drop everything until he's cleared up a fatal accident with very embarrassing implications for the police. And then he discovers that this death was no accident . . .

'Kramer and Zondi are two of the most attractive policemen in modern fiction. They are funny, human and vigorous . . . An enjoyable murder mystery and a wry picture of South African life'

*The Mail on Sunday*

'Sharply observed glimpses of apartheid . . . plus red herrings by the shoal'

*Guardian*

'A distinguished crime novelist who has created in Tromp Kramer and Sergeant Zondi two detectives who are as far from stereotypes as any in the genre'

*P. D. James*

'A rattling good detective story'

*London Standard*

'Mr McClure is an exceedingly skilful writer'

*New York Times Book Review*